Welcome to Renaissance Village, the plush new condo community for today's young elite. There are a few drawbacks the realtor forgot to mention: infants are being bizarrely murdered; women are being sexually terrorized from within their bodies; and an ancient mystery peering forth from a little girl's eyes is about to escape in a whirlwind of horror . . .

"WITH *THE SEARING*, JOHN COYNE PROVES HIMSELF THE MASTER OF OCCULT-IN-TRIGUE . . . *THE SEARING* WILL KEEP YOU AWAKE ALL NIGHT, IN MORE WAYS THAN ONE."

—*CLIVE CUSSLER, author of RAISE THE TITANIC!*

Berkley books by John Coyne

THE LEGACY
(Based on a story by Jimmy Sangster)
THE PIERCING
THE SEARING

JOHN COYNE
THE
SEARING

BERKLEY BOOKS, NEW YORK

This Berkley book contains the complete
text of the original hardcover edition.
It has been completely reset in a type face
designed for easy reading, and was printed
from new film.

THE SEARING

A Berkley Book / published by arrangement with
G. P. Putnam's Sons

PRINTING HISTORY
G. P. Putnam's Sons edition / September 1980
Berkley edition / July 1981

ISBN: 0-425-04924-8

A BERKLEY BOOK ® TM 757,375
Berkley Books are published by Berkley Publishing Corporation,
200 Madison Avenue, New York, New York 10016.
PRINTED IN THE UNITED STATES OF AMERICA

acknowledgments

For their help in the research and writing of this novel, I would like to thank Derek V. Goodwin, Tom Hebert, Susan Goodman, Gerald Allan Schwinn, Misty Kuceris, John Payne, and once again, my editor, Judith Wederholt.

For Al Montesi, my teacher

prologue

Fall, 1608

In the patch of woods above the river, the white-tailed doe woke with the sun. She raised her delicate head and sniffed the wind. She caught the scent of rabbit a hundred feet higher on the hill and heard a beaver slap the water as it slid from the shore into the river. These creatures she did not fear.

Yet she hesitated, camouflaged in the brown brush and short grasses of a thick stand of trees. She sensed no predators and, unfolding thin legs, she gracefully stood, a young deer, barely four feet tall, brown, silky and fragile as she picked her way from the bed of leaves.

The sun had cleared the horizon and was high enough to shine on the water that ran from Fairfax Stone in the Appalachian mountains down to Point Lookout in the Chesapeake Bay. The young deer did not know the source or length of this river, or that the Algonquin Indians called it Patawomeck.

Nor did she know, this bright fall morning, that a

white man named John Smith was sailing up river to plot the unexplored territory of the New World for European settlers. The year was 1608 and this anonymous white-tailed doe had less than one hour to live.

Only the unexpected snapping of a dry twig or the fluttering of quail from grass startled her, and then she stood perfectly still, hidden by natural camouflage in the wild woods, her heart throbbing against her side.

When her fear subsided, she stepped out of the woods and into the meadow. The grass here was taller than she, and swept down to the river's edge in a smooth, unbroken yellow patch. This meadow was contained in a natural amphitheater, formed as if a giant thumbprint had been pressed into a half-mile of soft soil above the riverbed.

The white-tailed doe moved tentatively forward. This meadow was new to her, but she had picked up the scent of a buck and, excited and frightened by the urge that raced through her, she pursued the scent, moving deeper into the meadow and disappearing finally in the long grass, her progress marked only by the irregular wave she caused in the still field.

He stood in the woods beyond the open field and the strong scent of him filled her damp nostrils, which quivered at each rush of wind. Intoxicated, she leaped forward, racing across the field, her fair brown body leaping clear of the grass with each long bounce; her sharp hooves barely touched the ground and she was up again in a graceful leap.

It was while she was in midair, in that long split second of sailing over the tall grass, that she was struck. The unseen, incomprehensible bolt of pain and passion pinned the doe in midflight and ripped through her brain.

She fell to the ground in an awkward scramble, flattening the grass as she tumbled out of control and rolled to a quick death. No marks punctured her skin and only a bubble of blood dropped from her nostrils. She lay abandoned in the long grass, wide eyed and innocent.

The buck had seen the doe falter in flight and he turned away abruptly, raced into the dark woods, and ran for miles along the shores of the Patawomeck. He never again returned to that meadowland.

The deer lay abandoned and untouched, her slight body gradually stiffening under the sun, and by late afternoon the scavengers of the woods had found her carrion and begun to tear away the flesh. Later rodents and ants and a variety of field insects picked the bones clean, leaving behind the skeleton of a white-tailed female deer.

Those remains lay perfect in the meadow, disturbed only by the changing weather, rain and snow storms, and the annual growths of flowers and grass that grew up between the thin bones and the finely shaped rib cage.

In time, of course, even this skeleton disappeared as the bones shifted, broke apart, and sank into the soft soil, leaving no witness or reason of death.

It was simply an unaccountable death in nature, the killing of a female deer on a fall morning in 1608, in the middle of an empty meadowland shaped like a thumb and pressed into the bank of a river the Indians called Patawomeck. It was not the first death in this odd shaped tract of land, nor would it be the last.

September, 1973

The child had been with her in the kitchen, playing on the linoleum floor of the farmhouse. It was a hot afternoon and she had opened the back door to catch what little air there was in the day. She could see across the sloping yard to the barn, where her husband moved slowly in and out of the dark shadows, doing a few odd jobs around the place. It was too hot for any hard work. The heat hung in the air like wet sheets.

She paused in her own work of canning to glance down at her daughter. The child was rocking back and forth on the floor, her attention concentrated on her right hand, which she held close to her face. She kept turning her hand, endlessly fascinated by the mystery of this small part of her own self. The woman sighed. Just to look at the child made her sad.

At the age of six, the girl was not like either of her parents. She did not have her father's dark and blunt body, nor her mother's thin, hollow looks. Her skin was

5

clear and soft and as translucent as china. Her eyes were dark, and her features perfectly shaped and very fine.

"Cindy?" The woman spoke, but the child continued to be absorbed with her hand, turning the open palm back and forth, inches before her eyes. She knew the child did not hear her. The doctors had told them that much.

She was in her own world, safe and secure, and completely cut off. The doctors gave them a word for her illness and books to read, but she had not read them. She did not need a doctor to explain the consequence of her sin.

She was being punished for her sin. God had given her a daughter and then taken away the child's mind, leaving her as dumb as one of the farm animals. It was her punishment for what she had done.

The woman went back to work, losing herself in canning. She kept busy. She drove herself every day on the farm so at night her exhaustion forced her to sleep. She kept at her work for another fifteen minutes, boiling the mason jars in hot water and then filling them with the first of the fall fruit, and did not think of Cindy until she glanced up from the sink and saw that the child was no longer on the kitchen floor.

The woman glanced around the kitchen and under the table. She peeled off her rubber gloves and turned down the gas flame. She wasn't worried. Cindy had only just begun to walk, and her progress had been slow. She knew the child couldn't have gone far.

But Cindy wasn't in any of the downstairs rooms or the closets. Her mother even opened the basement door and went down to search the dark cellar. They had found Cindy before hiding in a damp corner, curled up in a fetal position and rocking slowly to the beat of her heart.

But Cindy wasn't down there, or anywhere in the house, and the woman ran out and across the yard to tell her husband.

"She ain't here," he said quickly. He stood in the bright sunlight of the barn door, looking toward the giant sycamore and the white farm house. He had bad eyesight and he squinted into the distance, squeezing his expression into a tight, fierce grimace, as if he were making a fist of his face.

"She'll get into the fields," she said to her husband. "You know she don't know about cattle. She'll get hurt in those fields." Her husband looked at her, at how the worry consumed her face. She was only twenty-four, but the child had made her an old woman.

"You go into the cow pasture," he told her. "I'll look in the field." And then he struck off, moving slowly, deliberately, toward the open field beyond the farm road. He walked with his head down, as if bent against the wind, but there was no wind. He planted each foot as if claiming the space with his footstep.

The green alfalfa field swept in a clean, unbroken pattern from the country road that paralleled the river, up the hillside to the crest of the hill. It was only a quarter of a mile wide and less than a mile to the ridge, and the hay field fitted snugly inside the natural amphitheater.

At the top, where the farm road ran left and circled the cow pasture, he set off and followed a foot path to the Indian burial mound. Standing on the old rocks would give him a high, clear view of the field below. As a child he had played there himself; he and his brothers had made the mound into their fort and fought Indians in the oak grove beyond.

Weeds and wild flowers had grown up to obscure the structure, and plowing along its banks had further disguised its shape.

He came up behind the mound, climbing through the thick brush until he was on the flat dirt roof of the rectangular rise. Then he saw the child below him, digging furiously.

He climbed down, went around the piled mound, and came up behind her. She was kneeling in the long grass, digging into the bottom of the mound, and already she had exposed the corner stone of the burial site.

"Cindy," he said. He was behind her, an arm's length from his daughter, and he could have easily reached out and enveloped her into his arms. Yet he waited. This sudden, unexpected behavior of hers puzzled him. The child had never left the house before.

"Cindy . . . ?" He spoke again, but she continued to dig, scooping out the dirt with her small hands, clearing away the face of the flat cornerstone.

The stone, he saw now, had been cut. A few rough-hewn marks were carved into the face and Cindy had begun to clean them of dirt. She worked carefully, taking meticulous care with the carved lines. When she was finished she sat back on her haunches and began to rock, the slow, steady monotonous movement that filled her days.

He studied the crude marks in the flat stone. It wasn't any kind of language, just a set of awkwardly slanted, meaningless gashes made, he supposed, by the edge of an old plow glancing against the rock. Reaching out for Cindy, he wrapped his arms around her and hugged her closely to him.

But Cindy wouldn't be held. She struggled in his arms until he let her free. Then she leaned forward again, closer to the rock, and carefully touched the crude inscription, ran her fingers across the lines slowly, almost reverently, as if she were trying to memorize them:

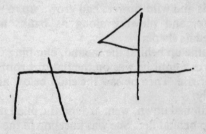

one

May, 1980

Doctor Sara Marks spotted the child standing in the shadows of the barn doorway and was struck immediately by the girl's exquisite beauty. She could not have been older than twelve and had the thin, long-limbed body of a preadolescent. Her dark eyes, however, suggested she was older. They implied sadness, perhaps even tragedy; it was this look of suffering that made the girl so beautiful.

In spite of her striking appearance, her face and arms were unnaturally white, and Sara thought she might be ill. She seemed apprehensive, standing in the shadows and staring with hostility at the crowd of people circled around the auctioneer. But then Sara realized, with the intuition gained from years of medical training, that the young girl was not normal, that she was retarded in some way.

"Doctor Marks!"

Sara glanced over her shoulder and saw Lewis Magnuson walking toward her, pushing through the crowd to where she stood alone in the shade of the barnyard's great sycamore.

"I was thinking you might come," he said, his loud voice attracting attention. His hand was extended and she reluctantly submitted hers to his grasp. He shook it violently, and she was thankful that soon she would have nothing more to do with him.

"Find anything that's caught your eye, Doc?" He winked.

His country boy come-on she had experienced before, but it always angered her. Her face flushing, she looked across the yard and saw the young girl rush out of the dark interior of the barn and around the corner. She ran awkwardly, arms and legs flying out in her haste.

"Who is that child?" Sara asked.

Lewis Magnuson glanced up to see the girl disappear into the field of corn, thrashing through the stiff stalks, stumbling forward as if pursued.

"That's Cindy, Bruce Delp's girl. She's got that autism. Can't talk. Lives in her own little world. No one knows what causes it." He would have continued, but Sara quickly silenced him, saying, "Yes, I know."

"Well, yes, I guess you would." The big man chuckled. "Is that your specialty, Doc? Children, I mean? You're a pediatrician, aren't you? Or one of those gynecologists?" He was grinning good-naturedly, as if her medical degrees were all a joke.

"I'm a pediatrician doing research in endocrinology."

Magnuson snapped his fingers and responded. "You work for the government?"

"At the National Institutes of Health." She replied curtly, but her coolness was wasted on him.

"Well, there's so many of you moving out here, it's difficult remembering who's a doctor, or an undersecretary, or a White House aide. I'm just a country boy myself, and we're not used to so much importance." He kept grinning and now there was perspiration above his lips and across his forehead. It made his face shine like silver.

"And just when will we be moving out here, Mr. Magnuson?" Sara gestured toward the meadow beyond the barnyard. "Those houses don't seem anywhere near completion."

"Another three or four weeks at the most," Magnuson declared, his voice booming again. He was being expansive once more, taking credit.

"Now have you found anything among all this old farm equipment that you'd like for your new home?" He gestured toward the crowd gathered in the yard between the barns and the farm house.

The crowd was getting larger, and people were getting restive, waiting for the auction to begin. Most were farmers from farther south in Virginia, and from across the river in Maryland. Sara could see the license plates of trucks and cars parked in the open field below the farm house.

"It seems a shame," she remarked.

"What's that, Doc?" Magnuson had taken out an enormous handkerchief to wipe the sweat off his face. He used the handkerchief like a wash cloth and it left his face polished.

"That he had to sell the land, give up his farm."

"You can't make a living today with a small place like this, but old Delp did all right. It's about the last farm left on the Potomac within commuting distance of Washington. He got himself top dollar for these acres, and all you people got yourselves a new co-op village."

"But he lost his land! I would think that a man like Delp, whose family has lived right here for generations, wouldn't be happy just to make a quick profit. It seems to me he's being *forced* off the land, and no amount of money can ease that."

Sara was suddenly furious at Magnuson, and for the first time she wasn't concealing her feelings from the developer. She moved to brush past him, but he stood his ground and said quietly: "Delp doesn't give a damn about this farm. It's always been a losing business for him, just like it was for his old man. None of the Delps have ever amounted to much.

"Besides, he's not giving up all his land. He wants to keep working. I guess because of that child of his, the young girl who ain't quite right. So we've hired him as the maintenance man of the Village. He'll keep his farm house and one or two of the smaller buildings for equipment. The barn itself we'll make into indoor tennis and squash courts, and the swimming pool—but you've seen the plans for that.

"And you people have done real nice," Magnuson added pointedly. "Even if old Delp does lose his farm, you people with the new administration have yourselves an exclusive country estate. And one of the best views on the Potomac." He waved once more, sweeping his arm in a wide arc.

From where they stood under the sycamore, they could see the length of the river above Mason Island, and across the water into Maryland. It was a beautiful view, Sara admitted. The trees on the banks of the Potomac were already turning green, and in a few more days most of the river would be lost from sight, hidden behind the thick foliage. But today the bright spring sun sparkled off the cold water.

"And you're sure I'll be moving in here by the end of the summer?" This time she spoke pleasantly. She would try harder to get along with the man.

"You have my word, honey." The grin returned to Magnuson's round face.

"Thanks, but I'll hold onto my contract." She couldn't be nice; he brought out the worst in her. The only answer was to leave and she stepped into the sun, saying, "I have to meet the Volts. We've planned a picnic."

"Say hello to them for me, Doc, and it was nice

seeing you again. Now don't worry about your new home. Everything is going to be just fine. We'll have all you bright, young people into Renaissance Village before September.'' He kept smiling, but there was no warmth in his eyes. He watched her disappear into the auction crowd, thinking that she was one fine-looking woman with her cornsilk hair, her long legs, and her small, tight ass.

Peggy Volt followed her husband up the slope. They had already left the paved streets and the building site, and were climbing straight through the tall grass toward the ridge of the meadow. They had passed what she thought were perfectly fine picnic spots, but she knew Kevin: he had some mystical place in mind, some perfect location that only he could see with his mind's eyes. His friends laughed over his secret system, treating it as just a silly idiosyncrasy. But she saw it as manipulation, and resented it accordingly.

Kevin was carrying everything: the wicker picnic basket, the car blanket, and the small ice chest full of wine and beer. She could see the perspiration on his neck, and already the back of his cotton shirt was damp with sweat. His exertion made her feel momentarily guilty, yet she was the one who was six months pregnant and had to struggle lopsided up the steep hill.

Peggy stopped, winded from the steady climb. ''Kevin, isn't this good enough?'' she asked. Her face was red from the heat, and she wanted him to look around and see her exhaustion, but he only yelled over his shoulder, ''We're almost at the top. I spotted a place the other day that's flat and in the shade.'' He kept walking, lengthening his stride as he gained the crest of the hill.

The picnic spot was perfect: A patch of ground at the top of the meadow and just inside the stand of trees that edged the field. Kevin always did everything right, and that annoyed her. When they had first started to date, she had been awed by his intelligence and sense of detail; she had not realized then how difficult it would be to live with someone who was nearly perfect.

"Sara will never find us here," Peggy complained. It was not like her to bitch, but the exhausting climb had put her in a bad mood.

"Yes, she will. I told her where to look." Kevin calmly set about arranging the picnic area, spreading out the car blanket and opening the wicker basket. "She won't be here for a while, though; she said she wanted to look around the barnyard for something to buy, and then to stop by her house."

"Maybe we should've tried to buy something."

"I did," Kevin answered, setting down a stack of plastic dishes. "I drove out yesterday afternoon when Delp was cleaning out his barns and bought a few of the better items before they were picked over." He glanced up and saw his wife staring at him. "What is it?" he asked. He slipped his arm around her, but there was little warmth in his embrace. The gesture was calculated and precise, like a military drill.

He was not an affectionate person. Peggy had always known that about him, but she had been attracted nevertheless to his clean Nordic looks. There was a neat efficiency to him that she found irresistibly sexy. He was slim and tall and bald. Even before she had met him, he had begun to completely shave his head.

On the first evening they were at his apartment he had asked her to shave him, using a safety razor and cream. And when she was done, and had wiped his scalp dry with a soft blue bath towel, she was so intoxicated with desire that she made him make love to her there, on the cool, damp tiles of the bathroom.

"What is it?" he asked again.

"Nothing."

He sat back and sighed, letting her know that her adolescent behavior perturbed him. Then he reached into the wicker basket and finished setting out the food.

Peggy looked down the hill and saw Sara. She was at the last village road, standing at the entrance to a cul-de-sac. She spotted Peggy and waved.

Peggy managed to wave back. Sara would notice that she was crying and blame it on the pregnancy. Everyone thought that was why she had been so moody and tearful these past weeks, and she let them believe that. But the child had nothing to do with her hysteria. It was Kevin who drove her to tears; it was her husband, whom she hated.

"What is it now?" he demanded.

Peggy shook her head, not answering. She raised her head and blew her nose, then wiped the streaking tears off her face. She was looking away from her husband, looking into the dark trees that framed the valley and thinking clearly for the first time in her life. When the baby was born, she would leave Kevin. He could keep the child; she didn't care. She wanted to be free of him, free of these new friends, and free of this co-op village they all thought was so wonderful and clever and special.

She turned her head and said quickly. "It won't work, Kevin. I'm going to tell the others."

"No, you won't, Peggy." He didn't even bother to raise his voice. "It will work and you will keep your mouth shut. If you do say anything about it, I'll have you killed. And I mean that, darling." He smiled, his face half-hidden in the shade of his Eddie Bauer cap.

Sara left the blacktop village street and walked across the field to her house under construction. The sides and roof were built, but the windows and doors were vacant and the house looked as if it had been bombed out. It was a two-story frame house with a fireplace in the study and a double garage.

The house was too big for her, and she hadn't wanted to be tied down to living in the country, but Kevin Volt had lectured her about how necessary it was to make good investments, now that she was over thirty.

Sara stepped on a plank that stretched from the piled excavation dirt to the back door and went into the house. It was cool inside, refreshing after the hot day in the open fields. She could actually feel a breeze through the doors and windows, and she moved from room to room, not seeing the unfinished construction, but envisioning how it would look with all of her things in place.

She did not have enough furniture, she realized, walking slowly through the thirteen-by-twenty living-room. Perhaps what she should do was rent out the house and find a one-bedroom apartment somewhere in the District.

She stood still and looked around the huge, empty house and felt the sadness rushing through her. It didn't have to be this way, she kept thinking. It didn't have to be this way at all.

It had been snowing all that week in Boston and again she had put off seeing the gynecologist. It was after one when she finally telephoned him from the Harvard campus and he told her what she already knew.

She had left the university then and gone out to walk alone across Harvard Yard, plodding through the deep snow, disregarding paths and sidewalks.

There were only a few students outside, and they were like dark shadows moving against the driving storm. Any other time she would have found the scene charming: the red brick walls, the snow, and the clean white look of the campus. She might even have stopped in the Yard to lean against a black tree and enjoy the scene, for this was when she loved Harvard the most: when it was deserted and snowbound, and seemed to be all hers.

But she didn't stop. She kept walking aimlessly through Cambridge, past Appleton Chapel, along Quincy, then onto Divinity Avenue and back to the biological research labs. It wasn't until she reached the labs that she realized she had been crying.

Inside, she went to the faculty lounge, where she washed her face and put on makeup—something she never did during the day—and only then did she return to her tiny office in the laboratory.

It was the next several hours that counted, she knew. If she could make it through the afternoon without breaking down, without becoming hysterical, she'd be all right. Then she'd be strong enough to tell Sam.

"Hey, Sara, what happened to you?" her graduate assistant called out. "We're an hour late already with the trials." He was across the room, standing in among the cages of white mice.

"It's snowing outside," she answered back, "haven't you heard?" She kept walking, carrying her notes and files in one hand, and trying to tie the belt of her white lab coat with the other.

Her office was a small cluttered room at the opposite end of the lab, hidden behind dozens of small metal cages. She made it to her desk and sank down into her seat, almost disappearing behind the stacks of reports, then closed her eyes and took several deep breaths.

"When do you want to run those benzodiazepine trials?" her assistant asked, stepping quietly into the doorway. He was holding a clipboard and jotting down notes.

"Go ahead without me, Terry," she answered slowly.

He looked up, surprised.

"Hey, are you okay?" Behind his glasses he had a small, cute face, and Sara liked to kid him that he resembled one of the grandfather rhesus monkeys they kept in the laboratory.

"I think so." She forced a bright smile. "I may be coming down with the Ethiopian flu, or whatever they're calling it this season, but I'm fine. Where are we on the schedule?"

"I ran that experiment with chlorpromazine and haloperidol this morning on section X-43."

"And what happened?" Each question forced her to pay attention, to concentrate on her work.

"What we expected. It increased the amount of the metabolites of dopamine in the mice's brains."

Sara nodded. "I guess Carlsson was right." She smiled wryly.

"Then we'll run the benzodiazepine series?"

"Sure. But not on X–47. I don't want those mice to have any trace of antipsychotic drugs in their system. We might want to test that group later with meprobamate."

She stood up quickly and a wave of nausea struck her. For a moment she thought she would vomit right there in the office.

"Sara, hey, sit down." Her assistant came around the desk and eased her back into the chair. "You're dead white," he said, sounding surprised, and pressed his palm against her forehead. "And you have a fever." Now he was worried. "Are you sure you're okay? Maybe I should call Sam and have him come get you."

"No, that's not necessary." Sara sat up and brushed his hand away. She was uncomfortably warm and she did not want to be touched. "Would you get me some water, please?"

"Sure." He was eager to help. "Don't move!" He hurried from the office, rushing through the long laboratory filled with glass cages of experimental white mice.

Sara relaxed and took deep breaths to regain her composure. It was best, she thought, that he and everyone else at Harvard think it was the flu. At least for now, at least until she decided what to do about the baby.

At six Sam telephoned.

"Still working?" He sounded annoyed.

"I'm afraid so. We ran some new benzodiazepine tests and I. . . ." She stopped apologizing. It was an unspoken agreement between them that they did not have to justify their actions, but the habit was hard to break.

"Well, I was planning to start cooking, but if you're going to be late, maybe I should just rustle up something for myself. I'm famished." He sounded put-upon.

"I'll be home within the hour." Sara glanced up at the wall clock. "Is there anything you want me to pick up at the store?"

"No, I did the shopping. Traffic is terrible. You'll probably be caught. . . ."

"I'll take the bus and leave my car here," she interrupted quickly, annoyed now at Sam's petulance. "I'll be home by seven, a quarter after at the latest." And then she hung up, her whole body trembling from the confrontation. She was overreacting, she realized, and she knew why. She was afraid of what Sam would say when she told him.

In the end she did take the car. She would tell Sam she'd wasted half an hour waiting for the bus, but the truth was she wanted the car at home in case he became impossible and she needed to get out of the house. She knew she was being paranoiac, but she couldn't help it. If she knew anything at all about him, she knew what he thought about having kids.

The traffic was as impossible as Sam had predicted and it took more than an hour to reach Watertown. Even then Sara had to leave the VW by the high school and walk up Barnard Avenue to their house.

Sara could see him reading in the livingroom as she tramped across the yard and up onto the porch. She took her time and stamped her feet on the wooden steps, hoping he would come to the front door and welcome her home, but she could see through the windows that he wasn't moving. When she couldn't stall any longer, she pushed open the door and barged inside, showering snow in the wide foyer.

"The door!" he shouted, annoyed by the sudden draft of icy wind.

He had eaten; Sara could see the dirty dishes on the end table. He had even opened a bottle of Beaujolais and was finishing it. A full glass of wine reflected the soft light from the table lamp.

She crossed the room, tracking snow on the carpet and stood over him, still wrapped up in her coat and long wool scarf, waiting for his attention. He looked up again, frowning, unsure of what she wanted. Above the scarf he could see only her eyes and cheeks, still red from the raw wind.

"Sara," he said quietly, "you're getting everything wet." He moved his long legs away from her dripping clothes. "What's wrong, anyway?"

"Sam, I'm pregnant." Damn, she thought, even her voice sounded guilty.

"Oh, shit!" he whispered. The book in his hands slipped from his fingers.

Sara didn't move. She stood above him, waiting for him to look up, waiting to see the look in his eyes, but he kept staring off. It took all her strength to keep from breaking down. Finally he asked, "How long?"

"Six weeks."

"Well, at least there's still time."

"Time for what?" Sara asked, but the cold ball of dread deep in her stomach told her she knew what he meant.

"To have an abortion," he said calmly, watching her. "I can telephone Greg at the clinic and he'll set up an appointment for tomorrow. You have a section to teach in the morning, don't you? Well, I'll have Greg arrange for an appointment in the early afternoon. It's really nothing more than a simple D and C."

Only then did he stand. He was wearing jeans and he shoved his hands into the back pockets and leaned forward from the waist as he walked. He was very tall, over six feet, but slim and rangy, and he wore large glasses that made him seem like a caricature of a professor.

Sara had never found him handsome, but she was attracted to him nevertheless, fascinated by the way his mind worked, the intensity he could generate. He was the best young researcher at the Med School. She missed the warmth and friendliness she had found with other men, but was drawn to Sam by the sheer power of his intellect.

Now she couldn't look at him. She stared down at the shabby livingroom rug.

"You don't need a child," he announced. "Not when I'm just beginning a book and you're finishing up your research grant. It will only complicate our lives."

Sara shook her head, still unsteady on her feet. She had known he would be difficult, but his cold-blooded response stunned her. It was as if he had stripped her bare before an audience.

She turned away, nauseous again, overwhelmed by his blunt reaction. He had made up their minds as if solving a household dilemma . . . should they have the porch painted? No, not till she'd finished her research and he'd outlined his book.

"What's the matter?" he finally asked, seeing the dazed look in her eyes.

"I haven't decided what to do, Sam." The answer exhausted her.

"Sara!" he reprimanded. "Let's be realistic." His voice had gained its edge once more. "We don't need a child. I have two years before tenure and even with a book there's no assurance I'll get it, not with all the cutbacks." He sat again and made a slight display of settling down once more with his book and glass of wine, showing with his deliberate behavior that the discussion was over, his decision final.

Sara managed to walk to the stuffed chair across the room and sat precariously on the arm. She did not answer, only remained perfectly still, trying moment by moment to maintain control, to let the first wave of his response sweep by. She had not realized until he said the word abortion how much she wanted the child. It was as if it were a secret she had kept from herself. The thought of an infant alive inside her made Sara feel immensely secure, as if she had discovered a great wealth.

And Sam had spoiled everything.

Sara looked up and saw him watching her. His book lay open in his lap and his face was in shadows, hidden behind the bright lamp. When he moved, the silver frame of his glasses flashed.

"I'm going to keep the baby," she said, and this time her voice was strong and resolved. Saying it out loud, declaring her intention, made it seem possible. "I want to have a child, Sam."

"Your work is more important, Sara. You don't have to prove anything by having your own kid. Just think how many children you save by your research in endocrinology, research that will suffer if you go off and be a mother." He spoke slowly, carefully, as if he had thought it all out.

"My research isn't enough," she answered softly. "I need something more. I realize that every time I go into the children's hospital. It hurts to see the children in pain—but it would be wonderful to know a child that you'd saved. To save him with your own hands, instead of with a drug you tested one day in the lab. I need to share my life—with you, with patients, with a child of my own. Don't you understand?"

Tears blurred her vision but she could see he was coolly shaking his head. He did not need that kind of feedback, that kind of human contact and love. His research, his laboratory work was enough; individual patients would only drain him and tie him down. She had always known there was this fundamental difference between them, but before it had not mattered, and now it did.

"Unlike you, I don't want to have a child," he answered, disregarding her plea. He was angry, and when he sat forward, moving his head into the bright light, the reflection off his glasses made him look sinister.

"Sara, you're being irrational. I'm not prepared to marry you. It's not a decision I've had time to process."

"I'm not asking you to marry me." She stood and took off her coat. She would not need to flee the house. She knew exactly what she had to do.

"We'll talk about this later," he announced.

She went to the hall closet and hung up her coat. "I've made up my mind, Sam. I'm having it."

He threw the book across the width of the room. He hadn't aimed at her, but the heavy textbook flew right past, smashing against the front door.

"We're not having any goddamn kid," he shouted. He was out of the chair, standing, holding onto his rage with the thin edge of self-control. He did not like confrontations, Sara knew; she had learned how to adjust her remarks, to keep quiet when he became upset, but now walking back into the livingroom, facing him again, she was resolved in her decision.

"Sam, I'm having this baby."

"I'll leave you, Sara."

She managed to shrug. "I'm sorry, Sam. I don't want you to leave me." She kept her eyes on him, kept searching his thin face for some explanation, a reason for this hostility, and then his face swam out of focus as more tears flooded her. She was trembling, shaking violently from his abuse. It was all over, she realized.

"Sam," she pleaded, "please understand."

He hesitated for a moment, as if to contemplate once more his decision. Then he walked past her and out of the room.

A week later, while crossing Mount Auburn Street on her way to lunch at Ferdinand's, Sara slipped on the icy street and miscarried.

Sara took one long look around her new house and was turning to leave for the picnic when a fine spray of dirt filtered down from the temporary plank ceiling on the second floor.

"Oh, God!" she swore, moving quickly aside and ducking her head to shake off the construction dirt from her hair and shoulders. She had no business, she now saw, wandering through the empty house.

A plank overhead moved again, stopped and more dirt showered the room. A fist of fear flew up Sara's throat and she caught her breath.

"Who is it?" Sara shouted.

Another plank moved and more dust and construction dirt seeped down from between the cracks. No one answered.

Whoever it was upstairs was not walking, only stepping back and forth. The same two planks moved again.

Sara rushed to the front door, but stopped before stepping into the sun. It was her house; she would not be chased off.

At the first step of the stairs she halted and standing on her tiptoes tried to see through the loose boards into the second floor. The squeaking came from the area that would be her dressing room and walk-in closet; she couldn't see into that far corner of the second floor.

Oh, God, she thought, it must be some animal. She leaned against the wall and breathed deeply. The tension had taken her breath away. She should just leave. Whatever it was would go or the carpenters would chase it into the fields on Monday morning.

Yet she hesitated. She was frightened and that angered her. Whenever she found such a weakness in herself, she fought back.

On the first floor she found a short piece of two-by-two and went back upstairs, thumping the steps as she walked, hoping to scare it out of the house before she reached the second floor. At the top of the stairs she stopped once more and shouted, "You better watch out—I'm coming up," then giggled at the absurdity of what she was doing.

She stepped into the upstairs hallway, holding the length of lumber like a club. The walls had been finished with plasterboard and the rooms were closed off; she had to peep around an open doorway to see into the dressing room. It was empty, except for a stack of lumber that had been left behind, and in one corner a small workhorse.

Then she heard it, inside the walk-in closet. She stood quietly, listening to the steady creaking of the floor boards. It would not be frightened out; she would have to go into the closet and chase it away.

Sara went into the room, keeping her distance from the closet, giving herself room in case it charged at her. She was very scared now and the lumber trembled in her hands. She would see what it was before approaching.

It couldn't be anything too big, she told herself. There were no brown bears or bobcats this close to Washington. At worst, it would be a beaver or muskrat from the river. But it was neither. Sara sighed thankfully and let her arm drop.

Sara recognized the child. It was the girl she had seen earlier in the barn, Bruce Delp's daughter. The girl had her back to the opening of the closet and was sitting on the rough planks, her legs pulled up and her arms wrapped tightly around them, as if she were in a fetal position. The child did not look up at her, just kept rocking back and forth in a slow, steady cadence.

Sara thought briefly of just leaving. The child would be all right; obviously her parents let her run wild in the fields. But Sara could not walk away. She had a responsibility, as a woman and as a doctor. She set aside the wooden stick and stepped inside the closet, moving carefully so as not to surprise the girl.

"Hello, Cindy," she said, but the girl did not respond.

Sara took a few more steps forward, stopping in front of the child. There was very little light in the closet, but she could see the girl well enough.

She was more beautiful than Sara had realized, and it was not a child's beauty. This girl had grown out of her fresh, innocent look, and her fair face was serene and reserved. She had the look of a woman in her twenties, a look that was mysterious and romantic, as if she knew certain secrets. It was not the face of a child, but of someone with a past.

Sara knelt down in front of the girl and said softly, "Cindy?"

There was no response. Sara watched closely to see if the child registered her presence, but the girl still swayed back and forth, her large round eyes staring blindly at the dark, bare wall of the closet.

Sara could smell the child's body odor and it shocked her. The girl needed to be washed. Her dress was soiled and her body stank of sweat and barnyard filth. The child had been playing with pigs. Where was her mother? Sara was immediately enraged that the girl was not better cared for. Still, this was rural Virginia. What more could she expect?

"Cindy?" She kept her voice soft, but even that, she knew, was an intrusion into the secret, silent world of this child.

The young girl stopped her gentle swaying and very slowly turned toward Sara. There was no fear on her face. Sara reached out and touched the child's shoulder and the girl scuttled away on all fours and sat hunched over, her back to the corner, her black eyes fixed on Sara. She was angry now. Her breath came quickly, in thin, rapid puffs.

It was a mistake to have touched her. She had not built up enough trust with Cindy, and now Sara was disappointed with herself for not being attuned to the child's emotional condition.

"Cindy, I won't hurt you," Sara began once more. "I think we should go home. Your mother will be looking for you." Sara was still kneeling on the floor though her knees hurt from the hard wood.

In the dark corner of the closet the child had curled herself up again, her long, thin arms wrapped around her legs. She stared mindlessly ahead.

"I think we should go home to the farm house, Cindy. Your mother and father will be looking for you. I'll go with you; you won't have to go home alone. I'm going to stand up and walk toward you. I'll help you stand."

Cindy did not respond. She continued to rock gently back and forth, her eyes unfocused.

Sara knew she towered over the girl, that in the small closet her size was threatening, but there was nothing else to do. She moved slowly forward, talking softly as she walked, watching the girl's eyes.

She came within two feet of the crouched child and still the girl did not react, but then Sara's body blocked Cindy's view, the bright space of light from the outside room, and Cindy screeched and, bolting from the floor in one smooth violent motion, struck Sara with her arms as she passed. Her forearm caught Sara in the stomach and doubled her; Sara cried out from the unexpected blow, and the girl was out of the closet and the room, running wildly.

Sara could hear her footsteps on the stairs, then across the first floor and out of the house. She slid to the floor gasping for breath. She would be all right in a few minutes; the girl had not hurt her. And it was her own fault. She should have gone for help. The child was ill, seriously ill, and she had been stupid to become involved so cavalierly.

Sara knew better. She always knew better, but that did not stop her from repeating the same mistake. It had happened before. It would happen again. She could not keep herself away from anyone who was suffering or in pain. Others saw it as her special strength, but she recognized it for what it really was, her greatest failing.

two

Kevin Volt stood before the fireplace in his new family room and rocked back and forth, as if adjusting his weight to the gentle roll of a ship.

His left hand was in the deep pocket of his gray flannel slacks and his right hand was around a tall glass of Perrier water and ice. While he talked, he gestured with his right hand, clicking the ice against the thick glass. He liked the sound the ice made and he gestured more than was necessary, feeling that the sound effects added importance to what he was saying. He was talking to his dinner guests, telling them how he had improved his new house, and he had been talking for a straight fifteen minutes.

"This model is called Locust Grove. It's styled after one built during the colonial period. The original house was occupied by Major Samuel Wade Magruder. I've made some changes, naturally. What would have been a guest room upstairs I've turned into a nursery for the baby, and I've made a small workshop in the basement.''

Kevin was uncomfortable standing with his back so close to the fireplace. The blazing fire was too hot against his legs but still he did not move. He could see himself in the hall mirror and he knew he looked commanding and attractive. Peggy had shaved his head that morning and, in the soft glow of the fireplace, his scalp reflected golden in the mirror.

Distracted by his reflection, he lost the point of his story. He stopped to sip his Perrier and then abruptly said, ''Neil, what about your place?''

''It's the Portsmouth,'' Neil Cohoe replied, speaking too forcefully, as if he'd been called on when he wasn't paying attention. ''That's the split-level colonial.''

''Four bedrooms, right?''

Neil nodded, sipping his drink.

''Do you have plans for the other three?'' Kevin kept grinning and glancing back and forth between Neil and Marcia Fleming, who finally stared down at her hands, embarrassed.

''What's your house, Marcia?'' he asked next.

''The Rambler.'' She jerked up her head and answered his question coolly, establishing some distance between them. Then she smiled as a compromise. She had brilliant, perfectly white teeth, brown eyes the color of wet suede, and olive dark skin.

''That's the two-bedroom ranch house, isn't it?'' He raised his chin, as if making a point.

''Yes.'' Her smile was gone.

''Little tight for you and the boy, right?'' He sipped his Perrier as if camouflaging the question.

''We don't need much space.'' The smile returned like a cold sunrise.

''Well, in that case, why don't you move in with Neil?'' Volt continued relentlessly. ''A single guy like him must be rattling around in all those rooms.'' He laughed aloud and alone. Neil and Marcia, on the sofa, glanced at each other without comment, and Sara Marks, sitting in a deep leather armchair, looked away, toward a vague, empty mid-distance in the long family room. Peggy sighed, exhausted from tension. And then the baby cried, and she was on her feet immediately.

"We have to do lots of adjusting because of Amy." She smiled apologetically, but her eyes flashed with pride. "We'll eat as soon as I look at her."

"May I come with you, Peggy?" Marcia Fleming quickly asked.

"Yes, of course. Sara?"

"I'd love to see the baby." Sara was out of her chair, eager to get away from Kevin Volt.

"We'll be back in a few minutes," Peggy said, her face flushed from the heat.

Her anger toward him built quickly, racing through her like a speeding ball of flame. By the time she reached the second floor, she was clenching her teeth to keep from screaming.

"Are you okay, Peggy?" Sara whispered, touching Peggy's arm reassuringly.

"I'm fine, Sara; It's only the baby, I guess. I get nervous, you know, when Amy cries." She managed a small laugh as she went down the dark hall toward the nursery. The soft night light had been left on and the room was filled with gloom.

Peggy flipped on the overhead light and went to the crib in the far corner. The room smelled of a child, of soiled diapers and baby powder. It was a smell Peggy had come to love.

She lifted the infant carefully from the crib and cuddled Amy to her, patting the baby and whispering softly. The baby's face was red and wet with tears.

"She's really wonderful," Peggy said, turning to face Sara and Marcia. "She's asleep all the time, except when I need to feed her."

"Then everything is okay with you?" Sara asked. It was the first time the women had been by themselves all evening.

Peggy shrugged.

"And what about Kevin?"

Peggy shook her head and immediately tears rushed to her eyes.

"I'm sorry." Sara stepped closer and briefly hugged Peggy and the child. The baby had quieted, but now all of them shared a silent, muffled moment of crying.

"It will be all right," Sara whispered, trying to reassure her.

Peggy pulled away. Amy was again fast asleep, and Peggy set her gently on the mattress, then stood and sighed.

"No, it won't be all right," she answered, still looking down at her child. "I was going to leave Kevin after Amy was born. I didn't know what I was thinking; I mean, where would we go? What would we live on?" She turned and stared at them, searching the women's faces, as if they had the answer.

"I'm trapped here in this house, this phoney country village, trapped here in Virginia until Amy is old enough for me to leave her with someone. But then, I don't know. Where will I get a job? I'm going to be two years out of the job market. And you know how Washington works. You have to know someone to get a job. I don't know anyone. Everyone is Kevin's friend, not mine."

"Peggy, you're just suffering from postpartum depression. You'll be fine in another few weeks," said Marcia.

"No, I won't," Peggy answered back. She knew what was wrong with her life.

Her husband and Neil Cohoe had come upstairs. She could hear Kevin at the top of the landing, explaining in detail what changes he had made in the construction model. He was more involved in this new house than with their child.

"We better leave," Peggy whispered. "I want to shut the nursery door before he wakes Amy."

Kevin and Neil were in the front bedroom now, the master bedroom of the house. For the last several weeks Peggy had not slept with her husband. Instead she had moved into the guest room, telling Kevin she wanted to be nearer the baby. It was a lie. She could no longer bring herself to be in the same bed with him, to be close enough to smell his body.

"Is there anything I can do to help with dinner?" Sara offered. She wanted to help Peggy, to see her through this terrible time.

"No, thank you. We're just having veal stew with red wine. It's really quite simple to make. Have you ever tried it?" She started to talk again in a surge of forced enthusiasm; any kind of conversation to keep her mind off Kevin.

She led the way down the back stairs to the kitchen. She was concentrating on dinner now, moving back and forth between the stove and the butcher block table. Marcia and Sara wanted to help, if only to slice the warm bread fresh from the oven, but Peggy would not let them.

Peggy's behavior frightened Sara. She was manic, rushing around the kitchen, talking incessantly. The woman was seriously ill. Sara could see it in the tension on her face, in the odd look in her blue eyes.

"There!" Peggy stepped back from the bowl of veal stew. "It's done." She was perspiring from her effort, from the rush of talking and work.

"Would you two please put this on the diningroom table for me?" Peggy forced a quick smile. "I'm going to run upstairs to change my clothes—I just can't sit down to dinner feeling so sweaty and overheated." Her words came all in a rush as she turned abruptly and almost ran from the kitchen.

Upstairs Peggy called Kevin and Neil, then went back to the guest room and locked the door behind her. Over the last few days she had moved all her clothes and toilet items there, separating her private life from Kevin's. There was a bathroom adjoining the guest room, and she let Kevin have the big one off the master bedroom. This room and the nursery were her sanctuaries. Kevin didn't even venture down the hall any more.

Peggy took off her blouse and sprayed on deodorant and perfume. She would have liked to take a bath. To just forget about Kevin's guests downstairs and soak. The baby suddenly began to stir in her crib. Peggy had become so accustomed to the child's sound that even when she was asleep Amy's slightest noise would wake her.

She went through the bedroom and into the dark nursery, her footsteps softened by the deep carpet, to where the small crib was situated away from the windows and against the inside bedroom wall.

It was not a real baby crib, but part of a hayrack that Kevin had bought from the old barn. He had wanted it for his workshop, but Peggy had taken it for the baby. With the farmer's help, she had cut the rack down into a crib and then packed the high sides with quilts.

Peggy bent over and looked closely at her daughter. The child seemed so vulnerable when asleep, her eyes squeezed shut, her delicate fingers clutching the air above her. She lay on her stomach, a tiny bundle wrapped snugly in her pajamas.

Peggy placed her open palm before Amy's mouth and felt the puff of breath, warm against her skin. The helplessness of the infant, Amy's total dependence on her, frightened Peggy. Whatever happened to her now, she was no longer alone. She could leave Kevin, but not Amy. Amy had changed her life irrevocably.

She had to go. She had already been upstairs fifteen minutes, and Kevin would soon be summoning her as if she were an errant child. Peggy sighed and, calling up her reserves of willpower, went downstairs to have the last normal meal of her life. It was almost ten o'clock and one-month-old Amy Volt had less than an hour to live.

Amy slept peacefully, her mind a white cloud of unconsciousness. She knew nothing beyond a few simple sensations, the gratification and warmth of being cuddled, the hours of peaceful sleep. She was fed and changed and lay softly in her bed. The world beyond her crib was a fog of the unknown. She knew only the smells and touches of the one woman in her life.

Amy woke abruptly. Her blue eyes were not yet able to focus, nor did she see the shadow of the figure, or understand the threat to her life. She felt only the presence of a strange sensation and, fearing it, cried out instantly. But her voice was muffled and her tiny body made immediately a victim. In a moment she was unconscious. She gasped for air as her body shook and stretched out rigid in the hayrack crib. A small bubble of blood broke in her nostril and then her short life was consumed by incomprehensible pain. It ripped like an electric bolt through her mind and destroyed her brain.

Her tiny arms and legs jerked and stiffened and her eyelids popped open, as if she were only a child's toy doll. Peggy found her rammed against the crib's high quilted side, her eyes frozen open and her round, pink-cheeked face marked with her violent death.

three

"Mrs. Volt, I know this is a terrible time for you, but please understand we have to ask certain questions." The young Virginia detective spoke carefully. He had never before handled a child's death and it was all very new to him, like an exercise in his police training course.

Peggy did not respond. She sat in the livingroom chair, staring ahead. She seemed to be shrinking away, disappearing into the chair. He wondered if he should stop his questioning for the moment, but then he asked, "At what time did you find the baby?"

"Amy! Her name is Amy!" Peggy shouted.

"Easy, darling." Kevin came over and sat on the arm of her chair, but when he tried to put his arm around her, she brushed his hand aside.

Joe Santucci watched them both, his eyes jumping back and forth from the husband to the wife. There was trouble here, he saw, but it might be just the reaction to the baby's death. He had to be careful; he couldn't let his imagination take over. Still, the palms of his hands were sweaty and that was always a good sign. He was getting close to some answers.

"Mrs. Volt, would you mind telling me how you found Amy?" He tried again, this time lowering his voice, keeping her calm. Interrogating her the way he had been taught.

"We were having dinner," she began, whispering her reply. "We were having dinner . . . we had just sat down, and I had this strange feeling that something was wrong with Amy." There were tears in her eyes. She had been crying continually since the child was discovered.

"Did you move Amy?" the detective asked. He was matching her soft voice, listening to her response, and the room had quieted down. There were others present. The Volts' dinner guests, several policemen, the crime lab people from Alexandria, and a reporter from *The Washington Post*.

"She was on her side," Peggy Volt answered slowly, ". . . as if she were sleeping on her side. But she couldn't: She wasn't able to turn over; she was too young." Peggy looked up and stared at the detective.

She knew now, he realized, and there was terror in her eyes. The look on her face was so frightening that he glanced at his notes to break her hold on him.

"You said you left the table around ten o'clock and went upstairs. Could you be more precise on the time?"

She was shaking her head, unable to continue.

"Officer, how much longer are we going to be subjected to these questions?" Kevin Volt stood, as if to make his objection more forceful. "You can see my wife's condition. This has been a terrible, terrible thing. . . ."

Santucci did not immediately respond. He had been watching Volt, and the husband's behavior had been peculiar. In the midst of the tragedy, when his wife was hysterical with grief, Volt had appeared to physically withdraw from her. It was as if this had happened to someone else's family and he was not involved.

"They killed my baby," Peggy whispered. She kept staring ahead, not seeing anything, only remembering how Amy had looked in the crib, her face pressed against the quilting. She could not breathe; she wasn't able to move herself. And she hadn't been dead for long. The body was still warm when she lifted Amy from the deep hayrack. For just a moment, Peggy thought everything was all right, and then Amy's tiny head flopped over and the blood ran out of her nose.

"We're going to request an autopsy," Santucci continued, still speaking softly, addressing himself to the wife. "If what you say is correct, we might have a homicide here."

"Wait a minute! Wait a goddamned minute!" Kevin Volt moved toward the detective. "You're not doing an autopsy on that baby. No one killed my child. What are you talking about?" He glanced at the other police officers, as if trying to gain support, and then focused on Neil Cohoe. "Tell them, Neil. We were together all evening. Tell this cop!"

"Mr. Volt, would you please sit down?" Santucci asked.

"This is my house, Lieutenant. Don't go telling me what to do!"

Two of the uniformed policemen at the doorway straightened up, but the detective motioned them to be still. Then he looked up at the husband towering over his chair.

Volt was not a big man, but he had the slight, compact body of a natural welterweight. Santucci wondered what Volt did for a living, and why was he in such fine physical shape. The army, he thought; the man had the look of the military.

"I apologize, Mr. Volt. Yes, this is your home, but I am conducting a police investigation, and it's possible your daughter was murdered."

"We were the only ones in this house!" Kevin Volt

shouted. He was leaning over the detective. "Are you accusing me of murdering my own child?" Volt was almost out of control. His shaven scalp was flushed with excitement, the blood vessels standing out and visible.

The detective was a big man, a former Virginia Tech basketball player, and his body filled the leather chair. He said quietly to Volt, "It is possible, perhaps likely, your daughter died of natural causes. Or at least the causes surrounding a crib death. I don't know the answer to that question, and that is why an autopsy is necessary. We have to find out why she died. But I want you to know it is possible your daughter was killed."

"By whom?" Volt shouted.

"By the person who broke the glass door on the basement entrance and tracked mud across the floor and up your kitchen steps." Santucci stopped to let his statement register. The husband was unprepared for that reply and it surprised him. He stepped away from the detective, unsteady on his feet as he turned, confused by the sudden news.

"Here, Kevin, sit down for a moment." Neil Cohoe moved to make room for Volt on the couch. He took him by the elbow and made him sit, then he asked the detective. "You mean someone broke in here last night while we were eating and killed the baby?" He sounded relieved, as if any suspicion of him and the others was over.

"Please be quiet, Mr. Cohoe, and we'll straighten everything out in a few minutes. I just have a couple more questions." Santucci smiled. For the time being, he would be nice to all of them.

In the kitchen Tom Dine stretched. He had been leaning over, looking through the alcove into the crowded livingroom, watching Joe Santucci question the five people. It had been a long night for him, too, and he was tired.

Santucci had telephoned after midnight, calling to say

he had a murder at the new village development on the Potomac. For two months Dine had been following Santucci, researching how a young detective learned his job. It was to be a series of articles for the *Post*, and he had everything he needed except a murder case, a focal point around which to build his story. Now he had it—the murder of a one-month-old child. It was exactly what he needed to make his series dramatic and the realization nauseated him.

Earlier that night, upstairs in the nursery, Joe had pulled back the tiny blanket and showed him the child, saying. "I thought it might just be a crib death, you know, but see the neck? It looks twisted. I think someone tried to twist the kid's goddamned head off."

"Jesus Christ!" Tom turned his face away. He had a brief image of someone creeping through the dark room and grabbing the helpless baby, muffling her mouth and strangling her with the ease of an adult's strength.

"One of them?" he asked. He glanced back at the child. She made such a tiny mound at the bottom of the crib.

"No, not them. There's muddy tracks all over the basement floor, and the back door has been jimmied. It seems someone came into the house and snuck upstairs while they were all having dinner."

Tom Dine took out his notebook and jotted down details of the nursery. It was an odd-shaped crib, and it took him a moment to realize what it really was, a hayrack cut down to a child's size.

"Look, Tom, you got to be careful about what you write. It's gonna cause me trouble, you know, if we go to court and too much of this case is in print. Whoever it is will say he couldn't get a fair trial."

"I understand. And I appreciate that you're letting me get this close to a case. I'll protect you, I promise. But you've got to remember. This is a hot ticket."

Joe Santucci nodded and looked satisfied. He wanted

Dine to do the story about him. If handled carefully, it could help his career, but he still had to keep the reporter under control.

"Okay, let's go interview these dinner guests. It's shitty, ain't it, to have a kid killed while you're sitting at the dinner table? I don't know why this Volt woman isn't out of her fuckin' mind."

Santucci led the other police officers out of the nursery and down the hallway to the stairs. The detective was too big for the house. He had to stoop because of the low ceiling, and his frame darkened the passageway, like a huge rock closing off the light at the end of the tunnel.

Tom Dine hung back. The crime lab people were still working in the nursery, and the police ambulance had arrived to take away the body. He stepped aside to let them into the room, but he did not want to go downstairs right away. This would be the last time he'd be upstairs in the Volt house and he wanted to see how they lived their private lives.

He crossed the hall and looked into one of the bedrooms. There were women's clothes in the closet, perfume and a jewelry box on the dresser. The room had twin beds, but only one was being used; the sheets were wrinkled and the bed was carelessly made.

Tom turned and went to the front of the house and into the master bedroom. It was twice the size of the other rooms, and had its own bathroom and dressing area. The room was lovely, painted in soft pastel colors and carpeted wall-to-wall with a deep brown rug.

Tom was envious. It was the kind of place he'd like to have if he could ever afford to get out of his city apartment. The bedroom had a fireplace and a fire had been lit earlier in the evening. Now only a small pile of embers glowed in the dark, and the large room was lit softly by the lamps of the village streets.

Tom thought of how perfect these people's lives had

been: a new house in the country, a new child. Then the sight of the infant came back to him. He couldn't get over her small, perfect hand, the miniature fingers squeezed into a tiny fist.

The light was on in the bathroom and he crossed to it through the dressing room. The police had probably left it on when they searched the house, and he wanted to see what they had seen, however insignificant.

It was a large bathroom, bright with mirrors and lights. The room had two sinks, and both a glass shower stall and a deep, wide tub. Tom stepped inside and heard his own footsteps for the first time, unmuffled by the deep rugs that covered all the other floorboards.

Looking around, he was impressed by the orderliness of the bathroom. Above one sink were two bottles of aftershave lotion, shaving cream, sticks of deodorant, Q-tips, mouth wash, talcum powder, and a brown leather manicure set.

The articles almost seemed coordinated, each of the colors, shapes, and shades complementing the others. Compared to the jumble of his own medicine cabinet, this one seemed as carefully composed as a still life by Vermeer. A neat bathroom was a woman's touch, he thought—but none of these toilet articles were for a woman.

Peggy Volt did not use this bathroom, he suddenly realized. Her husband used it alone, and the bottles and jars were arranged with a military precision. The Volts did not share a bedroom, nor did they sleep together. The wife, he now understood, slept in the back of the house, next to the nursery, and for some reason that fact struck him as important. Flipping off the bathroom light, he went downstairs to hear Joe Santucci interrogate the guests.

And in his haste he never saw the girl crouched into the tight corner of the shower stall. Her long legs were drawn up tightly, and her beautiful, dark eyes were wide open. A truly exquisite child who stared blankly ahead as if she were looking toward and listening to some faraway world.

In his reporter's notebook, Tom Dine scribbled: "Peggy Volt was too small for the leather chair. She sank into the deep cushions like a weight. In the crowded, intense room, she was lost. The investigation left her untouched, as if it were being conducted in some foreign language."

Tom glanced once more at Doctor Sara Marks. All night he had kept watching her, all the while pretending to be intent on the dynamics of the investigation. He had rarely seen a woman so beautiful. Her blond hair swept to her shoulders in thick, cascading curls, and her wide, flashing eyes were as bright as blue Limoges. But her mouth captivated him. It was wide and wet-lipped, and when she smiled, even sadly, the smile crossed her face like a silent explosion, leaving him stunned by his awkward longing.

Tom flipped his notebook closed, unable to concentrate. Santucci was finishing, giving instructions to the dinner guests. He stood and again his height and build dwarfed the room.

Men built like Santucci did not threaten Tom. He was six feet tall himself, but his body was stocky and square, and it gave him the appearance of a shorter man. And he looked tough as well. His face was flat and blunt, like a punk fighter's. His nose was too thick and his mouth too large, but his smile and gray eyes softened his look. He seemed younger when he smiled. The smile disarmed people and made them trust him. He had learned to use his smile to get ahead on his job and with women. He used it the way other people used family money.

There was something else that made Tom attractive to women, a certain suggestion of danger. He was not sure why, but women said he frightened them. "There's something low-class and sleazy about you," one lover had said. "It implies you're up to no good. I think you're going to take advantage of me." Then she had shrugged and confessed, "But I like it. I know what to expect from you."

Tom slipped his notebook into his jacket pocket and went out of the house, pausing on the front stoop in the cold morning. He stood a moment looking across the cul-de-sac. Lights were on in several houses. He saw people at the front windows, staring across the street.

What a terrible thing to happen in a neighborhood. Once they learned of the death, all of them would be frightened—for themselves and their children. He couldn't blame anyone. Most of them were strangers to each other. And half of the houses were still under construction. He wondered what this bizarre baby murder would do to the real estate value.

The Washington Post had called the new people arriving to fill government positions the best and the brightest since the Kennedy years. A group of these political types had purchased the land and built the co-op that they called Renaissance Village. It was a novel undertaking and the smartest money in Washington thought it would succeed.

Joe Santucci came out through the front door, buttoning his raincoat as he walked. He shuddered at the sudden cold of the morning, then mumbled, "What a fuckin' way to make a living." He glanced at Tom and asked, "You don't need a lift, do you?"

Tom shook his head. "I'm parked down the street." They moved off the stoop, following the curving sidewalk. The lawn was still only piles of dirt. The Volts hadn't yet gotten around to planting grass, Tom Dine thought, and already they had lost their first kid.

"What will you do about this murder?" Santucci asked.

"File it. A baby has been murdered in the new

Renaissance Village. It's a front-page story, Joe," Tom added as a warning. He didn't want Santucci trying to suppress the crime.

"We're not positive it's murder."

"Joe, you showed me the baby, the way her neck had been twisted like a pretzel."

"There's got to be an autopsy. Whenever you have a death like this, you gotta do one. Don't write anything until I get the coroner's report. It could be, you know, accidental."

Tom stopped on the sidewalk. "What are you trying to say, Joe?" He watched the young detective, watching to see if this was a ploy to put him off the story.

"It's Volt," Santucci answered, speaking softly, though they were standing by themselves on the empty sidewalk. "I just got a call from the office. Volt's a spook. The FBI and the CIA are both getting involved, you know, just in case."

"What does that mean, just in case?"

"In case there're any international implications."

Tom smiled wryly and asked, "Do you think the Russians are killing our kids? Is that it, Joe?"

Santucci answered quickly, earnestly. "This Volt, he's pretty big stuff in the CIA, and they want to make damn sure the kid didn't die mysteriously."

"She did die mysteriously, Joe. Some goddamned pervert twisted her neck."

"Okay! Okay!" Santucci motioned Tom to be calm. "Look at this from my position. If they find out in Alexandria that you're privy to this investigation, my ass is grass."

"Joe, you're not going to keep this murder quiet." He nodded toward the houses in the subdivision. "Those people are going to find out about it fast, if they don't know already." He shook his head. "It's bad enough that the baby was strangled, but do you think it's going to be less frightening once they hear the CIA thinks it's a Ruskie?"

"This isn't your usual beat, Tom. Most of these people are federal. They've been overseas with the State Department. They work at the Smithsonian and at the White House. I know this area; these people are in my district." He said it proudly, as if he could count on them to keep the story quiet.

Tom unlocked the door to the Volvo, but before he stepped into the driver's seat, he turned and answered Santucci.

"These people are also human, Joe, and a one-month-old baby has been killed. Now I guess most of these couples have children of their own, and they're going to want to know who killed Amy Volt and why.

"And they're going to want to know damned fast." The reporter shook his head. He did not smile and his face looked tough again. "It doesn't matter whether they work in the White House or the CIA. A baby has been killed by some lunatic. It doesn't matter if he's a mental case or a Russian infiltrator. These parents want him caught before he kills their kids.

"And that's your problem, Joe." Tom smiled so his small lecture would not seem too pedantic. "You're the Man." Then he slipped into his car and nodded goodbye to the detective.

four

Sara Marks left the Volt house through the kitchen door, cutting across the yard and walking up the hillside to her house on Petrarch Court. She had not realized it was daylight until she stepped outside and saw the cold, gray dawn. She would go home, she decided, shower and go to work. This was not the time to stay home and obsess about the murder. She had to stay busy, to keep her mind off Peggy Volt and the death of her child.

She had left her front door unlocked—this was not Washington or Boston, after all—and when she came through the door she realized immediately that something was wrong, that someone was already inside the house.

The throw rug in the front hall had been pulled to one side and she could see mud on the waxed hardwood floor. Someone had walked into the house and through the livingroom toward the kitchen. And then she remembered what the detective had said, they had found a muddy trail of footprints on the Volts' basement floor.

She left the front door open behind her and moved inside, glancing into the livingroom on her right to see if anyone was there, but the room was empty.

"Who's there?" she called out. Her voice was tense, and she had begun to shiver from her own fear.

There was no answer. She stood quietly, listening for any sound, and then she thought she heard a single soft footstep from the kitchen. Her heart jumped and left her breathless.

"Who is it?" she demanded. She was almost hysterical, and her voice screeched in the silent house. If someone did attack, she could not defend herself; she would be too frightened even to run through the open door.

She glanced out front. There was no traffic on the cul-de-sac. A few of the houses on Petrarch Court were occupied, but no one was up this early. She could, however, run back to the Volt house. Still, she did not move. It was her house and she would not be driven from it. Her pride made her daring and she carefully pulled an ancient shillelagh, a gift from an old boyfriend on a Boston St. Patrick's Day, from the tall ceramic stand that held her umbrellas, and went into the diningroom. There were more muddy tracks on the creamy white rug.

The door into the kitchen was open. She saw a sliver of the large room, a corner of the butcher block table, the copper stove, and the back door. The door was open. She saw a wedge of cloudy sky and felt the draft whipping through the house.

She relaxed some and sighed, thinking: he's gone. She was safe. It was all right. She sighed again. The tension had left her weak. She went to the front door and locked it, then put away the shillelagh. What was she doing with that? she thought. She could never have hit anyone.

Sara returned to the dining room and, taking out the vacuum cleaner, worked it quickly over the rug. The mud had dried and it cleaned away easily. Then she put away the vacuum and locked the kitchen door, pausing a moment to see that everything was in place.

The kitchen was her favorite room in the new house. She had had the builder modify the model design so the breakfast nook was open to the rest of the kitchen. As a result, people congregated there. She liked that. When she had a dinner party, or neighbors came over just for a drink and crowded into the kitchen, it gave her a sense of family. She was an only child and a crowded kitchen, for some psychological reason, satisfied her notion of what a family was.

Sara began to strip off her clothes as she went upstairs to get ready for work. She was late, and if she didn't rush through her shower, she'd be caught in the long lines of traffic on the Beltway. She was not sure yet whether it was worth living so far from the city. It would have been much simpler to have bought a place in Bethesda. Then she could have walked to work.

Once more she had doubts about her job at NIH. Perhaps it had been a mistake to leave Boston, to walk away from Sam and come to Washington. She sank down at the end of the queen-size bed and slipped off her shoes. Well, it was too late now. She had made a commitment to the others and had invested her savings. She couldn't afford to leave, even if she wanted to.

She had never owned anything before in her life. In college and medical school, and even when she was working at Harvard and living with Sam, her apartment had never had any good furniture. She had owned only secondhand stuff and castoffs from her parents' old farm house.

Now her house was elaborately decorated, like a feature in *Better Homes and Gardens*, and she was self-aware enough to know why her style had suddenly changed. It was her way of separating herself from Sam and their life together. Their ascetic lifestyle. It was silly, she realized. She was only trying to get even with him in some crazy way. To show that she could live independently from him. And this was what she had gotten herself into! She shook her head at her own foolishness, then threw herself into her stretching exercises, doing her deep knee bends, sit-ups, and a half dozen others to tighten her stomach muscles.

Exhausted and out of breath, she got up and walked into the bathroom. Why was she thinking of Sam, she scolded herself, when it only made her feel miserable? It was the reporter at the Volt house, she realized suddenly, who had triggered her recollection. But why? He and Sam were not alike. Sam was thin and tall and tweedy, as fastidious as she was.

The reporter was different. He had seemed intense. And too muscular. And then she realized what it was about him that reminded her of Sam. It was how he had kept watching her all night, that look of adoration, a surrender to her beauty. Perhaps it should have thrilled her, but it did not. She was frightened by men who seemed so taken by her, who succumbed so quickly. Frightened because she had come to realize such sudden passion was not to be trusted. That it meant men loved her beauty, and not herself, and that their commitment to her was shallow and misdirected.

She slipped her hand under her long hair and piled it on her head, pinned it, and pulled on a bright yellow shower cap. Well, she wouldn't let it happen again. She would keep that reporter out of her life. She could keep out the world, and thinking that reassuring thought, she opened the frosted shower door and screamed when she saw the child crouched in the tight corner of the small stall.

Sara's fright was only momentary. Recovering from the surprise, she grabbed the white terry-cloth bathrobe off the door and, pulling it on, went back into the bedroom to telephone the child's parents.

"Oh, thank God!" Mrs. Delp exclaimed, then shouted to her husband, telling him that Cindy had been found. "Is she all right?" she shouted at Sara.

"Yes, I believe so." Sara looked up to see the child standing in the doorway. She was staring at Sara, but her eyes were unfocused. Sara lowered her voice and whispered, "Would you please come immediately?"

"Bruce is coming, Miss Marks. We've been half-crazy, looking for her. She's been gone all night, and then this baby getting killed . . ." Mrs. Delp's voice broke and Sara said quickly, "She is all right. She is right here with me."

Mrs. Delp quieted down and Sara hung up. Then she said to the child, "Cindy, it's all right. You can come into the room."

The child stepped forward. Her head was cocked, as if she was listening to someone far away, and she began to slowly walk in a tight circle, standing on her tiptoes. Sara saw then that Cindy was barefoot, and that her feet were muddy with the red clay dirt of the housing excavation, and wet from the shower stall. She was tracking mud across the rug, as she had done downstairs.

"Cindy, please," Sara said, going to her. The child was dirty and unkempt. If nothing else, Sara decided, she would clean her up before her father came. But at the first touch of her hand Cindy flailed out with her arms, as she had done the last time, but now Sara caught her arms by the wrists and held them.

The girl was stronger than Sara had expected, and she knew from the hospital that distraught people were often capable of unusual strength. Still she held the struggling child, whispering calmly, "I won't hurt you, Cindy. I am your friend."

The girl had twisted around in their struggle so now Sara held her from behind in a bear hug. It was easier to contain her that way, but Sara could hardly stand it. The girl smelled of barnyard filth. Sara turned her head away and gagged. God, she thought, how did these people live?

Sara could feel Cindy tiring and finally giving up. The little girl sank against her, then slipped to the floor and lay in a heap on the soft creamy bedroom rug.

Sara let go of the girl's arms and Cindy curled quickly into the tight fetal position that Sara was coming to recognize as her favorite pose. Her blank black eyes were open and she stared vaguely at the floor.

Sara knelt beside her.

"Cindy?" she whispered and touched the girl's thin, bony shoulder. Again the child recoiled.

Sara pulled back, let the girl calm down, and then asked, "What is your name?"

The girl did not respond, but Sara saw the question had alerted her.

"Is your name Cindy?" Sara settled down on the rug, stretched out near the child so she could see her face. "Is your name Cindy?" she asked again.

The child took a deep breath and screeched into Sara's face. It sounded like words, but none that Sara could understand. Then Cindy screeched again.

"I'm sorry, Cindy, I can't understand you."

The front doorbell rang. Thank God, she thought. Now Cindy was no longer her problem. Wrapping the white terry-cloth bathrobe tightly around her body, Sara went downstairs to let the farmer in.

Bruce Delp did not look her in the eye when she opened the front door. He stood on the walk, not even on the cement stoop, and said, "I've come for Cindy."

"She's upstairs, in my bedroom. You'll have to carry her, I think; I left her curled up on the floor."

The farmer nodded and started up the steps. Sara moved back, out of his way, and said, "The bedroom is at the top of the stairs." She waited in the foyer, so her presence would not cause another outburst from Cindy. Delp was downstairs again almost immediately. For a short stocky man, he moved quickly. Cindy was walking on her own, but she clung lovingly to him, her small hand in his thick fist.

"Thank you, Miss," Delp muttered as the two of them swept past her and out the door. The odor from their bodies and clothes floated back to her as they passed.

"Mr. Delp," she called after him. "What's the matter with Cindy?"

The farmer stopped. He had his arm wrapped protectively over Cindy's shoulder, and the girl still clung to him.

"They tell me she's autistic," he said, and now he did look at Sara. His eyes were small and cold, and as dark as his daughter's. "You know about that?"

"Yes, of course. Do you have her in a special school?"

The farmer shook his head. "They can't do nothing for her. We keep Cindy at home. It's best."

"Mr. Delp, I am with the National Institutes of Health. If you'd like, I could telephone my colleagues and see if we can find a good school for Cindy. Doctors understand a great deal about autism today, and. . . ."

"Don't you do nothing. I'll take care of my own." And then he pushed Cindy ahead of him and into the truck.

"I was just trying to help, Mr. Delp." She felt as if she had been slighted and misunderstood.

"I don't need your help with my kid," Delp answered, sliding behind the steering wheel. He stared at Sara for a moment, than said, "You keep away from her and she'll keep away from you people." Then he slammed the door and turned over the engine.

Sara closed the front door firmly and leaned against it, shocked by Delp's reaction to her offer. She was unprepared for such hostility; it frightened her. Who were these people? she asked herself. And why were they so strange?

She turned the lock on the front door and, as an extra precaution, slid the chain bolt into place. Then she went upstairs to shower and dress, but was so uneasy that she locked the bedroom door behind her as well.

Still the uneasiness remained. She paused and took several deep breaths, but her heart was racing. She was momentarily dizzy, from the excitement, she thought, and her own nervousness, and she slumped down on the end of the bed. And then she realized that something more, something frightening was happening to her.

She felt the tingling up the back of her thighs, and she fell onto the soft bed as her leg muscles tightened and the blood went rushing to her center. Her body seemed out of her control; the muscles of her rectum contracted and her hips and pelvis jumped involuntarily, thrust forward, as the warm blood burst through her body, flooding her groin and exploding into her limbs.

She let the rush spread out in a long, slow wave. There was a moment of peace, then another wave tore into her and held her tight for a moment before slipping away. Another shuddering. Another rage of thick pleasure. She was dizzy and confused and the temples of her brain hurt from the relentless charge of electricity.

She clung to the damp mattress, trying to keep her sanity as the bombardment continued. And then, just as suddenly, it was over. She lay still, breathing fast and hard for a moment, before she rolled on her side and clutched a pillow in her arms, trying to shield herself from the terrifying realization that something truly extraordinary had just happened to her.

five

"It wasn't murder," said Santucci's voice over the telephone.

Tom Dine swung his legs down from his desktop and reached for his notepad.

"What do you mean it wasn't—you told me! I wrote it up for tomorrow's paper. It's already typeset!"

"I just got the medical report. The baby wasn't strangled." Santucci spoke offhandedly, as if the whole business now bored him, but Dine could hear the disappointment in his voice.

"What killed her?"

"They're not sure yet. I guess it's a little too technical for a county coroner. He's calling in a neuropathologist, but his preliminary examination is that the child died from a brain swelling, not strangulation. He's not sure yet, but it looks like meningitis."

"Ah, shit!" And this guy calls himself a detective, he thought.

"I guess we've struck out again, Tom." Now Santucci sounded guilty.

Tom leaned forward, picked up the folder of newly typed notes and dropped them into the basket. A wasted morning. And he had to call his editor and tell him to kill the story.

"Look, I'm sorry, but I coulda swore that kid had been strangled. Did you see her face? It looked, you know, like she suffocated. That kid suffered before she died, I swear."

"Yeah, you're pissing in my ear and you're telling me it's raining. Give me a call when you've got a murder, Joe," and he hung up the phone.

There was no school bus to Renaissance Village so the mothers had organized their own car pool. On the day Amy Volt died in her hayrack crib, Marcia Fleming left the Smithsonian early to take her son Benjamin and four other third graders home from the Virginia Day school.

"I want you to play indoors this afternoon, honey," Marcia instructed Benjamin as she unlocked the front door and let them into the house.

"Oh, Mom!" Benjamin protested. "It isn't even dark and I told Debbie we'd go hunt for flowers." He threw his bookbag down on the hall table and went on, "Miss Maness told us all to bring in three different kinds of flowers for class tomorrow." He stood in the hallway with his small hands on his hips, blocking Marcia's way to the livingroom. He had the same dark looks as his mother, and at his age it made him adorable-looking.

"Miss Maness will have to do without your flowers. I don't want you wandering through the fields, and I'm sure Debbie's mother won't let her go out either." She moved around her son and continued through the house, going into the kitchen.

"If I'm the only one without flowers tomorrow, Miss

Maness is going to kill me. When Derek Nevins didn't do his homework last week, she made him bring his parents to school.'' Benjamin tagged after his mother. There were tears in his eyes and he let them stream down his face so his mother would see how much she'd hurt him.

Marcia put on the kettle for tea and went to the refrigerator and took out the milk. "Benjamin, would you like a snack?'' she asked calmly. She was immune to his nine-year-old theatrics.

"No!''

"No, thank you.''

"No, thank you, I don't want a snack.'' Benjamin plopped into a kitchen chair and buried his head in his hands, crying uncontrollably.

Marcia had to force herself not to go to him. It was times like this that she realized she had to be strong. It was the only way she could put discipline into her son's life. As it was, Benjamin was already spoiled by her permissiveness, by her continual guilt at not having a father for her son.

"If you want, you can have Debbie come here and play, or you can go and play at her house until supper. But you are not to go into those fields! Do you understand?'' She let her voice be sharp.

"I don't want to go play at Debbie's house. I want to play outside.''

Marcia did not respond. She knew his tactics, the way he pouted. It was not the time to try to reason with him, and besides, she didn't have the strength. Since the evening at the Volts', Marcia had had a headache and, though she had been taking aspirins all day, the pain was still there, lodged like a long knife in her forehead, low and sharp between her eyes.

Marcia poured boiling water from the teapot, but her trembling hands spilled it all over the oven top and the hot water hissed when it touched the flame.

"What's the matter, Mom?" Benjamin asked.

Marcia shook her head. "Nothing, sweetie." She knew that she would have to tell him about Amy Volt. He would learn about the death soon enough from the other children in the Village. It was not something that could be kept from them, and she wanted Benjamin to hear the true story from her. Still she hesitated. Benjamin had visited Amy and even held the baby in her arms. How would he feel when he found out Amy had been murdered in her cradle?

The telephone rang in the kitchen and Benjamin scrambled off the chair to answer it.

"You can't go outside, Benjy," Marcia repeated.

"Yeah, Mom!" He sighed, picking up the telephone. "It's for you," he said, stretching the lengthy cord across the kitchen and handing the receiver to Marcia. "It's Neil," he whispered, grinning.

Giggling now, Benjamin skipped away, grabbing a cookie from the plate.

"I'm going upstairs to watch T.V.," he called back over his shoulder.

"Don't go out!" Marcia shouted after him; then she said nicely into the phone, "Hello."

"Marcia, it's me."

She sat up straighter in her chair. Neil's voice always excited her.

"Have you spoken to Peggy?" he asked.

"No, Why? What's the matter now?"

"The baby. She wasn't murdered. I went by the house on the way home and the police had come. That detective didn't know what he was doing last night. They did an autopsy and found the child had died from some sort of brain dysfunction that caused swelling and oxygen starvation. It only looked like she had been strangled."

"Oh, thank God," Marcia whispered, and immediately she felt guilty, realizing it was Benjamin's safety that preoccupied her mind. And then, as if to make amends, she asked, "And how's Peggy?"

"No better than anyone could expect. She's being sedated."

"And Kevin?"

"Who can tell? I never know what he's thinking. Besides, they're both still in shock. The implications of all this won't hit them for another few days. She lost her child, Marcia."

She heard his voice crack on the telephone, and then a muffling sound as if he had put his hand over the mouthpiece. Marcia was a little surprised that the baby's death had affected him so much, but his vulnerability made her love him more.

"Why don't you come over for dinner? There's just us, nothing special."

"Thanks, I'd love to. I've got to meet with Magnuson this evening, but I'll be done by six." He sounded happy that he had somewhere to go for dinner. "I'll see you then."

"Whenever you can, don't hurry."

"Well, I want to hurry. I want to see you."

She smiled, touched and briefly overwhelmed. "Thank you," she whispered, and hung up. It had been so long since she had really been loved that she had forgotten how the emotion could knock her for a loop.

She pushed herself from the wall, only to be startled by Benjamin standing silent at the doorway.

"Are you okay, Mom?" The little boy's brown eyes were wide with apprehension.

"Yes, darling." Marcia opened her arms to him and Benjamin rushed forward and hugged her.

"You know what?" Marcia said into his hair. "I think it would be all right if you went out and collected those flowers, after all. Why don't you call Debbie and have her meet you here?"

Benjamin scooted from her arms, giggling and escaping. "I'll go by Debbie's house and pick her up," he said, running into the foyer and pulling down his coat. "We haven't got much time. It's almost dark."

His voice shrieked with excitement.

"Benjy, darling, please don't shout; I have a head-ache."

"Oh, sorry, Mom." He zipped up his jacket, and then went to his mother, kissing her on the cheek. "Can I take the farm wagon? We'll need something to carry the flowers."

"Yes, dear, take the wagon." She had bought it at the Delps' auction and Benjamin played with it whenever he could.

"I'll be home before dark," he added, anticipating her question.

"Be sure you are. And please don't invite Debbie for dinner. I've asked Neil over, and I just want a quiet evening, the three of us."

She waved good-bye and closed the storm door. Her life, she thought, was turning out all right. After the terrible years since she left Jeff, her life was finally getting back on course. She and Benjamin, her work at the Smithsonian, her new home in the Village. And now, perhaps, she had Neil. She smiled to herself and went upstairs to take a nap before dinner. It was four o'clock and within the hour another child would die in the valley.

In the thick stand of woods at the top of the thumb-shaped valley, the man walked up the hill and away from the river, his heavy footsteps crushing the dry dead leaves of fall. Now before dark he was searching for his daughter, moving quietly through the black trees.

At the crest he stopped and, still hidden in the trees, looked across the open fields above the Village. He did not see his daughter, but he could hear children, their voices carrying clearly in the late afternoon, that last hour of the day when the sun was down and the land-scape lit only by the soft light of fall.

He could not see the children in the tall grass, but he followed their voices like a trail as they climbed the hill.

Then their heads appeared on the hilltop. They were like spring calves, he thought, the way they rushed about, picking the wild flowers from the long grass.

The two children had Debbie's textbook with them, which showed color illustrations of the plants and flowers they wanted, but in the high weeds of the hillside it was difficult to find the right ones. When they did find one, they shouted out their discovery and pulled the old battered farm wagon across the field to cut away the patch, leaving an unnatural bare spot in the thick foliage.

It was too steep a climb for the livestock of the farm, and as a result only pheasants and the small white tail deer used the ridge as a sheltered spot. But now the children of the new village threatened the seclusion of the rocky citadel at the crest of the hill.

"It's a Wild Pink," Debbie shouted, pointing toward the tuft of flowers that grew thick in the fissure of the rocks.

"No, it isn't," Benjamin insisted, angry that he hadn't seen it first. He checked the textbook, hoping to prove she was mistaken.

"Yes, it is!" Debbie shouted again and, without waiting for Benjamin, scrambled onto the mound at the top of the ridge and crawled across the rough surface, moving quickly toward the beautiful wild bouquet.

It was their joy that made him angry. He was always that way with other children when he saw how bright and sane they were, and then he saw Cindy standing at the edge of the wood, near the children, close to the ancient burial site.

Sara saw the women running as she drove along the farm road, up toward Petrarch Court. Then she realized they were carrying a child and she pressed on the accelerator, speeding up the curving drive, reaching the women at the entrance of Erasmus Court. She skidded the car to a stop and jumped out.

The child lay limp in Helen Severt's arms. Sara gave her one practiced look, then rushed back and unlocked the trunk of her car. She was ill-equipped, she thought frantically, for emergencies. Her medical bag was full of the new experimental drugs she was researching, and she had little to help an injured child.

"What happened?" she called to the two women.

Helen Severt said nothing. She hugged her daughter to her, and did not take her eyes from Debbie's quiet face.

"She was playing up on the ridge with Benjy," Marcia Fleming shouted. "He came running back and told me that she just fell down and didn't move again. That's how we found her."

Sara pulled the car blanket from her trunk and tossed it to Marcia. "Spread this on the lawn and stretch Debbie out on it."

It was getting cold, she realized; they would have to get more blankets if they were going to keep the child from going into shock. But she didn't send Marcia home to get them. In her heart she knew she would not need them.

Falling to her knees, Sara knelt on the blanket beside the child and quickly, gently helped Helen settle the girl. Both of the women were talking frantically, explaining how they had found Debbie at the base of the mound, but Sara wasn't listening. She reached for the little girl's wrist and deftly probed for a pulse. Then, leaning forward, she lifted the closed eyelids and admitted to herself that the child was dead.

The breath went out of her and her hands began to tremble uncontrollably. Carefully she touched the white face of the child and then, there, in the open yard above Erasmus Court, she collapsed into the storm of tears that had been frozen inside her ever since that icy day on Mount Auburn Street.

• • •

"The mothers found her," Joe Santucci explained. He was sitting in his car with the reporter outside of the Severt home.

"What time?" Tom asked.

"Sometime around five. Fleming telephoned Helen Severt, Debbie's mother. There were no husbands around. Richard Severt works at the White House, some sort of energy advisor, and Marcia Fleming is separated, no divorce."

Tom Dine could not see the detective's face, but the tone in the man's voice told him that Santucci had suffered in the last few hours. "Did they move the body?" Tom asked.

"Yeah. The mothers went crazy, of course, and grabbed the child and came running downhill looking for Doctor Marks."

Tom Dine's head jerked up, but he let the detective continue.

"She had to tell Helen Severt that her child was dead. Oh, she made a stab at reviving her—mouth-to-mouth resuscitation—but it didn't do any good. The kid was dead. When I got here she was still stretched out on the grass, covered with a car blanket."

"Jesus H. Christ!"

Joe Santucci stirred again behind the wheel. "It's a fuckin' bitch."

"Where's the body?"

"At the morgue. They're doing an autopsy."

"Any marks?"

"She had hit or scraped her right cheek, and her front teeth had been chipped. And there was blood in her nostrils."

"Like the Volt baby?"

In the dark interior of the front seat, Joe Santucci turned to the reporter. Tom could see flashes of the streetlight shine in the detective's eyes.

"That's right," he whispered. "Like the Volt kid."

"Is there some kind of connection? Do you think maybe they were both killed?"

"We've got the coroner's report on the baby. She died from massive brain swelling. It's tragic, but it ain't murder." He nodded toward the hill behind the Village. "That little girl was murdered. I don't know how, and I sure don't know why, but she was murdered. That's one thing I'm sure of."

"What do you mean, sure? Has the little boy told you something?" Tom did not look up from writing his notes.

"For the moment I'm not saying." His whispering made it all sound mysterious.

"Come on, Joe, what's all this bullshit? What did you find up there?"

"We found tracks. Several good impressions. It might mean something. We'll know more tomorrow."

"Then we're back to the muddy tracks on the basement floor."

"Yeah, we're back to them."

"Okay, then what do we have? How do I write this up? A murder in the field. A little girl dead, but as to how and why, we have no clues yet. And another death. A baby death thought to be caused by a brain dysfunction, and for the time being the police aren't making any connection linking the killing and the crib death."

"It's all under investigation," Joe added.

"That's just great. I haven't got shit, Joe, and you know it."

Santucci did not move.

"Off the record, Joe. Deep background. Come on, what gives? What do you guys know?" He could feel himself getting uneasy. He was always that way when he began to push for a story.

"I think it's the farmer."

"The farmer? What farmer?" The news surprised Tom. He hadn't heard of any such person.

"Bruce Delp. His family owned all this land, about a

hundred acres since the Civil War. He sold out to Lewis Magnuson, the guy who put together the co-op village, but only under heavy pressure.

"Magnuson owns one of the banks that Delp owes money to for farm equipment. So Magnuson cut a deal with him. He wiped out the loan, gave Delp his house and a job as handyman, and let him keep the family burial ground up on the ridge. And Magnuson! He got himself a goddamned real estate bonanza."

"Have you arrested this guy . . . Delp?"

"I've got him under surveillance," Santucci said.

Tom stopped writing and looked at the man. Santucci was grinning as if he had just done something clever, and Tom realized then that Santucci was simply a big, dumb ex-jock. For the last few weeks, he had foolishly thought that behind Santucci's flat dull face, there was a reservoir of downhome common sense, an innate knowledge, but he was wrong. Santucci was a fool. A dangerous fool.

Tom closed his notebook and said softly, "Joe, two little girls have died mysteriously in the last twenty-four hours and you've got a suspect. What is this, 'I've got him under surveillance'?"

"I've got nothing on him, Tom," Santucci snapped back.

"Then why's he a suspect?"

"Look, Dine," Santucci tried to shift his bulky body in the tight space, but there wasn't room and the confinement only frustrated him more. He was someone who needed room to move around. "You don't know this Delp family," he told the reporter, lecturing him, pointing his thick finger at Tom. "They've been in trouble with the law before. Bruce Delp himself, his old man Hank, uncles and cousins. An older brother killed a girl out here back in '52. The Delp people take up one whole file drawer over at the office. They've always been in trouble with the law, one way or the other."

"And that makes him a suspect."

"You're damned right!" Santucci was still fuming. He stared out the front window and for a moment neither one of them said anything. Then Dine cleared his throat.

"What about that coroner's report? Any chance of it being available to the press?"

"You can have both reports—the Volt kid and this Debbie Severt—but they won't mean shit."

"Thanks, Joe, you're all heart these days."

"I got a fuckin' killer loose, Dine."

"Well, drive down to the farm house. I'll help you put him under arrest."

"Never mind, we'll do it my way." And then he reached over and turned on the ignition. "I've got to go," he said, closing off their interview.

"The coroner's reports?"

"Come by the office tomorrow morning."

"See you in the A.M.," Tom got out of the car, then he leaned back inside and added, "Joe, you got an explosive situation out here. I just want you to know I'm on your side on this one. I'll help you, but I've got to do my job."

"I understand, Tom. Thanks." He reached over and shook the reporter's hand, his enormous fist squeezing Tom's fingers in his grip. "And I appreciate everything you can do for the case."

"I want to make you a hero," Tom said lightly, trying to put some humor into the situation.

"If I don't come up with some results soon, they'll bust my ass back to highway patrol."

"Cheer up, Joe, it will come." But Tom knew this young detective was lost on the case. And that if someone else didn't intervene there would be more children killed in Renaissance Village, because someone, for some reason, had gone crazy on the banks of the Potomac.

six

Benjamin Fleming leaned forward, pressed his forehead against the window, and turned his face back and forth. The glass was cold and wet on his skin.

"What are you doing, darling?" Marcia asked from across the room.

"Nothing." He kept his head where it was; he liked the chilly feeling of the wet window on his face.

"Come away from there," Marcia asked.

"Why?" Benjamin asked, finding another cold pane of glass.

All day Marcia had been guarding Benjamin. When he played outside she came along, saying that she felt like playing on the swings, too. But then she only stood in the park, freezing in the slight fall chill, her body shivering while he swung alone. Now she was afraid someone was outside in the dark, watching the house and her son, framed in the window.

"It's cosy here, honey, by the fire," she tempted him.

"Why don't you get some popcorn and we'll make it on the fire?" But Benjy didn't move to join her. She was sitting on the rug before the fire, her back propped up against a chair and paperwork from her office spread out on the floor.

Marcia had telephoned the Smithsonian that morning explaining what had happened at the Village, and saying she was taking annual leave for that week. She had also been on the phone all day trying to reach her husband in California, hoping to have Benjamin fly out to Los Angeles and stay with his father until the village killer was caught.

"Benjy? All right now, come away from the window. Please." She tried to say it nicely, offhandedly, as if it wasn't an order.

Reluctantly the boy hopped down and ambled over to the fireplace. He made a small game of it, slapping each piece of furniture with his hand as he came across the room. Marcia suppressed telling him to stop.

He was bored, she knew, and lonely. Perhaps she should have let him go to school, but the night before he had woken up several times, crying out in fear. She had taken him into bed with her, but still he woke up screaming with nightmares. Marcia knew what he saw: Debbie Severt, her tiny body bloody and stiff in the tall grass at the top of the hill. And maybe Benjy saw something more, something Marcia hadn't seen—the face of the killer.

"Why don't you bring the small T.V. in here and watch something? Isn't it about time for *Happy Days?*" She smiled at him. He looked so adorable, dressed in his jeans and green soccer shirt, and she wanted to pull him close and hug him for a moment, but he was at that stage where any physical display of affection made him pull away and say, "Oh, Mom." She kept her hands off and he plopped down into the cushioned chair across from her. He was so small that the upholstery seemed to swallow him up.

"I saw someone outside." Benjy said it casually, but she could see him watching her.

"Who?" she said calmly.

A smile crept slowly across his lips, then burst out, lighting up his face.

"Benjy! That's not funny!" Her sudden fear caught in her throat and left her trembling. The early sunset of late fall filled the livingroom with shadows. But instead of enjoying the dusk as she usually did, Marcia felt she had to resist the gathering darkness.

"Turn on some more lights, Benjamin," she ordered, then added, "I can't see what I'm reading."

"Can I go over to Michael's?" he asked, getting off the couch.

"No!"

"Why not?" He moved around the room, affecting a limp as he went from lamp to lamp.

"Because I said so."

"Oh, Mom! It's only across the street. You can see his house from the front door."

"No." She began to collect her books and papers, stacking them together. "Let's go make cookies for dessert tonight," she offered enthusiastically. Maybe that would keep him occupied.

"No!" he snapped. There were large tears in his brown eyes and he wiped his nose with the back of his hand.

"Please, darling, use your handkerchief."

"I don't have a handkerchief," he shouted back.

In a moment, she realized, there would be a flood of hysterical tears and a crying tantrum. She picked up a small package of tissues and went to him, knelt down, and wiped his nose. He tried to twist away, but she seized his thin shoulder and held him.

"I know it's hard, Benjy, to have to stay inside by yourself all day, but I don't want you playing outside, not until that man has been found."

"What man?" Benjamin asked innocently. The tears

were gone. His round brown eyes looked puzzled.

Marcia had not discussed with him what had happened to Debbie. The police had only questioned Benjamin once about the death of the little girl, and she did not want to quiz him again, to dredge up more terrible memories of the afternoon.

"I didn't see any man kill Debbie." His voice was calm and certain. "She just climbed up onto the mound, and then she fell down." He said it matter-of-factly, as if it were just an accident.

"Well, let's not worry about it, honey." Marcia stood. "How about helping me make those cookies?" she asked quickly. If he wanted to escape the fact of Debbie's murder, that was fine with her. He was too young, too impressionable, and she did not want his life full of terror. In a few weeks the murder would be solved, and the child's death forgotten in the Village.

As they walked into the kitchen, the telephone rang.

"I'll get it!" Benjamin shouted excitedly, running ahead to grab the wall phone. "Hello?" he said.

Even from across the room Marcia heard the screeching, and she paused at the counter and glanced back at her son. Benjamin was holding the receiver away from his ears. He held it up, saying, "It's making a funny noise."

"That's all right, darling. Just hang up. It's probably broken."

Benjamin hung up the receiver and climbed down off the stool. The phone rang again immediately, loud and insistent in the quiet kitchen.

"I'll get it, Benjy," Marcia directed, picking it up before her son could climb back onto the stool. But before she could say hello, she heard the frightening, high-pitched screeching, and over the noise, she shouted, "Who is this?"

The screeching went on, chilling her with its fierceness. The sound curled around her like a snake, blocking out everything else. She slammed down the receiver and took a deep breath, relieved to escape the maddening sound.

"Who was it, Mommy?"

Marcia looked down at Benjamin. He was standing perfectly still, his tiny hands made into fists with both thumbs squeezed between the fingers. His small dark face was consumed with fear.

She went to him immediately, knelt down, and pulled him into her arms. "It's all right, honey." She could feel his slight body trembling in her grasp. She whispered that everything was fine. That it was just some child playing on the phone and he shouldn't mind.

Then the phone rang again, and a thin sliver of panic ran along her spine. It was like being watched, she realized; there was nothing she could do.

In her arms, Benjamin began to cry; his arms tightened around her neck. "Mommy, I'm scared."

"Don't be, honey. Now be a big boy, and I'll make that person stop telephoning."

On the next ring Marcia jumped up and pulled the receiver off the hook, yelling, "Stop calling this number. I'm going to telephone the police."

"Marcia . . . ?" The voice on the line was puzzled.

"Oh, God! Neil, I'm sorry." She sighed and sank down on the top step of the kitchen ladder.

"What's going on? Are you okay?"

"Yes, I'm—we're—okay, I think. It's just that someone has been telephoning the house and screeching into the phone."

"Anyone you recognize?"

"No. It's a fierce, terrifying sound. Actually shattering to hear. The range is very high, almost the sound you'd expect from a wild animal."

"Some crazy."

"Yes, I think you're right, but I don't know how he or she could have gotten me."

"Why?"

"My telephone. . . . It's unlisted."

"Christ, that's right." He paused, as if sorting out what to do next. "Listen, I just got home. Why don't you two bundle up and come over for dinner? Plan on staying the night."

"Thanks, Neil, that's very sweet of you, but I want to reach Jeff in California. I've left messages for him at his office and on his service. If I can reach him, I'd like to have Benjy fly out to L.A. for a few weeks."

"You can place the calls again from here. Marcia, get out of that house." He had raised his voice and was pleading with her.

"All right, we'll come." She sighed. It made her uneasy to agree to leave the house. She didn't like the notion of being driven from her own place, of having to go to Neil for rescue. But it would only be for one night, she reasoned. If it happened again tomorrow, she'd have her phone number changed.

"I'll come get you," he said.

"No, that's not necessary. We'll drive over. It's still light out."

"I'm coming over," he ordered, then quickly said good-bye.

He thought he was being kind, but his presumption irritated her. Since leaving Jeff, she had prided herself on taking good care of herself and Benjamin, without a man, without anyone else running interference.

The phone rang. The quiet, urgent ring left her breathless.

"Don't answer it," she shouted at Benjamin, but the boy was on the other side of the kitchen, nowhere near the phone, and Marcia's unnecessary command only scared him. He began to cry.

"It's okay." She rushed to him and let the phone go, but each long ring seemed louder and louder, and she kept count. It wouldn't last long, she thought; whoever was calling would grow tired and quit. But after twenty rings Marcia couldn't bear the sound and she rushed to the telephone, jerked the receiver off the hook, and shouted, "Stop it! Stop it immediately!"

"Hello?" she demanded.

She could not even hear breathing from the other end.

"Goddamn you!" Marcia slammed down the phone, then called to her son. "Come on, Benjy. We're going to spend the night at Neil's. Let's go pack your things. You can take your sleeping bag, too." She tried to make it seem like a small adventure.

"I don't want to go outside," the child whined.

"Oh, Benjy, darling, please don't make a fuss, okay? Just do what Mommy says."

"They'll kill me," he yelled back and then began to sob hysterically. He fell to the kitchen floor, his feet slamming the tile.

"Oh, dear God," Marcia sighed, exhausted from her own tension and fear. She wished now that Neil would arrive, and admitting that to herself did not make her feel inadequate. There was only so much she could do alone, and now, at this moment, she could not handle Benjamin. The child needed someone to take care of him; she needed someone to take care of her.

The telephone rang.

Marcia whirled around and stared at the white wall instrument. It rang again, its persistent, short, measured rings striking her, ripping through her mind.

"We won't answer," she told her son. "Come on!" Marcia gathered Benjamin into her arms, held him tucked to her body as they circled the kitchen, avoiding the telephone as if it were a rattler and ducked out of the room.

There was another phone in the hallway. It, too, kept ringing. She would unplug them both, she thought, take them off the hook until she had the number changed.

Then Benjamin said, "Maybe it's Daddy. Maybe it's Daddy telephoning from L.A." A sudden surge of joy and anticipation broke through the child's crying and he pulled from her arms and raced toward the hall phone.

"Wait, darling . . . let me." Marcia raised her arm, as

if to signal him to stop, but the child had reached the telephone and lifted the receiver. Please, dear God, she thought frantically, let it be Jeff. Let it be his father.

She heard the screeching from where she stood frozen in the middle of the livingroom. Benjamin dropped the receiver and screamed, and all she could think of in some odd, calm corner of her mind as she ran to the hall phone and yanked the plug from the wall, was that whoever was telephoning wanted her child and it was up to her alone to save him, and she swept her terrified son into her arms and ran out into the cold night and the dark cul-de-sac of the new Village.

seven

Tom Dine rang the bell of Sara Marks's home on Petrarch Court and listened to the peppy jingle ring through the big house.

How could she stand such a corny bell, he thought, and stepped away from the front door, scanning the other new houses on the cul-de-sac. It was a warm September afternoon and half a dozen neighbors were working on their front lawns. A perfect suburb, he thought. The people of Renaissance Village had no reason to be living in the middle of farm land, and the whole notion of this planned community disgusted him.

The door opened and he turned around, smiling, determined to make her like him.

"Oh," she said in surprise, recognizing the reporter.

"I'm sorry. Were you expecting company?"

"No, not really." She had been reading on the back terrace and had come to the door with a medical book still in her hand, keeping her place with her forefinger.

She was barefoot, with a white terrycloth robe over her swimming suit and her long cornsilk hair loose off her shoulders. Tom Dine thought she looked absolutely beautiful.

"I'm sorry to bother you," he said hesitantly, "but Detective Santucci said you saw Debbie Severt, and I was wondering if we might talk for a moment." Through the storm window door, he could see her frown.

"I spoke to the police and signed a statement. I really don't have anything to say for publication." She managed a quick tight smile.

Tom looked off, as if confused and embarrassed for the moment, then he said, "Well, think of it as off the record. Deep background. No names. No statements. It would help me understand what has happened if we could talk for a few minutes." And then he smiled.

It was infectious and she couldn't resist. Involuntarily she grinned and pushed open the storm door.

He was wearing a suit and tie and standing with the weight of his body on his right foot. His body was slouched forward, leaning precariously to one side, as if he were a tanker listing toward shore.

His odd helplessness suddenly struck her as sweet and innocent. This man could do her no harm, she thought, and then asked, "Would you like to come inside and have a cup of tea?"

"Coffee?" he asked. He smiled once more and his eyes sparkled.

"It's coffee, then." She felt suddenly weak in her legs as she led him through the house into the bright sunny kitchen. "Go to the terrace. I'll put on the water."

She kept talking, hoping she wouldn't say something outlandishly foolish. In spite of her beauty, she had never really known how to behave with men. At the hospital or the lab she thought of herself as an equal—as more than an equal—but in social situations, even in her own house, she was always uneasy and unsure.

Instead of going out to the terrace, Tom stopped at the glass door and stood watching Sara fuss over the coffee. Her surprising shift in manner made him curious. All her poise had slipped away.

Then he began to talk, to volunteer information about himself, to tell her why he was doing the story on Joe Santucci. He told her what Santucci had said about the killing of Debbie Severt.

As he talked he moved away from the back door and walked around the butcher block table. His flood of information spared her the burden of making small talk while she prepared a tray, and she obviously appreciated it.

She was going to some trouble now, getting out packages of cookies and arranging them all on the tray. She did not look up from her task, nor stop him to comment on his story. Tom couldn't tell what she was thinking. She would not even glance at him.

Still it gave him a chance to look at her, to see if she really was as beautiful as he had first thought. She looked older. Her face had lost that freshness of a twenty-year-old. It was a serious face, and through the years she had developed certain expressions with which to deal with others. It was those careful, orchestrated looks that she had used to respond to his questions at the front door. But he could see by the way her lips froze at the corners of her mouth that she was slightly frightened. He could see it as well in her blue eyes, and in the way she did not meet his glance.

He was tempted to confront her, to see what it was that frightened her. It had nothing to do with the death of Debbie Severt, he knew. The look in her eyes, her vulnerability, was not something that had happened overnight. But he wasn't going to tamper with her psyche. He was lucky she had even invited him for coffee. In time he'd learn what it was that frightened her. In time women always told him their secrets.

"There!" she said, arranging the cups and pots on the tray. "Would you please open the sliding door, Thomas?" Even as she teased him she did not look up.

He slid open the door and stepped away as she passed him. The strong aroma of the coffee came back to him, mixed with the smell of burning leaves from the next backyard, and the scent of her shampoo.

The sun was lower on the horizon so the chairs and tables were now in the shade. He carried them away from the house, into the last bright wedge of afternoon sunlight. It was warm in the sun, and he took off his suit coat and loosened his tie.

"I really don't have anything more to tell you about the little girl," Sara said, handing him a cup of coffee. "What about the autopsy? Did they find out anything from that?" She finished pouring her own cup of tea and finally looked across at him.

"The coroner says the girl wasn't murdered." Tom kept his eyes on her, watching for her reaction.

Sara straightened up in the lawn chair. The white terry-cloth robe had slipped loose, and he could see the top of her two-piece bathing suit.

"What, then?" she asked.

"The doctor said a seizure like the Volt child. I've got a copy of the coroner's report. Would you like to see it?"

"Yes, please."

He set the cup down and reached into his suit pocket. "Perhaps you can make some sense of this," he added, handing it to her. "It's over my head."

The medical report was several pages long, including a detailed description of the physical appearance of the dead girl, and Sara scanned it quickly, looking for details on the seizure.

"This isn't too clear, but there seems to have been a breakdown in the hypothalamus due to brain swelling."

She glanced up at Tom Dine. He was sitting perched on the edge of the chair and leaning forward. She hesitated a moment to study his face.

He was dangerous-looking. It was this look that had initially struck her, and even now, sitting safely in the bright sun of the afternoon, in full view of a half-dozen other houses, he still frightened her. But then he smiled abruptly and she saw again how charming he could look.

"What is the hypothalamus?" he asked.

"The hypothalamus is in the brain. It's under the thalamus in the cerebrum. The hypothalamus is what regulates a lot of our motivated behavior like eating, drinking, and even sex—it's our so-called 'pleasure center.' " Sara held up the report and added, "This is sketchy, but the coroner says that the child's brain suffered massive assaults in the region of the hypothalamus, destroying the tissues around the third ventricle. This doctor says it appeared as if the cells had been burned."

"You didn't see any physical damage to Debbie when you tried to revive her?"

Sara shook her head. "There was a small quantity of blood in her nostrils, and bruises around the face, but nothing significant, certainly not enough to kill her."

"Then what caused her death?"

"I have no idea. I might be able to tell more if I had done the cerebral autopsy myself, but from what this doctor tells us, I couldn't say for certain. It would only be a guess."

"What would you guess, Sara?" He was still leaning forward, eager for any sort of information.

"This isn't for publication?" She looked at him, frowning again.

"No, not if you insist," he agreed reluctantly.

Sara looked again at the typed report and answered slowly, thinking out her reply as she spoke. "There is a type of neurosurgery in which tiny electrodes are implanted in the brain and used to destroy a small number of brain cells. This is usually done instead of a lobectomy. You implant the electrodes in the amygdala region, then apply radio frequency current. This current generates enough heat to destroy the diseased brain cells. It once was a standard operating technique for certain patients with violent epilepsy.

"Now, the coroner says that the cell tissues in the hypothalamus region were destroyed within a half-inch radius. It's as if her brain had been hit by a massive bolt of lightning."

"Incredible!" Tom stood and began to pace on the open terrace, walking in a wide circle around Sara's chair. "What you're suggesting is that this child was somehow electrified?"

"I'm not suggesting anything," Sara resisted his assumption. "I don't know how the girl was killed."

"Well, let's speculate," Tom said, eager now to come up with some answers. "How could you destroy this hypothalamus without an operation?" He paused before Sara's chair.

Sara hesitated before replying. She was looking away, concentrating, trying to think how it might be done. "Well," she said slowly, "you'd have to make the incision here"—she paused to demonstrate, indicating a spot on the nape of her neck—"through the cerebellum and into the hypothalamus."

"Could the coroner tell if such an incision had been made in the neck?" Tom asked quickly.

"I wouldn't think so. It wouldn't be any more obvious than a tetanus shot."

"But it would have to be done by someone with training, right?" he asked immediately, anxious now to fit the first corner of the puzzle together. He was on to something solid; he just knew it.

"Yes, some training, I'd guess. The incision isn't the complicated part; it's the electronics. The searing." She was frowning, unsure what conclusion the reporter was drawing from these few bits of medical information. "Mr. Dine, I'm not suggesting any of this happened."

"Right! Of course!" He began to pace again, and as his mind worked, his pacing picked up. There were no marks on the child, he thought. It wasn't sloppily done.

Now he was excited at the possibility the child, and perhaps Amy Volt, had been murdered by an electrical force. He spun around and abruptly asked, "Would you examine Debbie Severt yourself?"

Confused, Sara shook her head. "That's impossible. I haven't the authority. I can't. . . ."

"Couldn't you get it?" he asked next. "Couldn't you get her parents to let you?"

Sara shook her head and began to gather up the cups. The sun had left the back terrace and now the late afternoon air was chilly.

"How can you not *do* something?" Tom protested, returning to the lawn chair. The tone of his voice was accusing, but Sara looked at him coolly, her eyes icy blue and angry. Her sudden, blunt reaction silenced him.

"I'm sorry," he said quickly.

"Mr. Dine, my diagnosis is merely speculative. There are thousands of doctors in this area; I'm just one of them. I have no more right than you do to tell the coroner what to do, or to suggest to Peggy or Helen that their children need another autopsy." She stopped and, picking up the tray, moved toward the back door of the house.

"Here, let me help you," he offered.

"No, thank you. I have it." She was polite, but he could see she was angry. He kept quiet and only went ahead to open the screen door. She passed him without a smile and, as he turned to follow, he spotted the child.

She was standing beyond Sara's property line at the edge of the Village. Here the valley came flush against glacier rocks and small, tough evergreen bushes that grew wild at the edge of the farm land, encasing the

Village within a natural boundary. The young girl was in among the trees, crouched down and watching.

"Who's that?" Tom asked, closing the kitchen door.

Sara looked over, unsure of what he meant, and he nodded out the windows.

Sara set the tray down on the kitchen sink and looked across the terrace to where her property line buttressed the rocky slope fifty yards away. She could see her clearly. The child made no attempt to camouflage herself in the thorn bushes on the steep slope.

"It's Cindy Delp," Sara answered. "The daughter of the local farmer. She's autistic." Sara spoke slowly and did not take her eyes from the girl. She could see, even from that distance, that Cindy's expression was passive and nonthreatening. Yet having the child so close to her house and brazenly spying on her was upsetting. She would have to talk to the Delps. They had to exercise more control over their daughter.

"Delp?" Tom Dine asked quickly.

"Yes, do you know him?" Sara turned away from the windows, surprised at the reporter's sudden reaction.

Tom shook his head. "No, but Santucci mentioned his name," he said vaguely, backing off from his initial reaction. He debated whether he should tell Sara about the detective's theory on Bruce Delp and decided it would be a mistake. Instead, he asked, "Do you know the family?"

"Slightly. I see Bruce Delp most often. He's usually around working on the property. Pearl, his wife, does some light housekeeping in the Village and is a part-time aide at Chestnut Lodge. That's the psychiatric hospital over in Maryland."

"An aide?" Tom blurted out. He made the connection immediately: an aide, someone knowledgeable enough to make the incision. Perhaps it wasn't Delp. Perhaps it was his wife—or, for that matter, both of them. The notion of a husband and wife killing small children sent a chill through him.

"What is it?" Sara asked. For a moment she had seen his tough posture slip away and she saw clearly that he was excited.

For a split second in the still kitchen they stared across the table at each other. The look in their eyes told them that they were in danger.

"What is it?" Sara demanded. The last few days had left her weak and irritable.

Tom shook his head. "Nothing really."

"What do you mean, *nothing!* I can see on your face something is wrong." Her voice was high-pitched and insistent.

"It's Delp," he said quietly, "Santucci thinks he may have killed the girl. He found a footprint near the Indian mound." The reporter shrugged, then went on. "When you said his wife was an aide at a hospital, I. . . ." He shrugged again.

"Oh, God," she whispered. She swallowed fast and turned around abruptly so he wouldn't see her gag.

"Are you all right?" he asked.

"Yes," Sara answered, nodding as she looked out the window. Cindy was still crouched in the rough outcropping of rocks, her arms wrapped tightly around her knees as she stared across the lawn at the new house. Her beautiful face was blank and expressionless.

"This is ridiculous!" Sara exclaimed. "I'm going to take that child home."

She was reaching for the back door when she was struck, hit again with that sweet mixture of pleasure and pain. Lightheaded and hot, she stumbled against the butcher block table as her muscles contracted and the blood rushed to her center. Her legs went weak and she slid down slowly to the cool tile floor of the kitchen. The strong, pulsating sensation spread through her limbs, leaving her spent and dreamy.

Tom dropped down beside her and pulled her quickly to him. She slipped her arms around him and buried her head against his chest. For a moment neither one spoke.

She felt safe in his grasp and allowed herself the luxury of being held as the powerful current ran its course through her body.

"What is it, did you faint?" Tom asked.

Sara nodded, still unable to speak. For the moment she was frightened and inarticulate, and she did not want to leave the security of his arms. Through her panic and confusion filtered a comforting thought: she had forgotten how wonderful it was to be held.

Tom kept his arms wrapped around her and pressed her head gently to his chest. Then, taking her by the shoulders, he moved her away so he could look at her face. The pupils of her eyes were dilated and wet with tears and her face had softened and lost its tenseness. She gazed up dreamily into his eyes. He leaned over and kissed her once.

"No," she said, but she did not turn away or struggle.

"Why?" he asked.

She shook her head. "This isn't what you think."

He frowned and stared at her, puzzled by her reply.

She pulled out of his arms then, gently, for she really did not know how she felt about him.

"I didn't really faint. It's just . . . something I can't explain," she said.

"Well, are you okay now? I mean, you stumbled. . . ."

"Yes, I'm fine . . . now." She smiled nicely at Tom. "I'm not trying to be mysterious, but lately my body has been reacting rather oddly."

"You mean one of those mysterious female ailments?"

"Yes," she answered, "something like that."

"Well," he said lightly, "then you're not in love with me. For a moment I thought you had been felled by my irresistible charm." He smiled, and she realized that she did want to be nice to him, that finally she did like the man.

"No, not yet," she answered and let her eyes linger for a moment on his face.

Tom said nothing. He knew when to be quiet and not push his good luck. He had taken a chance by kissing her, but she was reacting to more than that. The odd look in her eyes, the shuddering of her body, the way she had clung to him—in another woman, under other circumstances, he would understand what that meant. But here, in Sara's kitchen. . . . He watched her as she stood at the sink, looking across the lawn to where the little girl still sat.

The sun had disappeared and a fall wind had picked up as evening approached. It was cold outside and Cindy was wearing only a summer dress. She must be freezing, Sara thought, and then she staggered again as the driving current tore through her womb.

"Oh, God," she whispered and grabbed the kitchen counter, supporting herself as the excruciating bliss jerked through her body.

In two strides Tom was beside her, but this time she scurried away, shaking her head. She clung to the counter, bent over and gasping. It would be over in a few seconds, she realized, and yielded to the pulsating flow, letting it be easier on herself. Slowly the roaring in her ears subsided, and as she inhaled she became aware of him again, of the two of them standing awkwardly in the middle of the huge kitchen.

"Sara?" he whispered.

She nodded, wiping the tears from her face with the back of her hand. "Sorry," she smiled apologetically.

"What the hell was that?" he asked.

"I don't know." She stood up straight and took several deep breaths to calm herself. "This happened once before. A couple of days ago. For no reason I can think of, I had this tremendous, overwhelming orgasm. That was the morning after Amy's death. Now it's happened again. Twice." Sara shook her head. She was leaning against the counter, and she pulled the terry-cloth bathrobe tighter around her body.

"No matter what you may think, it's not a pleasure or a thrill. It's more like . . . an assault. It's painful, and terrifying, too—your own body completely out of your control."

"And it's always like this? Unprovoked, so to speak? Spontaneous? I wouldn't have thought that was possible."

Embarrassed, Sara sought refuge in a clinical lecture. "Well, it's not entirely clear what causes orgasms. We do know that they are a product of our minds. An orgasm is triggered by a reaction in the hypothalamus."

Tom jerked his head up and Sara, too, realized what she had said. It was so obvious that she had almost missed the connection. It was Tom who said slowly, whispering as if they had stumbled on information that was important and delicate, "The children were attacked in the hypothalamus."

"Easy." She gestured for him to calm down. "Those child's brains were violently destroyed. The cell tissues were electrified. Fried. Nothing close to that has happened to me." Calmly, as if to reassure herself as well as Tom, she said, "Besides, I feel fine now."

Then she remembered Cindy Delp and looked out the kitchen window. It was almost dark, yet she could see the rocky perimeter where Cindy had crouched among the rocks and thorn bushes. The steep slope was deserted and the child was gone.

eight

"Sara, this is Marcia Fleming. I hope I haven't called too early. . . ." She sounded apprehensive.

"No, I've been awake for several hours. Is there anything wrong?" Sara stood in the front hall of her home. She already had on her coat and was on her way into Washington to begin looking for an apartment. She had decided she had to find another place to live. She could not live alone in this Village.

"I don't want to bother you, Sara, but. . . ." Marcia sighed into the phone. "Would you mind stopping by here for a few minutes. I have something that's bothering me, and I thought. . . ."

"Of course. I'll be right over." Sara tried to sound positive and cheery; she could tell by Marcia's voice that the woman was depressed.

"I'll put on some coffee," Marcia answered, as if offering an inducement.

Sara walked through the backyards of the Village to Marcia's place, below her on the hillside. She could see Marcia in her kitchen, and Sara went up the back steps and knocked on the door.

"Oh, Sara, thank you for coming over," Marcia smiled up at the taller woman and Sara saw the exhaustion in Marcia's eyes.

"Are you all right, Marcia?" she asked immediately.

"I don't know," Marcia whispered and moved away from the door to sit at the diningroom table, looking through the windows at the backyard. In the damp, misty, cold morning the grass was green and lush.

"Sara, I realize you're not a gynecologist, but . . ." Marcia hesitated, then added, "but you are a doctor, and a . . . woman."

"What is it, Marcia? If I can't help you, I can certainly put you in touch with someone who can." She smiled and waited for Marcia to tell her what was wrong.

"Something is wrong with my body," Marcia began, not looking up. She was holding the cup of coffee in her hands, as if warming them. "I don't know if it's because of Debbie's death . . . my body telling me something . . . overemotional, or what." She was crying, drops of tears splashing down her cheeks. "This week, since Debbie was . . . I can't control myself."

"How?" Sara asked softly.

"I keep having these orgasms. For no reason, you understand? Without any sex, or even any man around." She looked over at Sara, her eyes wild with fear. "When I'm alone, I'm suddenly hit by real, violent orgasms. Incredibly strong. But I'm by myself, doing nothing, and they hit me." She shook her head. "What is it, Sara? What's happening to me? It's happened three times now. I remember each one."

"Marcia, it's been happening to me, too. All this week." Sara clutched her arm.

"Oh, no, Sara! You, too! Thank God. I mean, I thought I was going crazy."

"It still doesn't explain them away. I had almost convinced myself that it was me. That I was suffering from some sort of mental disorder. Now how can we explain *both* of us coming down with schizophrenia at the same time?"

"Perhaps it's simply stress."

"I don't know, but I'm leaving. These last few days have been a nightmare for me. I'm going to find an apartment in the District."

"But, Sara, your new home!"

Sara shook her head. "I don't care. I don't want to live here alone. I'm afraid of my house. I'm afraid of being there alone. Last night it happened. It was terrible. My whole body was sore. They just kept coming, again and again." Sara's hands were trembling and her fingers around the cup shook, spilling coffee onto the table. "I'm sorry." She pulled her hands into her lap, embarrassed by what she had done.

"It's all right," Marcia said quickly, wiping up the mess with a sponge from the sink. Their roles had quickly reversed and now it was Marcia offering comfort. She brought Sara another cup of coffee. "Here," she whispered, "drink this." Marcia spoke comfortingly, as if she were consoling her son.

"I'm all right. Really." Sara straightened up in the chair. Now she was upset with herself for behaving badly. It was so unlike her to lose control, to react emotionally in such a situation.

"Sara, I don't mean to pry, but has anyone been with you when you've had them?" Marcia asked.

Sara shook her head, and then stopped. "Yes, Tom Dine was with me yesterday afternoon."

"Tom Dine . . . ?"

"He's the *Post* reporter who interviewed us at Peggy's that night."

Marcia shook her head. "I just don't remember. So many people have been here."

"Oh, it doesn't matter, but he came by the house yesterday afternoon to show me the coroner's report, which he'd somehow gotten his hands on. We sat out on the terrace and then moved inside when it got cold. That's when I was attacked."

"Was that the first time?"

"No, the first time was the morning of Amy's death. I had come back home and found Cindy Delp in my bathroom."

"Your bathroom . . . ?"

"It seems as if she's fixated on my house. She's always around. In fact, I spotted her on the rocks behind my property when Tom and I were in the kitchen."

"When was that?"

"Oh, I don't know, about five o'clock, I guess."

Marcia nodded, indicating she wanted Sara to continue. In the big, empty kitchen the two women were sitting together, and their proximity, the dark dampness outside, had brought them close together, establishing a trust and confidence between them.

"I didn't know how or why, but it was happening; I was having these intense orgasms." Sara was speaking softly, explaining what had happened. "What makes it even more incredible is that I never have them. I just accepted the idea that I was one of those women who never would. After all, I'm thirty-two and I've been involved with men since I was twenty and, well, it just never happened before to me."

"But you had more?"

Sara nodded. "I woke up at one o'clock with an attack."

"Sara," Marcia spoke slowly. "I woke up in the middle of the night, too. I don't know what time exactly, but it was after midnight, I'm sure."

Sara shook her head. "Tom Dine said something yesterday afternoon that I discarded, but now I think he might have a point.

"According to the coroner's reports, both Debbie and Amy were killed by a seizure in the hypothalamus region of their brains. I'm not sure what chemical was used, or how it got into the brain, but the coroner said that the cells and nerve fibers were burned—he used the word electrified.

"Now you and I are having violent, frightening orgasms for no reason. But those come from the hypothalamus, too. They've done experiments, for example, where this section of the mind was stimulated by electric current and it caused sexual aggression in castrated animals. It's our minds that cause orgasms, Marcia, not our bodies. And it is our minds that are being attacked. Whoever killed those children is after us."

"Why *us?*" Marcia cried. Tears of fright sprang to her eyes as she remembered how Debbie Severt had looked, slumped over in the grass at the top of the hill. "We aren't even those children's mothers. Why isn't this happening to Helen Severt and Peggy Volt?"

"Marcia, maybe it is." Sara paused and stared at Marcia, the shock showing in her eyes. She had not thought of the possibility before. "We have to call them and find out," she said quickly. "I'll telephone Peggy." Already she felt better, planning what to do next.

But Marcia sat frozen, paralyzed by the realization that something in the Village was trying to kill them.

"Sara, what is it?" Marcia grabbed her arm. "You're a doctor. You must have some idea." The fear in Marcia's eyes blazed like passion.

Her voice rose steeply and Sara saw she was near hysterics. It was too much—Amy dead in her crib, Debbie killed only a few feet from Benjy, and now these mysterious and brutal attacks. Perhaps she should give

Marcia a sedative and let her get some sleep.

"Marcia," she said softly, "we'll be all right. Everything will be all right, I promise you." Then she paused and looked out the kitchen window. The day had cleared, but she realized she wouldn't be going into Washington to look for a new apartment. Something terrible was happening in Renaissance Village and she could not run away.

Cindy Delp stood deep in the trees and watched the girl cross Wycliffe Drive and go to play by herself in the small park below the last row of houses.

But it was too cold and windy in the open field and, after only a few minutes on the swings, the girl left the playground and went back up onto the sidewalk and stood there, bundled up in a thick sweater, and watched several adults come out of one house and cross the newly sodded front lawn to the next house.

The woman waved to the young girl, and she returned the greeting, but did not run back across the street to join them. Instead she stood alone on the sidewalk, then bored and aimless, she continued up the hill, toward the trees beyond the Village.

Cindy moved silently forward, slipping quickly through the oak trees and, when she reached the clearing of the woods, she halted. The new girl had spotted her and waved tentatively, with the awkwardness of her age, then approached, smiling nicely and saying hi.

Cindy was frightened now. Her hands shot up to her forehead as the bright lights zigzagged across her eyes. Through her blurred vision, she could see the girl approach and then her head began to spin. She stumbled forward, losing her sense of balance as the whirling intensified. It was as if someone were whipping eggs inside her head, scrambling her brain. She gasped with pain and seized her head with both hands.

The girl stopped, shocked by Cindy's behavior, and

shouted out, asked if Cindy was okay, and then she started towards Cindy, saying she would get help. She reached out, as if to touch Cindy, and then she was struck. Her head felt the crushing attack, the whacking across the back of her skull, and she fell into the thick leaves, her blond head ricocheting off the huge stones, her brains spilling out onto the forest floor.

nine

Tom Dine opened the lot map of Renaissance Village and spread it flat on Sara's butcher block kitchen table, using the salt and pepper shakers to hold down the edges. It was a surveyor's map and Sara saw he had marked several of the numbered lots with large Xs.

"What are you doing?" she asked.

"I'm really not sure. Just something I've been thinking about. A notion, that's all. Look!" With a black magic marker, he circled the Xs he had already drawn. "I'm trying to see if there's a pattern here, if you women and the children are being attacked in any sort of a pattern."

"But what would that tell us?" She saw that he had already X'd her lot, as well as Marcia's and the Volts'.

"I have no idea, but if we think of the Village as sort of a mine field, and people only in certain locations are hit, then, at least, we have something to work with. Now among the women, who have been attacked?"

"We're not sure we've talked to them all. But certainly Kathryn Mackey."

"Where does she live?"

"Here, lot 67 on Boccaccio Court. And Rebecca Hunt on Montesi Court. This lot here, on the corner, number 68. And Jill Terracciano farther up the hill, number 74. She also thinks her daughter Michelle has had them, but her daughter is only eleven and Jill refuses to ask her." Sara shook her head.

Tom placed an X inside lot number 74. "Who else then?"

"Lynn Myers. She lives on the other side of the farm road, in either 52 or 53; I'm not sure. We can check by calling her."

"That's okay for now. It's close enough. Any more?"

"Joy Lang behind the Myers. Pam Finney on Chaucer Drive. That would be lot 54.

"How many have been hit?"

"About fifteen. Let me get the list to make sure we have them all." While she read off the names and lot numbers, Tom placed Xs on the map, then at the top of the map he sketched in the outcropping of rocks and Indian mound and added another X. Then he studied the map for a moment before he said to Sara, "Do you see the pattern?"

She shook her head.

Tom drew three black lines through the map and connected the Xs. They pointed like spokes of a wheel toward the Indian mound.

The pattern was unmistakable, and Sara was impressed. The chart was something that would never have entered her mind. "What does it mean?" she asked.

"I'm trying to see if the women in *certain* spots in the Village are being attacked, proving that it's the location that matters, or why no men out here are being hit."

The kitchen wall phone rang and Sara went to answer it while Tom leaned forward, bracing his hands at the corners of the table and studying the map.

"Oh, God, no!" Sara exclaimed.

Tom turned quickly and Sara put her hand across the mouthpiece and said, "It's Neil Cohoe. He says there's been another death."

"Who?"

Sara listened a moment and then said, "A couple out looking at houses . . . their daughter. She had gone off to play and they found. . . ."

"Where?"

"Neil, Tom Dine from the *Post* is here and he wants to know where they found the girl." Sara listened a moment and said, "In the woods." She paused again, listening, and then repeated for Tom, "Near his house. That's off Wycliffe Drive, beyond the Volts. Neil, what lot are you?

Tom picked up the magic marker and leaned over the map.

"It's lot 75, Tom," Sara said.

Tom drew an X in the wooded section beyond the development. It was still in line with the other killings and the attacks on the women, but outside the village. He moved the salt and pepper shakers and rolled up the map. Santucci would be in the woods with the police and there was a story to write.

"Neil said this child was brutalized," Sara explained, getting off the telephone. Her face was white and the fear had returned to her blue eyes. It made them look cold, like glass. "He said the child's head was smashed against some rocks." She picked up her coffee cup, but did not drink from it. The cup shook in her hands.

"I'd better go see what happened."

"Oh, don't," she blurted out. She did not want to be left alone in the house.

"I have to go, Sara," he answered softly. "It's my job. And I'll have to interview Santucci. He'll be there." Tom stopped talking. He set down the map and went to her, holding her first by the shoulders. He could

feel her body shaking beneath his fingers and he pulled
Sara gently into his arms, hugging her against his chest.

"We were wrong," Sara whispered. "Someone is
killing these children."

"We knew that, didn't we?"

"Yes, but this is cold-blooded murder. My God, the
child had her head smashed against rocks." She shuddered in his arms.

"I have to go, Sara."

"Are you coming back?"

"Yes, I'll get the story and phone it in from here. I'll
be back as soon as I can," he added.

She nodded, thankful that Tom was with her. "I'll be
here," she whispered, and leaning forward kissed him
quickly, embarrassed by her own forwardness.

At the dead end of Wycliffe Drive the half-dozen
police cars were jammed together, blocking access to the
murder site, and Tom Dine had to walk across several
front yards to reach the scene of the crime.

The child's body was still on the ground in the middle
of a cluster of oak trees that grew in a thick patch of
woods a dozen yards from the last subdivision lot.
The police had roped off the area in a wide circle around
the dead child, but Tom slipped under the line and
walked over to Joe Santucci, who stood away from the
body talking with two uniformed county policemen. He
nodded to Tom as he approached, then signaled that the
reporter should stay away. Tom stopped where he was
and looked at the dead child. The gray plastic shield had
already been slipped over the corpse and the body lay in
the fall leaves like a small package.

Tom took out his notepad and pen and began to jot
down a description of the murder scene . . . "The body
was found within shouting distance of Renaissance
Village, the latest victim of the bizarre child murders in
this new community of Washington intelligentsia."

He paused and glanced around, then added, "The

child's body was discovered in a small cluster of black, leafless trees. It lay on a carpet of soft leaves, her head within a few feet of a large boulder, one corner of the massive rock still wet with blood.''

Tom looked again at the murder scene. There were other rocks half-buried under the thick foliage, and a band of sturdy oak trees circled the murder site. There were more trees and thick green bushes beyond this small clearing and the whole forest would have appeared impenetrable, except that it was late September and the trees were bare. Tom had not realized such a dense corridor of trees existed this close to the open valley and the Village.

"This one is different," Santucci announced, walking toward Tom Dine. His big feet kicked up the ankle-deep leaves as he came across the clearing.

"That's what I've heard."

"The little girl had her face all smashed up."

"How bad?"

"It's hard to say without the autopsy, but her face was a fuckin' mess. The mother went berserk when she saw the kid."

"Who found her?"

"Some children. They said they were playing cowboys and Indians here in these woods."

"No chance they did it?"

Santucci shook his head. "Nope, these kids were maybe seven and eight. Whoever did this, you know, had to be bigger, stronger. The girl is eleven and tall for her age. You can see that much." He gestured toward the plastic gray bundle.

"Number three," Tom commented.

"Yeah, number three." Santucci sighed and, opening his suit coat, slipped his hands into his waist and pulled up his loose trousers.

"Are you getting much pressure at headquarters?"

"What the fuck do you think?" Santucci snapped. "Every day there's another of your goddamn articles about the murders in the *Post*. Believe me, I got them all screaming, from the governor's office on down.''

Santucci was not looking at the reporter as he spoke, but staring past Tom at the small crowd of village people who stood quietly behind the ropes. ''You know who telephoned me?'' he said. ''Lew Magnuson! He wanted to know when we were going to catch the killer. He said the murders were ruining sales. He said everyone was afraid of Renaissance Village.'' The big detective shook his head.

''Well, he's right.''

''What do you mean, he's right?''

Tom gestured toward the girl. ''Weren't her parents just looking for a new house?''

Santucci sighed. ''Shit, don't you give me trouble, too.'' He flexed his shoulders as if his suit coat was too tight, and then he nervously straightened his tie.

''Okay, I'm sorry, Joe. I know you're under the gun. What about the farmer? What about Delp?''

''We got him under surveillance.'' Santucci looked away.

''How many more kids does he have to kill before you lock him up?''

''We're still not sure it's him,'' Santucci admitted. The pushiness of the reporter got him angry. He did not need Tom Dine to tell him what to do. That was the trouble with investigative reporters. They all thought they were cops.

Tom shook his head in disgust and zipped up his green down jacket. He was ready to leave. There was a sudden distance about the man that made Santucci immediately wary, and he blurted out, ''Don't go taking this investigation into your own hands, Dine. Don't go making a lot of half-assed accusations in the *Post* or I'll have a judge clamp the lid on you.'' He sounded small-minded and mean.

''Have you heard about the women?'' Tom responded, baiting the big detective.

"What about the women? What are you talking about?" The man was immediately worried.

Speaking softly, as if embarrassed, and not looking at Santucci, Tom told him about Sara and what had been happening to the women in the Village.

"Jesus H. Christ!" Santucci shook his head. "Orgasms! Spontaneous orgasms. Now I've heard it all." He shook his head, and then, sounding annoyed, "How can that have anything to do with these murders?"

Tom told him what Sara had said about the hypothalamus region of the mind, of how it controlled the sexual response of women. "I can't tell you why," he explained to Santucci. "I don't know why, but there might be a connection between the deaths and the attacks on these women."

"What the fuck are you talking about, Dine?" Now there was real annoyance in Santucci's voice. He gestured to the damp spot on the leaves, to where the child's body had been found by the huge boulder. There was no sign of blood on the ground. It had disappeared, blending with the bright colors of fall foliage.

"The little girl was brutalized. Her face was smashed up. Whoever did it knocked a hole in her skull. You know how you can take a hammer to a Halloween jack-o'lantern and smash in the hollow pumpkin with one blow. Well, that's what happened to this kid. Her brains were all over the fuckin' forest." In his agitation, Santucci had moved away from Tom and had begun to thrash nervously through the deep cushion of leaves.

"There were no marks on the other children," Dine responded, defending himself. "I'm just saying there might be a connection between the orgasms and the deaths.

Santucci came back to him. "Look, Tom, what you see here is a progression. You're seeing a series of murders that are becoming more violent as the killer goes progressively madder. We're dealing with a psychopathic mind. I know what I'm talking about. I studied all this at George Mason University. We got ourselves a real psychopath loose in Loudoun County. Now get out of here with orgasmic stuff.'' He started to laugh, amused by the information.

Tom Dine flipped closed the pad, angry at how Santucci had reacted to his information. "You don't have shit, Santucci," he answered, defying the detective, and then he turned away and walked up the slight rise and out of the small circle in the woods.

It was a ploy. He wanted to force Santucci into telling him something, but the detective didn't call him back and Tom went under the police rope and through the crowd of villagers who still stood at the edge of the wood. He was right: Santucci didn't have anything on Delp or know why the children were being killed, and that gave him a sudden fear for Sara's safety. It meant that none of them knew who was attacking the women and children in Renaissance Village.

ten

Benjamin Fleming looked out his window and saw Cindy Delp playing on Dante Drive. She had a home-made slingshot and was picking up loose gravel and shooting stones across the empty yard, towards the new houses under construction.

It was an effort that required some skill, but Cindy was clumsy and uncoordinated, and her stones scattered harmlessly into the field.

Benjamin had his eye on the slingshot. He had never seen one so magnificent, and even from the second floor window, he saw it had been carefully carved from the wood of a tree branch, that the arms had been varnished, and then rope twisted around the handle to make a firm grip. His mouth watered. The slingshot was useless to Cindy Delp, he knew, and he abruptly spun away from the window, ran out of his bedroom and down the stairs.

"Benjy?" His mother heard him on the front stairs.

"What are you doing, darling?" she called from the kitchen.

"Nothing." He came to an abrupt halt at the bottom of the staircase.

"You're not to go outside," she reminded him.

"Oh, come on, Mom!" he shouted.

"That's final, Benjamin. No arguments. If you're bored, come into the kitchen and help me make dinner. Neil's coming over and, oh, he told me to tell you that he's got a small telescope from the Observatory. If it stays clear, you two can go up on the ridge tonight and look at the stars."

"I don't want to look for stars," Benjy cried.

"Don't whine, darling," Marcia said nicely. "It's unattractive."

Benjy jumped off the landing and hit the hardwood floor of the foyer with both feet.

"Please, Benjy, you're wrecking the house. Come out to the kitchen. I miss you, honey." She spoke sweetly, coaxing him.

Benjamin went instead to the bay windows of the livingroom and searched for Cindy. She had moved further up Dante Drive and was still looking for stones at the edge of the street. He should help her, he thought, show her at least how to shoot the slingshot. He wouldn't need to leave the street, he reasoned, and if his mother wanted him, she could easily see him from the front windows.

"Benjy?"

"Mom, for cryinoutloud! I'm just here in the livingroom."

"What are you doing?"

"Reading," he answered, glancing at a book left on the window seat.

"Okay. Fine. Just checking." Her voice was soft and amused.

He picked up the book, flipped rapidly through the pages, and leaving it open on the window seat, tiptoed to the colonial coat rack in the hall, took down his jacket, and quietly slipped out the front door.

He zipped up his jacket as he ran, yelling out loud with excitement, the sting of the cold September afternoon on his cheeks. At the top of the street Cindy Delp turned and cocked her head. Her black eyes watched the small boy run up the slope towards her.

It was too quiet in the livingroom, Marcia realized. Benjy wasn't a boy who read in silence, and she wiped her hands clean and went to check. She saw the book abandoned on the window seat and called his name.

"Benjy, are you in the bathroom?" She shouted from the bottom of the stairs and listened for any noise of him scurrying around upstairs. Where was he? she thought, angry with him for making her nervous.

She turned around then, to head for the basement, and saw that his bright red jacket was missing from the hall.

"Oh, Benjy," she whispered, "how could you." Her fear brought tears to her brown eyes, making them shine like copper.

She ran out into the cold afternoon. Within seconds she was shivering, but she kept searching, up and down the street. She shouted his name and it flew back into her face. Then she ran into the house and called Neil and Sara to tell them Benjamin was missing.

Cindy ran away from him. When Benjamin reached the top of the hill, she crossed the street and stood in the vacant front lawn of another new house.

"Do you want to play?" he shouted at the girl, then watched as she picked up another stone and aimed it right at him. But when she pulled the thick rubber sling, the stone popped out and flew harmlessly a few feet in the air. "You're not doing it right," he shouted at her.

She did not respond, nor pick up another pebble off the ground. The slingshot hung loose in her hand, as if she had momentarily forgotten its purpose. He kept his eyes on it. She didn't want it, he thought. She would throw it away soon and he could pick it up, keep it for himself.

He stepped off the curb and moved across the street, kicking a stone forward as he walked. It was windy at the top of the hill. The wind blew his long dark hair into his face, and he tossed back his head so he could see.

When he reached the middle of the street, she tensed up and drew back. Her head was cocked and her blank eyes stared vaguely at him, unfocused, but keeping him in sight. She wore only a light summer jacket and a short cotton dress. Her bony knees were red from the cold and her long, blond hair flew in a tangled web around her thin face.

When Benjamin reached the other side of the street, she backed away once more, moving farther into the front yard of the new construction.

"Do you want me to show you how to shoot that?" he asked nicely, but still she did not respond.

"Hey," he shouted next, "can you hear me?" Still she did not answer. She stood with her head to one side, her mouth open and her eyes unblinking.

Benjamin shoved his hands into his jeans and moved along the street, not gaining on her, but changing his position. She moved with him, turning not only her head but her whole body as she tracked him with her large eyes.

"Hey, what's the matter," he asked, "can't you talk?" He had never talked to someone who wouldn't answer him.

She bent over, picked up a tiny piece of limestone, and aimed it at Benjamin. But again the stone flew up harmlessly into the air.

"Hey! What's the matter with you?" He picked up several small pebbles from the edge of the sidewalk and threw them at Cindy, aiming low and trying not to hit her, but one bounced off the hard ground and caught her leg. Cindy screeched and backed off.

He grabbed another stone and squeezed it in his fist, held it ready, waited for her to shoot at him again, but she didn't react. Instead she turned and moved towards the open farm field.

"Hey!" Benjamin shouted, unsure of what he should do.

When she reached the field, separated from the Village by a barbed wire fence, she paused, looked back at Benjamin, then waved, as if inviting him to follow her.

"He may have just gone out to play," Neil tried to reason with Marcia, "and he knew if he said anything, you wouldn't let him go." He glanced at Sara and Tom Dine, soliciting their agreement. "Let's not panic," he added, and motioned with his hands for all of them to be calm.

"I can't just stand here," Marcia announced. "I have to go look for him." She zipped up her parka and checked the pockets for her gloves.

"We're all going, Marcia, but let's do it with some order," Neil said quickly, and again looked to Tom and Sara. He was as tall as Tom Dine, but thin, and he seemed weak in comparison. "Tom, you have a car, right? Why don't you go with Sara in one car, and Marcia and I will take mine." He spoke with his hands, and they flashed in the air like signals.

"No," Marcia protested. "We're not going to find Benjy by driving around. He's not on the streets, I'm sure. He's gone off somewhere, with someone, into the fields, or down by the river, or to the woods." She glanced nervously at the others. No one had yet said anything about Benjamin being in danger.

"I agree," Sara nodded. "It would be more effective if we split up. Neil, you take the car and tour the streets, and the rest of us will go into the fields." She, too, was already moving toward the door, ready to leave.

"Marcia," Tom asked, "is there any particular place

where Benjy might go? Somewhere around the Village where he likes to play?'' He did not raise his voice and his calm direct question momentarily eased the tension in the foyer. They waited and watched Marcia as she tried to think.

"We've been here such a short time. I mean, he doesn't know many places, usually he plays in the yard, or the small park. . . .''

"Would you check the park, Sara?'' Tom asked, and Sara agreed. She felt immediately better, seeing that Tom had begun to organize the search.

". . . And he has been fascinated by the barns. . . .''

"I'll go to the barns,'' Tom answered. "Let's plan on meeting back here in half an hour if we haven't found him.''

Cindy let Benjamin keep her in sight. She slipped through the fence and kept moving downhill towards the barns, but Benjy was able to stay with her. They were out of the Village, yet still in sight of the houses. He could see, over the tops of the corn stalks, the brown shingled roofs of the Village and he wasn't afraid.

Once in the field, however, Cindy began to run, cutting diagonally into the corn, jumping from row to row and increasing her speed. He had to run to keep her in sight, and even then she was only a bright flash of color among the stalks of high corn.

Then all at once he lost her. He had kept running as fast as he could, racing between the tall, thickly planted rows, out of breath and panting, his small feet stumbling on the plowed ground, and he suddenly realized he couldn't hear her thrashing up ahead of him.

He stopped and listened, but no sound came back to him on the cold wind.

"Cindy!'' he shouted and his voice rang clear in the empty afternoon. He shouted again and again, and then, exhausted, he fell sobbing to the dirt, a tiny figure lost in the forest of corn.

• • •

Tom Dine walked from Marcia Fleming's house down to the barns below Michelangelo Court. The cul-de-sac circled the giant sycamore and the Delps' white house seemed out of place and awkwardly big among the smaller and newer contemporary homes.

The barn was a hundred feet to the right of the farm house and up a slope. Renovation had already begun, but it still was an old-fashioned red barn, with its steep gables and wide doors. Tom followed the tractor tracks up to the wide double doors and went inside.

He searched the cattle stanchions and the horse stalls, then went upstairs to the loft, calling out Benjy's name as he moved through the dark, silent building. The loft was empty except for a half-dozen bales of hay left in one corner. It was best to make certain, Tom thought, and climbed up to look behind the stack.

Cindy was there, hidden between the bales, curled up into a tight ball with her legs drawn up, her face tucked against her body.

"Cindy?" he whispered and crouched down closer to the child.

He did not touch her. Her unapproachability made him wary, yet when she didn't respond to his voice, he gently moved his hand across her arm.

She curled tighter, like an animal, shrinking from his touch. He leaned closer to catch a glimpse of her face and now he could smell her unwashed body. It startled him and he edged away.

"Cindy, let me take you home," he said and took her arm, trying to pull her loose.

She hit him hard across his face. Her small fist caught him flush on his chin and knocked his head back, hurting him.

"Goddamn it!" He reached for her with both hands, but she slipped loose, flaring her arms and scrambling away.

Tom caught hold of her right ankle, and she kicked

wildly at him with her free foot and screeched out loud.
Her violent sounds were frightening and for a moment
he hesitated, slightly afraid that if he let go, she'd attack
him. Then he tightened his grip on her ankle and moved
forward.

She kept scurrying away, using her hands to grab hold
of the bale wire and pull herself forward. He reached
for her left leg and Cindy kicked out at him, missing his
face and hitting him on the shoulder. It momentarily
knocked him off balance and he lost his hold on her
ankle. She got up and climbed rapidly, out of the bales
and over the top. He pulled himself up and, jumping
over two bales, cut her off, trapping the child in the
dark corner.

"Okay," he whispered, breathing deeply to get his
wind back. "You're coming with me." He moved
slowly forward, realizing now that she was dangerous.
This was not just a helpless, retarded child.

He moved again and then abruptly halted. Her dark
eyes had found their focus and across the wide pupils
quick, sudden bolts of violent light flashed and blazed
in her retinas.

"Cindy!" Her eyes flamed up with color, beautiful
blues and greens and yellows, all blinding him with their
brilliance. "Don't!" He turned his head to one side and
raised his arm, shielding himself, and she pushed forward, ran by him and out of the corner of the loft.

Tom shouted for her to stop, but she had already
reached the stairs and was disappearing. He went after
her then, out of the empty building, out into the old
pigpen, then over the fence behind the stables and into
the corn field, the last remains of the working farm
land.

He kept gaining on her as she thrashed through the
field, hurdling the rows of stiff yellow corn stalks,
moving uphill and deeper into the five-acre patch of
corn.

It was deep twilight and his field of vision had been

reduced to only a few yards. She was almost lost to him, he realized. Already his side hurt and he was gasping for breath. He couldn't keep up with her. He stumbled forward, nearly falling, and when he glanced up, she was gone.

"Oh, shit!" He stopped at once and listened. Ahead of him, and to his right, he heard someone racing through the corn. He started running again, following the sound, and ran for another twenty yards, then paused. Once more he heard the frantic thrashing through the thick corn, but now from below him in the wide field.

"Goddamn it!" he swore and kept running, racing downhill, then cutting through the corn, pushing his way from one row to the next.

It was night in the field, the dark had rolled across the hillside, filling the rows of corn. The last light of the day was high in the sky, a pale, soft light sprinkled already with stars.

The wind had picked up, and it whipped through the corn stalks, ripping the stiff husks. The field sounded like an angry orchestra, swirling around him.

He had lost her, he realized, and he was exhausted, tired from his run, out of breath, and in pain. He turned around, started once more to walk uphill toward the top of the field. They would have to get more help, he decided, call Santucci and involve the police in the search. Then he looked up, checking to see where he was in the field, and caught a glimpse of Cindy crouched in the corn a dozen feet away.

"Cindy!" He jumped towards her, beating back the stiff stalks. She had Benjy with her, holding the small boy in her grip. Tom lunged forward, arms outstretched, reaching through the stiff rows, and she dropped Benjy and jumped away, slipped aside from his grasp. He fell forward into the corn, tripping on his own feet, and tumbled over.

The boy was crying and Tom quickly picked him up,

hugged the child to his chest, spoke softly, whispered that everything was all right, that he was safe, but realized as he spoke that Benjy was not safe, that none of them were safe in the Village.

eleven

Sara Marks woke after midnight with her hands inside her nightshirt, fondling her breasts. She rolled on her back and felt the rush of blood to her vagina. In the dark bedroom she moaned with pain, then gasped, as the orgasm tore through her. Her pelvis shook with each wave and she grabbed hold of her pillow, clutching it tightly and submitting herself to the driving thrust.

It was over in seconds and Sara panted as she struggled to the side of the bed, her white cotton nightshirt damp with perspiration. For several minutes she just sat and let herself recover her breath. The sudden, unexpected, and violent orgasms no longer shocked her; only in the aftermath of its violence was she again frightened.

She stood and walked unsurely to the bathroom, stripping off her nightshirt. She had to shower. Her body was soaked with perspiration.

In the dark Sara pulled a towel off the rack and wiped the sweat from her neck and body. Then she flipped on the lights and as the intense fluorescent bulbs blinked on, she looked in the mirror and saw the bubble of blood in her nostril.

Tentatively she touched the bubble with her finger and broke it. The blood beaded at the corner of her lip, then ran down her chin. She was trembling, confused as always by the blood. She opened the medicine cabinet door, took out mouthwash, and rinsed her mouth, then, stepping into the shower, she spent ten minutes letting cold water pound her body.

Sara shut off the shower and, wrapping a wide brown bathtowel around herself, went back into the bedroom. She had made it to the middle of the room when she felt the sudden, hot flash driving through her mind, splitting it apart, and tumbling her into another frenzied orgasm.

Sara fell onto the bed, but this time she tried to fight it. She fought to disassociate her mind from what was happening to her vagina, to the rush of warmth flooding the center of her body. She concentrated on work, on the experiments she had done that week, and she rolled across the bed and tried to stand, but in the end she could not resist the driving attack. She let the tide of passion overwhelm her and the sexual wave run its brief and intense course through her body. And when it was over, she sat up and, reaching for the telephone, dialed Tom at his apartment.

"I'm sorry," she said, whispering into the mouthpiece, "I know it's the middle of the night, but it just happened. Tom, please help me." She started to cry and, overwhelmed and frightened, she could no longer stop the tears.

"Are you hurt? Have you hurt yourself?" he asked immediately.

"No, but they're getting worse. They are more violent." She remembered the blood then and touched her nose. "And I'm bleeding."

"Sara, I'm getting dressed. I'll be there within the hour."

"Thank you," she whispered. She found it hard to admit to him—or anyone—that she needed help, but she secretly was grateful that he was coming to her. She hung up the phone and it rang immediately, before she lifted her hand off the receiver.

"Sara!"

"Yes, Marcia."

"It happened again."

"Yes, I know; me, too. Are you okay?"

"I am now."

"It must have hit us all."

"Should we call?"

"Let's wait. There's no reason to wake everyone in the Village."

"Sara, I'm scared." There were no tears in the woman's voice, just fear.

"It's all right, Marcia." Sara spoke confidently, as if she were sure there would be no more attacks that night. She wished that Tom weren't an hour away. She would feel a lot safer, she realized, if he were with her, and she even knew that was odd: What could he do? What could any of them do? "Marcia, I'm going to walk over to your place. Would you feel better if I did that?"

"Oh, God, yes, but I can't have you go outside alone. It's the middle of the night. I mean, we don't know what this is."

"It's okay, you're less than a block away. Besides, I'd feel safer, too, if I were with someone. We're not going to get any more rest tonight."

"Stay on the sidewalk," Marcia instructed. "Don't take any shortcuts through the backyards."

Sara smiled. "All right, no shortcuts." She felt better knowing there was another woman sharing the same fear and worried about her safety.

She hung up and again the phone rang immediately. This time it was Kathryn Mackey calling to say she, too, had been struck.

"Let's meet at Marcia Fleming's," Sara told her.

"Are there others?" Kathryn Mackey asked.

"There's us, and I suspect there are others, but we should wait until daylight before telephoning them."

"I see lights on in Rebecca Hunts' house."

"Call her. The two of you can go together to Marcia's.

Giving instructions made Sara feel better. It put her in control and meant there were tasks to accomplish. The telephone rang twice more while she dressed, more women awake and frightened. She told them where to meet, and finished dressing. Then she went downstairs and, unlocking the front door, left a note for Tom, telling him where she was, and let herself out into the dark.

Sara was not dressed for the weather. The overcast sky had cleared and the night was bright and cold. The wind chipped at her face and she turned the collar of the raincoat up to shield herself. She thought for a moment of going back into the house to get the car keys, but then realized how silly that was: she could see the lights on in Marcia's kitchen, and, instead of following the curving sidewalk from Petrarch Court, she cut through the backyard of the next lot and down the hillside.

Sara got as far as the property line, walking with her head bent against the wind and her hands burrowed into her light fall coat, and she never saw the young girl standing against the lone tree in Marcia's backyard until Cindy Delp reached out and grabbed her as she passed.

Sara stumbled forward in sudden fright when she felt the child's arm. Then, recovering, she grabbed the girl and shouted, "Cindy, what are you doing? Why aren't you at home?"

In the bright moonlight, Sara saw her questions did

not register. Cindy's face was blank and her mind adrift.

"Cindy!" Sara demanded, but she realized that gaining the attention of an autistic child took time, and was often impossible.

Cindy did not respond, but she slid her hand down Sara's arm and grabbed her fingers, then tugged and tried to make Sara follow her.

"Cindy, what is it?" Sara asked, resisting.

Cindy paused and stood perfectly still. She was concentrating and trying to speak. A word seemed to form on her lips and then it was gone, leaving only the anguish of the effort there on Cindy's face. Impatiently, frantically, Cindy flung herself at Sara, screeching wordlessly. Then she grabbed Sara's arm and pulled her. There was nothing Sara could do: she followed the child into the Village.

In the back bedroom of her home on Wycliffe Drive, Peggy Volt lay awake in the dark. The quick series of orgasms had passed and she had fallen asleep again.

It was a light, uneasy sleep and when she heard him leave the front bedroom, she woke immediately, alert and followed his footsteps through the house and into the basement. Now that he was working full-time on the project, he spent most of his time at home, downstairs with the new equipment.

Peggy had not asked him what it was. She knew better than to question him about his work. He wouldn't explain and he'd only become irritated by her prying. When she had married him, he had warned her about his job, telling her it was like his past, something which she would never know about.

She had accepted his explanation, and was even secretly thrilled that he had a mysterious background. It made him more romantic. But she had been much younger then, and in love. In time she realized the secretiveness was only his way of protecting himself, of keeping her from becoming too close to him. It was his subtle way of controlling their marriage.

Peggy sat up and reached for her housecoat, then in the dark she went to the door and carefully opened it. He had turned lights on downstairs. She could see shadows in the hallway and knew already where Kevin was. He had turned on the lights in the kitchen and gone down into the workshop.

She went silently along the upstairs hall and then down the stairs, moving quickly through the dark livingroom to the kitchen. At the kitchen door, she hesitated and peeped into the room. It was empty and he had left the basement door open. He was being careless, she realized, thinking she was sound asleep in the back bedroom. Peggy continued across the kitchen and opened a drawer. Now she was frightened. She watched her hand tremble as she reached forward and picked up the butcher knife.

Cindy Delp led Sara away from Marcia's house, out of the backyard and across the farm road. Sara went obediently, like a blind man following a guide, up the curving main road of the development, toward the Volts' house. She did not question the child.

Peggy Volt pulled the knife from the drawer and moved slowly away from the counter, backing into the middle of the kitchen, feeling as if she were outside herself, watching herself as she gradually turned, went to the basement door, and stood there in the shadowy light. She was out of control, her mind told her, yet she felt perfectly calm and rested. All the agonizing guilt she had felt after Amy's death was about to be washed away. She was going to revenge her death, kill him for destroying the mind of her baby. She moved quietly, the long butcher knife concealed in the folds of her heavy dressing gown.

• • •

Cindy Delp led Sara around behind the Volt house. She had begun to walk faster and she tugged at Sara's arm to hurry her. Kevin Volt had built a high metal industrial fence around his backyard, but Cindy expertly slipped her thin hand between the wire mesh and opened the gate.

"Cindy?" Sara whispered, but the girl did not hesitate. She pulled Sara after her into the backyard. It was darker here; the house blocked the moonlight and the yard was black. Sara moved carefully, trying to feel her way with her feet as Cindy, insistent now, dragged Sara to the locked storm door.

The girl kept directing Sara. Mutely, urgently, she signaled Sara to ring the doorbell. Sara could barely see the white, porcelain face of the child, but she saw that Cindy's black eyes were still unfocused and empty, like burned-out lights.

"Why?" Sara whispered, hesitating. Peggy had not been one of the women who telephoned, and Sara knew she would be waking her and Kevin in the middle of the night. "Come, Cindy," she said gently, "let me take you home."

Cindy jumped back, avoided Sara's grasp. As if by a fierce act of will she tried to speak, but her lips moved soundlessly and in the end she could only screech out into the empty night.

Kevin had encased the equipment along one wall of the basement, locking it away in metal cabinets so it was not visible. When the heavy, metal doors were closed it looked like a row of gray lockers.

Peggy had never seen it displayed and operating, and the shiny instruments, the several monitor screens, computers, and the rows of knobs and buttons looked beautiful, even thrilling. She felt as she did when she caught a glimpse of the control panel of an airplane's cockpit.

Kevin had his back to her and was bent over a console. Something was wrong. He had the panel off one piece of equipment and was working on the wire. A collection of small tools, miniature tweezers, and screwdrivers was set out in rows on the counter beside him.

Peggy stood at the bottom of the steps and watched him work. He was so engrossed that he had not heard her come down the stairs. It was as if he were a surgeon in the operating room, she thought, watching the sureness of his hands and the economy of effort. It fascinated and repelled her, and then, quite by surprise, she was overwhelmed by a wave of intense hatred for the man. Her rage made her dizzy and uncertain on her feet. Again, she realized, she was watching herself. She saw herself lift the butcher knife with both arms, pausing with the knife held high above her head.

She knew how simple it was: a dozen steps across the well-lighted basement, a quick, violent slash. She would aim at the slope of his shoulder, cut neatly, diagonally into his heart. There would be no blood, she thought. She would simply slice through his heart.

Sara saw a brief flash of terror in the child's eyes. They focused and froze and Cindy's pale face rippled with a moment of awareness. The long-legged girl wheeled awkwardly to the back door and slammed the bell, then hit the storm door, pounded it with her fist.

Peggy never heard the bell. Her small, slight body charged across the room, swinging the butcher knife in one long graceful arc, sweeping it down toward the slumped shoulder of her husband.

The doorbell surprised him. He jerked back, startled at the sound, and Peggy's knife missed his shoulder and smashed into the metal counter. She stumbled forward and he grabbed her before she fell to the floor. She had no strength to resist him, and she cried hysterically in his arms.

Sara grabbed Cindy. She wrapped her arms around the tall child and wrestled her from the back steps, afraid Cindy would wake up everyone on Wycliffe Drive with her pounding.

The girl resisted for a moment and then went limp. Instead of struggling, she turned to Sara and hugged her, burying her face in Sara's neck.

Sara moved the child away, pushed her back, and looked into Cindy's large, dark, vacant eyes. Then Cindy screeched and her face contorted in pain.

"What are you trying to tell me, Cindy?" Sara demanded. "Why did you bring me here?" But the child only stared blankly up at Sara, her mind once more adrift. "It's all right, Cindy," Sara sighed and hugged the hurt child to her breasts. "I'll take you home." She slipped her arm around Cindy's shoulder and led the young girl from the back door of the Volt home and down the farm road to her house.

In the basement, Kevin Volt kept his hand pressed against his wife's gasping mouth. She tried to twist away and he merely tightened his grip, locking her against his body. For a moment he didn't think about Peggy, but listened for more noise. The bell had stopped ringing and there was no longer pounding on the back door. He was curious about who it might have been, but not worried. His wife was his only worry, and she was now trapped in his arms.

twelve

"I've worked it out," Marcia Fleming announced, coming back into the livingroom with several sheets of paper.

The women had turned on her television set while they were waiting and were silently watching an old black-and-white movie. It was after three A.M. and everyone was exhausted. The attacks were over and they wanted only to get some sleep. Still, none of them had left Marcia's house. Without saying so, they were all afraid of being alone.

"There is some sort of progression," Marcia continued. She moved in among the others, and they made space for her on the sofa so she could spread the sheets of paper on the coffee table.

"If we were all accurate in our reporting, then the times imply that the attacks happened in a sweeping motion." Marcia raised her arm and showed what she meant. "Beginning first with the women closest to the river—Pam and Kathryn—and at the bottom of the development, the attacks have spread up the hill, and have hit Sara, who's the last female in the Village, five to ten minutes after everyone else.''

''What does it mean?'' asked Jill.

''It means we're being hit by some sort of wave,'' Sara replied.

''And there's another pattern,'' Marcia added. She shifted through the sheets and continued, ''Since these attacks began last week we're getting hit more frequently. Amy Volt was killed at ten o'clock on Tuesday. Sara said she experienced her first orgasm the next morning, around eight A.M. Debbie was killed at four P.M. that afternoon.

''Those first series of attacks,'' she went on, ''were ten hours apart. The next series were eight hours apart. And now the attacks are closer.'' She stared again at the women. ''By this calculation, some of us should be struck at 10 A.M.''

''Some?'' Rebecca Hunt asked.

Marcia nodded. ''According to the times everyone gave me, it appears that we're not all getting hit. Look, only half of us are here tonight. Peggy Volt, for one, told me she'd telephone Sara or myself if she had an orgasm. And Joy Lang never called. She said she would''

''Joy's not home,'' Pam volunteered. ''She had a date in D.C. tonight and she told me she was staying in town.'' Pam glanced around at the others, her eyes wide-open and innocent. ''She's afraid of staying in the Village.'' She sounded apologetic.

''We are all afraid, Pam,'' Sara quietly remarked. Then she turned to Marcia and asked, ''Where's Peggy?'' Sara had not mentioned to her or any of the women how Cindy Delp had dragged her across the Village to bang on the Volts' back door.

Marcia shook her head.

''Do you think we should call her?'' Now Sara was

nervous. The behavior of Cindy Delp had baffled her, and suddenly Sara felt she had made a mistake. Perhaps she should have awakened Peggy and found out if everything was all right.

"I think we should telephone Peggy," she blurted out.

"Sara, it's the middle of the night," Marcia protested. "She would have called if she was attacked."

Sara stood. She knew the other women were watching, and that her nervous reaction bothered them. She realized they needed her to be calm and collected during this crisis, but she was worried about Peggy Volt.

"I'm going to telephone her," she announced and, without hesitating, she went into the kitchen and dialed. She needed only to hear Peggy's voice, Sara reasoned, and she'd feel better.

Kevin Volt answered the phone on the first ring, as if he had been waiting. Sara excused herself for calling and asked to speak to Peggy.

"Peggy's asleep, Sara," Kevin answered coolly. "Is there anything wrong?"

"Well, no, not really." Sara paced away from the wall phone, stretching the cord. "I'm not sure Peggy mentioned anything to you, Kevin, but some of us women have been experiencing rather bizarre attacks."

"Attacks?"

"Well, no, not attacks really," she sighed. "I think Peggy should explain this to you." Sara felt flustered. She was not handling this well.

"Of course, Peggy has been having a difficult time. That's to be expected after the baby's death."

"I know and I'm sorry to bother you." Kevin was right. What was she doing checking up on Peggy?

"Sara, what is this about attacks?" He tried to seem merely curious, but his voice tightened.

"I really think Peggy should tell you, Kevin." Sara tried to back off from giving an explanation.

"Sara, my wife is ill. The doctor has her under heavy

medication. The woman isn't rational most days. You say she—and the other women—are being *attacked!*" His voice rose sharply and now he was afraid. Perhaps something had gone wrong.

"Kevin, I'm sorry for being so vague, but I'd rather not say anything more." Sara had gained control; she would not confide in him. "Ask Peggy," she said quietly.

"Thank you, Sara. That's exactly what I'll do." He hung up abruptly.

Sara's hands were shaking when she replaced the telephone receiver. She stood for a moment, calming herself, and then she went to tell the women that Peggy Volt was all right, at home in bed and asleep.

Kevin sat a moment on the bed beside his wife and gradually suppressed his rage toward Sara Marks. This was not the time to be careless and imprudent.

His immediate concern was his wife and she hadn't stirred since he had given her the injection. It was enough to keep her unconscious for another twelve hours, he knew, and he left her alone, locking the bedroom door behind him, and went downstairs to his workshop. It was not quite four A.M., and he had more work to do before daylight.

In his basement workshop Kevin Volt again adjusted his mini-wave Gunn diode, establishing the electro-magnetic field at 10 GHz. He then switched on the microwave generator and on his notepad scribbled down 10.2 GHz. Next he turned the receiving oscillator to 10.245 GHz, and mixed the two signals in the Schottky diode to produce 20.445 GHz. On his notepad he noted the 45 MHz displacement.

His hands were sweating as he flipped the transceiver switch and electronically tuned the Varactor bias, honing it in on section seven of the Village. He was working fast, and he glanced up quickly at the rough map he had pinned to the wall above the computer ter-minal and reset the Gunnplexer, adjusting it 0.35 MHz to allow for the colder night temperature. Then almost casually he flipped the switch and heard Sara Marks say, "I think we're all right for tonight. I don't think we have to worry about anything more this evening."

In his basement lab Kevin Volt sat down, exhausted from the tension. He did not bother about what Sara was saying; it did not matter. Finally the alignments were correct. He had focused the homemade microwave signal. Tomorrow, he decided that moment, he would begin to direct the laser beam at the houses. And by Monday, he reasoned, he would have the answers he needed from Renaissance Village. But by Monday there would be no Village.

thirteen

Sara cooked dinner for Tom Dine that evening and found she actually enjoyed doing it, taking the trouble to set the table with her mother's good china and a linen tablecloth she had bought on impulse on a trip to New York, in a small, elegant shop near the Plaza Hotel. She and Sam had seldom made the effort to eat dinner together and if they did, it was usually Sam who cooked. He had the time and he was better at it—or so he'd made them both believe.

Now, in her new house, Sara let Tom make them drinks, and had him sit and talk with her as she prepared chicken, sautéed, with lemon and parsley. Then while Tom built a fire in the livingroom she went upstairs to shower and change and comb out her hair. She reappeared wearing blue silk hostess pajamas, severely cut, one shade lighter than her eyes.

They had dinner by candlelight, and coffee and brandy sitting in the semidark before the warm fire.

Both were careful not to talk about the murders and what was happening in the Village, and for the first time since they met, they actually got to know something about each other, about how they had lived their lives before meeting on the night of Amy Volt's murder.

"I've always been too busy getting my medical degrees to think about marriage," Sara explained. "I was living with a man before moving here from Boston. He's at Harvard—entrenched at Harvard would be a better way of putting it—and when I got this opportunity to come to Washington and NIH, it seemed like the best thing for me." She shrugged her shoulders.

In the soft glow of the fire, Tom could see Sara's eyes, shiny with unshed tears.

"Do you think you made a mistake?" It was a question he had to ask, and he waited apprehensively for the answer.

"No, I don't think so," she answered slowly. For a moment she thought of telling him what had happened—the pregnancy and miscarriage—and then realized she didn't want to talk about it and said instead, "Sam and I were fine together, comfortable, but it wasn't much more than an easy living arrangement. In many ways, I think, we were both glad that this job with NIH came along."

"Are you lonely for him?"

"I am lonely, sometimes, but not for Sam. I just got used to living with a man, and, now, in this big house I feel lonely. Buying this house may have been a mistake. I should have done what most single women like me do in Washington, bought a condominium in the District."

"You wouldn't feel so bad about this place if it weren't for the deaths and those attacks."

She nodded, agreeing.

"Anyway, maybe they're over," he went on, trying to snap the gloomy mood of their conversation.

"I hope you're right," she replied, but there was no confidence in her voice. The thought of another attack made her immediately frightened. She sat up on the edge of the couch and began to toy with her hair, to comb her thin fingers through the fine, long, cornsilk strands. The fear returned again. It ran the length of her body until her arms and feet were trembling. She would have to do something, she knew, pour them both another brandy.

Still, before she could move, Tom got up and moved closer, sitting next to her on the couch.

"It's going to be okay," he whispered, and she turned her head and buried it in his shoulder.

The wine with dinner and then the brandy had made her feel sad, and once, during dinner, when she looked across the candle-lit table at him, she thought how nice it was to have someone there in the house with her and not be looking ahead to a long night by herself.

"Come on," he said, "let me take you upstairs."

She shook her head. "I'm afraid."

"I won't hurt you."

"I'm afraid of myself. I don't trust my own body."

Tom moved her away and looked at her face. The fear had crystallized in her eyes, making them look cold and hard.

"You're going to be all right." He tried to reassure her.

"No, Tom." She raised her hand and stroked his cheek.

He kissed her fingers. He knew he had to take control, to make decisions for both of them, and without giving her a chance to protest, he stood and, bending over, picked her up in his arms. She was lighter than he had expected, a child's weight, and he carried her easily across the livingroom and up the dark stairs to her bedroom. She lay quietly in his arms. His strength, the ease with which he carried her, was comforting. She could trust him. He would protect her.

Tom placed her on the bed and she lay still, watching while he closed the bedroom door and turned out the light. He stood in the shadows, taking off his clothes, and she could see his silhouette by the moonlight streaming in the front windows.

She had never been courted this way, fussed over and adored. Her romance with Sam had not been very erotic and she wondered about Tom, suddenly aware that she did not really know him. Perhaps he was peculiar and would make demands of her. She had at first been put off by his rough ways. He came across the large room, back to the bed, and she closed her eyes and waited.

Sara lay on her side in the blue silk dressing pajamas. Her face was in profile and locks of blond hair had fallen over her cheeks, hiding her face. She looked asleep and so lovely on the bed that for a moment just staring at her was a pleasure to him.

She had a rare beauty, he realized. Lovely without effort. She did not have to orchestrate her good looks. Her beauty was simple and casual, as if it were merely an accident of nature. Just looking at Sara overwhelmed him, and he couldn't get over his good fortune. When he touched her, his hand trembled.

"Would you mind if tonight we didn't make love?" she asked. "I think if I could get through tonight, I'd be all right again."

She did not open her eyes as she spoke. She was afraid of what he would think, of how he might react, and she did not want him angry at her.

"Of course," he answered. "Would you feel better if I slept in the guest room?"

"No," Sara shook her head. "Come to bed with me. I want you to hold me." She sounded like a child, afraid of the dark.

Tom went around the bed and slid inside beside her. He was nervous himself, excited by being in bed with a new woman, and unsure of how to behave. It had been a long time since he had slept with someone and not made love to her.

Sara slid out of bed and went into the bathroom and

closed the door. She did not explain what she was doing, but when she opened the bathroom door again, she was wearing a nightgown.

In the moment before she flipped off the light, standing in the bathroom doorway, he could see her outline beneath the sheer cloth of the gown. Her long, thin legs, the dark triangle of her sex, and the slight impression of her small breasts. Her hair she had combed out and it easily reached her shoulders. She looked like a woman coming to bed to make love, and he thought for a moment that perhaps she had changed her mind.

But her manner now was far from passionate. She sat on the edge of the bed and took off her jewelry, tilting her head to each side as she unfastened her small pearl earrings. She set them on the top of the night table and they clicked against the glass. It was the only sound in the bedroom until she said, "When I bought this house, my great fear was robbery." She laughed nervously. "Who in the world would have imagined anything as bizarre as this?" She shook her head.

Tom reached across the bed and stroked her arm. He wanted to say something to reassure her, but he would have to lie; he had no idea why she and the other women were being attacked. Instead, he said, "Come to bed, you need to rest."

She nodded, agreeing. It was late and she was tired, and tomorrow was a full day of work. He moved over and she slid in beside him. Now they were both tense, aware of each other and careful not to touch.

"I don't know if this is going to work," Sara whispered. She was facing him, and had pulled back her hair so her cheek lay flat on the deep pillow. She looked incredibly beautiful, he thought, so fragile and fair. He touched her, caressed her cheek with the tips of his fingers.

"You're not going to fall asleep as long as I'm here, are you?" he asked.

"I'm afraid not."

"Okay, let me hold you for a moment, and then I'll go into the guest room. I'll be close, in case you need me."

"Thank you," she whispered. "I'm sorry I'm being such a jerk about all this."

Tom pulled her into his arms and could see in her eyes that now she did trust him, that she was allowing herself to be comforted and held.

Sara's head was buried into his shoulder and she breathed deeply. She liked the smell of his body and the fact that he handled her so easily. She was always cautious around men who were physical with her, always afraid that she'd be accidentally hurt by their fooling around, but in Tom's arms she felt secure, and slowly she sank against him. He moved his hand and slipped it through the open folds of her night gown, touching her small breast. She moaned softly at the pleasure of his touch.

"Don't," she asked, but there was no authority in her whisper.

Tom did not rush her, only slowly, gently, he fondled her bare breast. She pressed the length of her body against his, arched her pelvis to his and he bowed his head and ran his tongue lightly over the arch of her breast. He could taste the salt of her sweat.

"Don't," she asked again, but they both knew he would not stop, nor did she want him to.

He moved his left hand up her thigh and slid his fingers between her legs. She was wearing panties and, through the fabric, he rubbed the ridges of her sex.

Sara reached out and ran both hands through his dark hair, grabbing hold, as she shook with each touch to her body. The fear she felt about an orgasm had passed, and Sara wanted him now to come inside her. This time, with him, she would be able to come. Sara was certain he could take her over the edge of her resistance. In his arms she felt both saved and threatened, and this odd duplicity, this mixture of love and fear, would make her come.

He had her nightgown halfway up her body, but would not stop to slip it off. She wanted to tell him to wait until she was naked, but he was in a rush. His hands and mouth were everywhere on her body and she could not stop him, nor did she want to. She put her arms around his neck and pulled him down on to her body.

The rock hit the window at that moment. It broke the glass in the bedroom window and crashed to the wood floor. Sara screamed and Tom pulled away, rolling off the bed. Another rock smashed the windows, and Tom ducked immediately, but the stone dropped harmlessly to the floor.

"Oh, God, what is it?" Sara was sitting up in bed, the blanket pulled high around her neck.

"Stay where you are," Tom ordered. A third stone struck the house, missing the windows while Tom, keeping away from them, moved around the room and out of the bedroom. He crossed the hall and went into the guest room. From there he could look down onto the front lawn.

"It's that farmer's daughter," he shouted to Sara. "She's on the goddamned lawn throwing rocks."

Sara threw off the blankets and stood. Another stone hit the windows, spraying glass into the room. The rock landed at the bottom of the bed and Sara screamed.

"Watch it!" Tom was standing at the bedroom door. He looked helpless without clothes and in his bare feet, and he was afraid to step into the room. Broken glass was everywhere on the thick carpet.

Sara slid into her slippers and pulled on her robe as she went from the room. A rock hit the house, missing the windows.

"This is absolutely ridiculous," she said, going past Tom. "That child is terrorizing this whole Village."

Whatever sympathy and understanding she had had for Cindy Delp was lost in her rage. The stoning and broken windows had frightened her and that fear had turned to an almost uncontrollable rage.

"Easy, Sara, she doesn't understand," Tom cautioned. But Sara did not reply. She had unlocked the door, turned on the front step lights, and gone out into the cold.

Cindy was surprised by the light. She stopped and stared at Sara standing in the doorway. In her hand was a rock the size of a soft ball. Again, she was not dressed for the weather. She stood on the lawn wearing a cotton dress and heavy, barnyard shoes without socks.

Sara wrapped the dressing gown tighter to her body and went across the lawn to the young girl. She could see there were more rocks at Cindy's feet, a small stack of stones that Sara guessed Cindy had carried from the fields beyond the Village.

Cindy watched Sara steadily as she approached. She did not change expressions. For a moment Sara wondered if Cindy would turn on her, raise her thin arm, and strike her with another rock. The child could kill her, Sara thought, slowing her pace and hoping to seem less forceful and threatening. She had no idea what delusions might be racing through the mind of this strange girl.

"Cindy?" Sara spoke softly and stopped within five feet of the child.

The tall, thin girl opened her hand and let the rock drop. She turned to Sara, moving with the awkward, jerky motion of a retarded person. She began to cry and tears ran down her pale cheeks in a steady flow. Sara stepped forward and took hold of Cindy, held her firmly by the shoulders.

"What is it?" she asked "Why did you throw those rocks?" She watched the face of the child for a flicker of comprehension. Cindy was staring up at her, but

Sara saw there was no recognition in the blank eyes of the girl.

Cindy tried to speak. Her slight body trembled as she struggled to make sound. A frown crossed her forehead and her wide mouth quivered as she attempted to utter a word. Then she raised her hand and, pointing across the lawn toward the house, screeched out loud. It was as if the sound was being painfully ripped from her lips.

"What is it, Cindy?" Sara knew what torture she was inflicting on the child by making her speak, but she realized also that Cindy was trying to tell her something, to warn her.

The girl kept staring beyond Sara, pointing toward the house. Sara could see the fear gather in the child's black eyes and she spun around to look behind her. In the doorway Tom Dine stood, watching them both.

fourteen

"What do you think she was trying to tell you?" Tom asked. They were both dressed and sitting in Sara's livingroom after Tom had taken Cindy home.

"I think she was trying to warn me. Warn me about you."

Tom's face paled, and he could feel his heart race angrily. The strange murders in the Village had not personally touched him, but because of Sara he was being drawn closer to the crimes. Now she was even suspicious of him. He had a sudden urge to leave the Village and these people, but when he looked at Sara, saw the worry in her eyes and the weariness on her face, he knew he couldn't leave her. She needed him, and he knew also that he could help her. He could save this woman's life.

"Why?" he asked.

Sara shrugged. "I don't know. Perhaps because she sees any sexual involvement for me as dangerous. Marcia Fleming has charted the timing of these spontaneous orgasms. They seem to be sweeping across the Village at predictable times. I should have had one about fifteen minutes ago. Maybe Cindy knew about these attacks.''

"But you didn't have one.''

Sara nodded, realizing he was right.

"Where were you fifteen minutes ago?''

"Upstairs, getting dressed, then I came downstairs to the kitchen.''

"And I was at the farm house with Cindy.''

"I've been alone before when I had the attacks. Do you think I'm imagining them?'' Her voice was immediately defensive, and she felt awful, thinking he did not believe her.

Tom shook his head. "I wish it were that simple.'' He leaned forward in the chair, speaking quickly. "But you haven't been alone, not at least from what you've told me.''

Sara frowned and shook her head. "Yes I have. There was the one time you were with me in the kitchen, but. . . .''

"So was Cindy. Cindy Delp was in the field behind the house. And the morning you had your first attack, she was hiding in your bathroom.''

"Cindy? But how could she be involved?''

"I'm not sure. What about mental telepathy? Do you think that kid could have triggered those attacks and killed those little girls?''

Sara sat stunned. She kept remembering Cindy, cramped in the tight corner of the shower, squatting in the rocky field behind the house, and then standing on the front lawn, throwing rocks at her bedroom windows. For the past week, every time she turned around, Cindy had been watching her, spying. Sara shook her head, "It's not possible. You cannot kill people or attack them simply by mental telepathy.'' Sara kept shaking her head, dismissing the notion. "It's ridiculous,'' she added, sounding angry at the idea.

Tom came to the couch and sat on the edge, turning to face her. "Let's interview that girl, give her an examination. Let's find out how severely autistic she is. I don't trust her parents. Have you talked to that old man? I mean, that guy is very strange."

Sara nodded, agreeing, but did not immediately answer. The whole experience of the night had been exhausting, and now she had developed a pounding headache. She rubbed her brow to try and ease the pain, but the ache was sharp, a series of jabs across her forehead. It was hard even to concentrate, but she answered Tom, saying, "I can't just examine the child. In the first place, I need her parents' permission and I won't get it. When I mentioned a special school for Cindy to Delp, he got very upset and as much as told me to mind my own business."

The pain was excruciating now, intense bolts of pain spinning in her head. She was going to be sick, she realized. This wasn't a headache at all. She grabbed the corner of the couch to pull herself from the seat. She had to stand; she had to get out of the house.

Tom was speaking to her, asking if she were all right and she could feel his hands grabbing her shoulders.

"My head," she whispered.

The pain had a life of its own. The sharp, piercing jabs had changed to swirling currents that whipped around her head. She could no longer see. Thin bolts of colored lights raced across her eyes in zigzag lines.

"Look!" She turned her face to Tom's. "It's my eyes. Do you see anything?"

Tom held her face steady between his hands. Her eyes were wide and blazing with colors. Microscopic bars of colored lights flashed across her irises and pupils in bursts of irregular lengths. And under his palms, Tom felt the temperature of Sara's skin change as her face became feverish.

"Help me, Tom." It was taking all her strength to stay conscious. She knew she couldn't stand; she couldn't get out of the house. And then she became sick and, jerking her head free, turned and threw up over the couch.

"Oh, God," she moaned as her body, out of control, retched again and she vomited what little fluid remained in her stomach onto the rug.

"Easy, darling," he said, trying to hold her steady in his arms, but she began to tremble and her rising fever dropped immediately. He felt her body turn icy in his arms. He kept talking, kept reassuring her as he moved her into a large wing chair and put her feet up on an ottoman. Then he pulled the comforter off the back of the couch and tucked it around Sara's shivering body.

"I'm going to telephone a doctor. Is there someone in the Village?"

Sara tried to shake her head, but the pain swirling around her skull made it impossible. "It's killing me, Tom. Please, dear God, take the pain away." Her face twisted against the torment. She took hold of him and her fingernails dug deeply into his hands, cutting his skin with her anguish. He grabbed her wrists and pulled himself free, and Sara's hands shot to her tormented head, digging her hands into her own scalp and drawing blood.

"Oh, Tom, please make it stop!"

He knelt beside her, tried to pull her hands from her hair. She was delirious, out of her mind with pain and helpless to tell him what to do. He had no idea where the closest hospital was located. He'd have to telephone Santucci. Santucci would get a doctor and ambulance and get Sara out of here, and then Tom remembered the murders. Sara was next. She was being killed right before his eyes, he realized, and then he remembered Cindy Delp.

She was here, he knew, in the house or close enough to cause pain, to kill Sara. He had locked the doors himself, and checked them after Cindy attacked the windows, but the bedroom windows were open and the broken glass still on the rug. It was possible that Cindy had gotten back inside.

Tom ran up the front stairs and pushed open the door. Sara had taped heavy plastic over the broken windows, but one sheet had been ripped off and was flapping loudly in the cold, dark room.

He stepped inside and closed the door. He did not turn on the light, but stood with his back to the door, searching the room in the moonlight.

She had to be there, hiding in the closets or the bathroom, and that frightened him. The child was deranged; she could do almost anything to him. Downstairs, Sara screamed in pain and her cry ran up his spine. Behind his back, he turned the lock on the bedroom door, locking himself inside with the young girl.

"Cindy?" he called. There was no answer, no movement in the darkened room. The only sound in the house was Sara's helpless screaming.

Tom circled the room, keeping away from the windows, moving along the wall toward the closets. He called Cindy's name again, but she would not answer.

He slid open the closet doors, moving quickly, pushing Sara's clothes aside as he searched. She was not there, nor, when he crouched down, did he find her under the bed.

Downstairs, Sara screamed once more and he pushed open the bathroom door and flipped on the light.

He could see Cindy's distorted figure behind the foggy glass of the shower stall and he yanked open the door. She was sitting on the tile floor, her legs drawn up tight, sitting in a tight ball and rocking back and forth. She stared at him, her face blank and expressionless, her eyes unfocused.

Again he heard Sara, her cry coming muffled through the house, and he reached forward and lifted Cindy off the floor, grabbing her beneath the arms and jerking her from the corner.

"Stop it!" he shouted, shaking the child. "Quit it, Cindy. Let her go."

The young girl stared dumbly at him, her mouth slack, her eyes empty.

Sara screamed again. The piercing cry rang through the house and tore at Tom. He could see her suffering on the couch, her mind being destroyed by this mute child.

"Cindy!" Tom shouted.

She was trying to speak.

"What?" he demanded and, with the strength of his arms, lifted the child, pulled her close.

Sara cried out.

"Goddamn it!" He shoved Cindy away and, with one quick, violent movement, slapped the girl across her face. Her head popped back with the blow. Tears flooded her eyes and a bubble of blood spilled onto her lips.

Downstairs, Sara stopped screaming.

fifteen

Joe Santucci stood before the fireplace and listened to their stories. He took notes and nodded, kept them talking, and, when they had finished, he paused a moment to flip through the pages and review his notes before he looked over and asked, "You said when you slapped the girl the headache stopped?" He sounded incredulous.

Tom nodded. "At the exact moment." He was positive about this. He could still see himself hitting the child, slapping her hard across the face, and then the silence from the livingroom.

"How can you explain something like that, Doctor? Explain it, you know, medically?" He and Tom Dine both looked expectantly at Sara, who sat across the room in one of the deep chairs. Tom had wrapped a blanket around her, and she looked small and afflicted.

"I can't," she said.

"But you think somehow this girl caused the

headache?'' Santucci glanced back and forth between the two of them.

"I do," Tom answered. "I have no idea by what process, but I know that girl had control of Sara's mind. And I think she was trying to kill her.'' He stood and began to pace the length of the large livingroom. There were only the three of them there; two county police officers had already taken Cindy Delp to her house.

"I also think," Tom continued, "that Cindy is responsible for these deaths. I think she killed the kids, and is attacking the women in this Village."

"How is she doing that, Tom?'' Santucci asked.

"Some sort of mental telepathy, maybe.'' He sounded uncertain now and his voice had lost its confident edge.

"Telepathy, huh?'' Santucci smiled coldly. He flipped his small notebook closed and moved away from the fireplace. "Is there anything else, Doctor Marks?'' he asked, towering over her as he buttoned his overcoat. "Do you want to press charges against her for those bedroom windows?''

Sara shook her head.

"I can't guarantee Cindy Delp won't do this again, but if I slap a court order on her, then we'll make her parents responsible."

"I'm not interested in punishing the child, Lieutenant."

The detective nodded. He knew the MO of these people: sophisticated liberals appalled by the notion of punishment. Well, they were her windows, he thought, her house and life. His experience told him it might get worse. Next time the kid might burn down the place.

"Wait a minute!'' Tom protested as Santucci headed for the door. "Aren't you going to do anything?''

"If you people won't press charges, then there's nothing I can do."

"I'm not talking about criminal charges.'' Tom knelt

and took hold of Sara's hand. Her fingers were icy cold in his grasp. "Sara, you have to do something. This kid almost killed you an hour ago. She's attacking you and the others."

"Tom, you don't know that." He was staring at her, his eyes wide and alarmed. "It's not possible for Cindy to be responsible. You can't accept not knowing, so you're blaming her. I understand that—but I won't press charges." She spoke calmly, trying to ease her fears with the smoothness of her voice.

"Can't you examine her? We know the girl isn't normal."

"We know she's autistic, but that doesn't give her superhuman powers."

"Examine her, Sara!"

"I can't. I am not the girl's physician. I haven't the authority." She kept shaking her head. "I don't want to be involved with these people." Tears flashed in her eyes. "Tom, I just want to leave this house, get away from this Village." She was crying and she turned her face into the cushion to smother her outburst.

Tom sighed and stood, letting her cry.

"I'm taking off, Tom." Santucci opened the door as he spoke. "I'm going to stop by Delp's place and see the kid."

"Are you going to arrest her?"

"That little girl didn't kill anyone, Tom," Santucci said quietly. "We're looking for a male, six feet perhaps, weighing about 170–180. That's who killed the girl in the woods. Not Cindy Delp."

For a few minutes after Santucci left, neither one of them said anything. Sara got up and made coffee and Tom fussed with the fire, building it with a few more cedar logs. It was only when the silence became too much that Sara said, apologizing, "I'm sorry, I can't agree with you about her, Tom."

He nodded, not looking away from the fire.

"I do know something about parapsychology and this mental telepathy just isn't feasible."

"Okay. Okay. You're the doctor."

"Thomas, don't be like that. Yes, I am the doctor. And yes, I happen in this particular instance to know more about psychic phenomena than you do." She was angry and disappointed at his adolescent behavior. Still, she hadn't liked siding with Santucci against him. She had seen the torment in his eyes last night when he watched her suffering.

Tom rolled over on the rug and faced Sara.

"You'd agree that mind control is possible. That some people can dictate our behavior?"

"Of course. It has happened throughout history. All charismatic leaders have that power. So do hypnotists, doctors, teachers, priests." Sara shrugged.

"And autistic children."

Sara frowned and shook her head. "I don't know what you mean."

"I've been reading about autism and there are a couple of things that struck me as having to do with mind control. These children have unusual abilities, and one of them is the power of concentration. In fact, they concentrate to such a degree that they lose touch with the world around them. Their concentration is like a flashlight beam in a dark room, narrow and intense on one spot. They're like geniuses in that regard.

"They tell the story of Isaac Newton, of how once during a dinner party he went down to the wine cellar for another bottle and didn't come back. The other guests finally went looking for him and they found Newton kneeling in the dust of the kegs, apparently seized by an inspiration and trying to solve an equation.

"The point is, these autistic children—like geniuses —can't turn it off. They're locked into a narrowly focused and intense beam of concentration, and it is this strange power, I think, that Cindy Delp has."

"And she used these powers of concentration to cause my headache?"

"Yes. I think she's trying to kill you."

"Oh, Tom!" Sara sat up, angry at his persistence, and at herself for listening to him. "Really, you're being absurd." She leaned forward in the chair, her face now only a foot from Tom. "Amy Volt and Debbie Severt had their brain tissues burned. The other child was brutally attacked; her head was smashed. Was Cindy there? Yes, I admit, she was around when I had some of my attacks. But Benjy Fleming never mentioned her. We have no idea where she was when these children were killed."

Tom sat up and seized Sara's hand, as if physically grabbing her attention.

"Sara, sure I'm making a wild guess. I know it's fantastic, but I think it's possible."

"It isn't," she answered flatly.

"Examine the child. Talk to her. See how she reacts to you. See if she is hostile to you."

Sara sighed. "Why are you so insistent?"

Tom paused a moment, remembering what it was that had given him this feeling about Cindy Delp. "I think it was the look in her eyes. It was a strange combination of fear and hostility. And then when I hit her—she didn't expect anything like that. I don't think her parents have ever physically touched that child. Well, when I hit her, she just crumpled against me. You stopped screaming at that exact moment, and I just knew you were okay, and Cindy. . . ." Tom paused again, trying to recall just how the child reacted.

"Then what happened?" Tom had not told her these details before.

"She got angry, fought to get away, tried to bite me. I really couldn't hold her. She may only be twelve, but she's a lot stronger than Santucci thinks. I know she's physically capable of killing that child in the woods."

Sara shook her head. "I'm not going to find out

much from her, you understand. I've tried to talk to Cindy before and it's impossible. She only screeches at me.''

"I'll go with you," Tom said quickly, encouragingly.

"Well, let me talk to her parents. They may not say yes." Sara tossed off the blanket and stood up. "Do you think we should go now?" she asked. "It's still dark.''

"Yes, while Santucci is with the family. I want him to see this." Now Tom was in a rush to see the child before Sara changed her mind.

"I'll get my coat," Sara said, and as she moved out of the room, the phone rang, startling her. She let it ring a moment, then turned away. "Tom, you get it please. I'm not up for more bad news."

Tom picked up the phone in the livingroom. It was Santucci calling, his voice low and hesitant, asking where Sara was.

"She's here. Why?" He knew from Santucci's voice that something had gone wrong.

"It's this Delp girl," Santucci said slowly, trying to seem casual and offhanded. "She's missing."

"I thought you had cops watching her?" Tom turned his back so Sara wouldn't hear. Now he was afraid. The child was loose in the Village. And he knew he was right about her; she was a killer.

"I don't think we've got a problem," Santucci went on, still speaking slowly, carefully. "Why don't you take Marks out of the village until we trace the girl down? You know, just in case."

"I thought there was nothing to worry about? I thought you said that little girl was harmless?" The anger that he had suppressed broke out once more.

"Look, Dine, I think the kid can do some harm. I mean, she might break a few more windows, but I'm telling you for the last time she ain't a killer."

"Then we'll stay right where we are."

"Suit yourself. I'm sending up a couple men anyway

to watch the house. But do yourself and the doc a favor and don't go wandering off. And keep out of the woods, for chrissake. As soon as it's light, I'm going to have my people sweep those woods.'' And then, without a good-bye, he hung up.

"She's gone?" Sara asked when Tom turned around.

He nodded. "Yes, and Santucci thinks she might come here. He's sending some cops up to stand guard."

"I'm beginning to feel I'm targeted somehow."

"So does Santucci. He wants me to keep you inside for awhile, and to tell him if we leave the Village."

Sara touched her forehead, as if she had forgotten something, and then in a daze wandered over to the bay windows of the livingroom and stood there with her arms crossed, looking out at the dark cul-de-sac.

"I wouldn't do that," Tom stepped up beside her. "I'm not trying to scare you, but she could be out there, watching the house. Why don't you come away from the windows?"

Tom slid his arm around her shoulder and Sara leaned against him. She was exhausted from being up half the night, and from the tension of her headache and its aftermath. It felt good to be held for a moment, to enjoy the safety of his embrace and she turned against him and, wrapping her arms around his waist, buried her head against his chest.

He kissed the top of her head, then lifted her chin to kiss her lips.

She responded. She linked her arms around his neck and pulled him toward her, enjoying the feel of the length of him against her. When they broke the embrace, they were breathless. Turning together so their bodies wouldn't part, they moved toward the stairs.

In the foyer, Sara asked, "Check the front door, Tom. I want to know those people can't get to us."

"I did, when Santucci left."

"And the basement?" Another wave of paranoia swept through her.

Tom nodded. "We'll check again, just to be sure."
He took Sara's hand and they went through the house to
the kitchen. Tom first made sure the door was locked,
then flipped on the outside lights to the terrace. The
backyard was empty and the flood lights spread across
the fringe of the fields beyond the lawns. No one was
crouched in the rocks beyond the property. He turned
off the outside lights, then said to Sara, "I went through
the basement earlier, but we can check it again." He
slipped the bolt to unlock the cellar door, but before he
could turn the knob, the door burst open and Cindy
Delp fell into the kitchen. Her hands and arms had been
gashed by glass and, as she tumbled forward across the
tile, her flaring arms sprayed them both with a fine mist
of warm blood.

Sara screamed and kept on screaming. The shock of
the bloody child and blood all over her had driven Sara
to hysteria.

The child crawled into the corner of the kitchen. She,
too, was crying, clutching her bleeding hands and arms
against her body. The blood soaked her torn dress and
spread in a pool around her body.

In Tom's tight embrace, Sara tried to stop shaking.
She understood the first symptoms of shock and
realized she had to control herself. Cindy Delp might
bleed to death if she didn't respond, if she didn't over-
come her terror.

"I'll call Santucci," Tom said, sensing she was back
in control.

"No, don't leave me!" Sara stared at her hands
trembling on Tom's arm. "We have to help her. She
needs first aid."

"Sara, you're in no condition. Let's get the cops.
They'll handle it. Please, Sara."

Sara shook her head. "There isn't enough time for
that. It's my responsibility. Get my bag by the front
door, and in the second floor hall bathroom there's a

first aid kit." She pulled herself up. The fear and terror had passed. She had summoned the last of her strength to save the child's life. She grabbed a dish towel from the rack and, ripping it swiftly into strips for tourniquets, moved toward Cindy Delp.

The child watched her. She, too, had stopped crying. Her face was ghostly, drained of the blood that gushed from the long slashes on her hands and arms.

"Hurry, Tom!" Sara shouted, seeing the severity of the injuries. And to the child, "It's okay, Cindy; everything will be all right."

The child did not seem alarmed at seeing Sara approach. It was only when she reached to apply the first tourniquet that Cindy avoided her grasp and instead leaned forward, as if doubled up in pain.

Then she dipped her forefinger in the shallow pool of her own blood and on the cream-colored tiles of Sara Marks's kitchen. She slowly, almost religiously, daubed six lines that looked more like scribbling than a message so urgent it had to be written in blood:

sixteen

"Do they make any sense to you, Marcia?" Sara asked, sliding the drawings over to her. "Tom made these sketches of the marks while I was treating Cindy." Sara looked across the table at Marcia Fleming. It was early morning and they had gathered in Marcia's livingroom. "I know that at the Smithsonian you work with languages," Sara went on, "and I think this may be one."

"You mean you think Cindy may know a foreign language?" asked Marcia. "That doesn't seem likely."

"Not a foreign language, more like . . . a personal language. Autistic children don't learn to speak the way normal children do—by mimicking adults. They can't seem to learn our language, but they are capable of an inner language that is difficult for others to understand."

Tom broke in. "For the last few days this girl has been shadowing Sara. She keeps hanging around the house, breaking into it, and I thought she was trying to

kill Sara. But maybe I was wrong. Maybe she was trying
to tell us something.''

"And since she can't talk," Marcia commented,
"she's using these marks to make you understand." She
looked at Sara and Tom and they nodded in agreement.

"Well, I think it is even *more* complicated than just
that," Marcia went on. "These marks do have significance." She kept talking as she moved to her
bookcase and took down several textbooks. "I've seen
this symbol before. I know what it means, and it's
incredible that Cindy would know it."

Marcia opened one of the reference books and placed
it on the coffee table before them. "These odd lines
which Cindy drew are actually part of the Ogam alpha-
bet, an ancient Celtic script. Ogam means *grooved
writing*, and there are about seventy varieties of the
script going back in America to the first millennium, B. C.

"Now we were taught that Christopher Columbus
discovered America in 1492, but since the 1960s we have
known differently. According to inscriptions found on
stones throughout America, we now know that America
was first settled by Celts, Basques, Libyans, and even
Egyptians over 2,500 years ago.

"These people built temples, left gravestones and
tablets, and married American Indians. They also left a
script called Ogam.''

On a blank sheet of paper, Marcia used a magic
marker to draw a few short lines. "The letters," she
continued, "are constructed from single parallel strokes
placed in sets of one to five, in position above, below, or
across a guide line.

"A stone from Vermont, for example, was inscribed
this way:

That inscription means 'Stone of Bel.' What is significant about the blood sketch by Cindy Delp is this—''
Marcia paused a moment to search through her books
on Ogam inscriptions, and when she found the page, she
turned the book around so Tom and Sara could see the
photographs and drawings.

"A linguist and epigraphist named Barry Fell
decoded Ogam in a place called Mystery Hill in North
Salem, New Hampshire. Mystery Hill is a twenty-four-
acre hilltop full of underground passages, standing
monoliths, drystone chambers, and inscriptions that
have never been fully explained.

"But within the last ten years it's been proven that the
standing stones have astronomical alignments. When
viewed from one particular spot, they line up correctly
for the winter and summer solstices, the point when the
sun reaches its furthest point north and south in the sky.''

"Like Stonehenge?'' Tom asked.

"Yes, but Mystery Hill has even more significance.
When Barry Fell visited the site in 1975 he decoded the
Ogam markings on a triangular stone tablet. When
translated it said, 'dedicated to Bel.'

"Now Bel was the Celtic sun god, but the Phoenician
name *Baal* also meant 'sun god,' so it's possible that
New Hampshire was visited by both the Celts and the
Phoenicians, and as far back as 800 B.C.''

Marcia pointed to one of the photographs in the
reference book. "This is the monogram of Bel or Baal,
that was found on a triangular stone in Mystery Hill.
It's the same symbol that Cindy drew. She wrote the
name of Bel in her own blood.''

Sara and Tom glanced at each other, then at Marcia.

"Do you think she found this picture in a book?''
Tom asked.

"I doubt that. There aren't many pictures of the
monogram. More likely she has seen a stone itself with
the inscription, found it somewhere here on the farm or
along the river bank.''

"How would that be possible?" Sara asked, frowning. "There couldn't be that many ancient stones in this country."

"Well, epigraphists have found examples of Ogam as far away as Oklahoma. I know researchers at the Smithsonian who have decoded second century, A.D., Hebraic script in Loudoun County, in Tennessee, and on prehistoric walls in Fayette County, West Virginia. So it is possible that there are some examples here on the banks of the Potomac, and if there are," Marcia's eyes widened, "I want to find them."

Tom stood and nervously began to pace around the sofa and chairs. "You mean that's all it is?" he asked, circling the women.

"That's enough for me," Marcia answered. "If Cindy has discovered prehistoric inscriptions here, in this Village, it's a major find for archaeology."

Sara pulled back the drawings and compared them again to the photos found on the triangular stone. Then she asked, "Do these inscriptions have any religious significance, Marcia?"

"Yes, they do. This triangular stone in Mystery Hill was located in the temple of the sun god. Usually stone tablets with such engravings were votive offerings. You would buy one from a priest near a sacred temple and then leave it behind as a gift to the god."

"Then there might actually have been a temple in the Village, or at least on the farm?" Sara asked.

"Yes, possibly. Or the stone might have been dredged up from the river years ago and used as part of the foundation for a building. No one would have thought anything of the grooves on the face of the rock. Until recently people assumed that grooves like that had been made by stone-cutting drills from colonial masons, or even Indians. I'm sure Cindy, or her father, or anyone else building this Village would have had no idea what these lines mean."

"Cindy knows," Sara answered softly. "And that's

why she drew them for me. She's trying to tell me something."

"Oh, Sara, that's not possible. How could Cindy know Ogam?"

"I'm not sure, but the child has nearly killed herself trying to explain. Now I'm going to try and help her tell me."

"Would you let me come with you?" Marcia asked quickly.

"Of course. I need your help."

"Let me go call Neil; he took Benjamin over to his place this morning." Marcia smiled wryly, "A vain attempt to keep him occupied." She stood and went upstairs to get her coat and to telephone.

Tom sat down across from Sara and whispered, keeping his voice low. "Why do you think Cindy knows anything about the killings? You told me last night I was absurd."

Sara nodded, agreeing. "I still don't think Cindy killed those children, or that she caused the attacks, but she may know something about the deaths. Autistic children, we know, are capable of extrasensory perception. There have been enough demonstrations of clairvoyant incidents to statistically show this ability isn't coincidental. She may be trying to tell me what she knows. The problem is that I can't understand her."

Sara raised her hands, knowing Tom would start asking questions she couldn't answer. "I realize it doesn't make any sense. But let me talk to Cindy; I think I'll be able to reach her. She wants me to understand her."

"You're wrong about her, Sara."

"I have to do this my way, Tom," Sara answered, resolved now that she knew what to do.

"She's trying to kill you," he went on slowly. "If you go near her again, she could destroy your mind."

Sara stared back at him. She was determined and her eyes lost their bright, shiny gleam and were now the color of slate. She was fighting her own exhaustion, his disapproval, and she knew she couldn't rationally explain her insistence on pursuing the child.

Tom was right: it was better to leave Cindy alone and let the police solve the murders. She could leave, sell the house, and move back to Boston. Perhaps it had been a mistake to leave, to walk away from Sam. She felt a piercing pain of homesickness for Boston, for the cool, damp cobblestones of Cambridge, for the ivy and dark brick of Harvard.

"It's something I have to do, Tom," she finally said.

"Why?" he asked.

"The child is tormented. I don't know why she's chosen me to communicate with . . . maybe it's because she senses I can feel her pain, even when she can't express it. It doesn't really matter why. I have to help her."

"Why, because you happen to be a doctor? This has nothing to do with the Hippocratic oath. You're getting involved with police work, not a medical problem. You're pursuing Cindy Delp for other reasons and I don't think you've thought them through." He settled back in the couch, staring hard at her.

"Why are you so angry? Are you afraid for me or are you upset because I won't listen to you? I don't think you know what's best for me." Sara spoke quietly and without raising her voice, but she let the tone show her annoyance with his attitude. She had spent all of her adult life studying the medical and psychological behavior of man, and she knew she was better qualified than Tom to deal with Cindy Delp.

"I think she's a killer," Tom answered, not responding to her hostility. "And, yes, I do fear for your life."

"Why?"

"Because I think I'm in love with you," he answered quietly.

"Oh, no," Sara sighed and looked away. She hadn't expected a declaration. It complicated everything, and the implications of all that came walloping home. She wanted to touch his arm, to show him some sign of affection, but she heard Marcia in the hallway upstairs, and she said quickly, "I don't like to depend on people." That admission surprised even her.

"What's so terrible about it?" Tom leaned forward and touched her arm.

"I find that when I depend on someone else, I only get myself in trouble."

They both started nervously at the sound of footsteps on the staircase.

"Well, here's Marcia," Tom said, too loudly.

"I'm sorry I upset you." Sara stood and began to collect her things, then whispered, smiling secretly to him, "I promise to behave."

"I think you're wonderful," he answered.

Sara stared down at the deep pile rug and blushed. His words made her feel warm and desired. She nodded, unable to respond, and walked toward Marcia in the foyer, her footsteps falling uncertainly on the carpet, as if she were slightly drunk.

seventeen

Cindy Delp sat at the kitchen table surrounded by adults but not conscious of them. She had become fascinated by her left hand, and she held her fingers inches from her face and slowly, endlessly, turned her hand before her beautiful black eyes.

While Cindy wandered in her own world, her father listened silently to what Sara Marks had to say. They had all crowded into the farm house kitchen, Delp and his wife Pearl, Sara, Tom and Marcia, and Santucci and two of the county police.

Only Bruce Delp and the women sat at the table. The men stood back against the kitchen cabinets, and kept quiet while Sara told the parents, "I think your daughter is trying to help us. I think she's trying to tell us something about the murder of these children."

Bruce Delp snorted and moved impatiently in his chair. He had been out working that morning and Santucci had brought him back to the farm house to meet

Sara Marks. He was dressed for the fall weather, heavy overalls, flannel shirt and denim jacket. Inside the house he had taken off the jacket, but not his Baltimore Orioles baseball cap. He kept it pulled down low on his face, as if to hide his eyes.

"I told the police here that Cindy didn't have anything to do with those kids. You've seen yourself my girl can't harm no one."

"We don't think she's responsible, either, Mr. Delp." Sara said softly. "But I do believe there's a reason for Cindy coming to my house. I think she is trying to tell me something."

Pearl Delp gestured toward her daughter. "Cindy don't know she ain't supposed to go up to the construction. She's been playing in these fields all her life, and it's hard, you understand, for me to keep her home." The wife's small, gray eyes looked guiltily at Sara.

"It don't mean anything, Miss, that she come by your place," Delp said, picking up from his wife. "About once or twice a day I have to fetch her from either the Village or the fields. She's been like that, you know, since she could first walk. I'm sorry she's been bothering you. The police here, they say she broke your windows. Well, I'm sorry about that; I'll be over there first thing this afternoon with new glass. We'll have you okay by evening." He tilted his head up to look at Sara and she stared into his eyes. They were small and watery-blue and full of pain. It hurt Sara to look at him.

She opened her bag and took out Tom's drawings. Unfolding them, she asked the parents, "Does this symbol mean anything to you? Have you seen it on the farm? Have you seen it cut into the face of any rocks?"

Sara held up the drawings so Pearl Delp could see, and the sudden motion of her hand attracted Cindy. Her head jerked back and she saw the sign and lunged over the table, grabbing it from Sara's hands.

She seized the drawing and held it tenderly, her

fingers softly tracing the lines. Then she placed the paper on the kitchen table and hovered over it. They were all quiet, surprised by her unexpected response. She began to hum softly to herself, a clear, simple child's lullaby, and, bending over the drawing, she smiled.

"Cindy, give that picture back to the lady," Pearl Delp ordered.

Sara raised her hand, motioned for the mother not to interfere. The roomful of people were silent, hypnotized by Cindy's fixation with the strange symbol of Bel.

"Cindy, what does this mean?" Sara asked, speaking slowly and softly to the child. She asked the question and then paused, waiting for Cindy to absorb the sentence and understand. After several seconds she asked again, "Cindy, what does this mean?"

It was as if the simple English sentence was a foreign language and Cindy was able to çatch only a few words. Sara waited, listened. Then Cindy answered painfully slowly, but her reply was incomprehensible.

"What did you say?" Sara tried once more.

Cindy spoke again, and Sara shook her head, frustrated that she could not understand. Tom motioned for her to remain sitting and he circled the table.

"Try to get it on tape," he said, handing her his small Sony recorder.

Sara leaned forward again and held up the tape recorder, but now Cindy would not even whisper. She sat quiet, still smiling, still gently touching the monogram of Bel.

Santucci and the other police officers stirred restlessly, and Pearl Delp came to stand at Cindy's side, as if to ward off Sara and her recording machine. Sensing that the meeting was about to break, Sara looked around the room as if appealing to them all. "Just give me a couple of minutes. She's not retarded; she can be reached, I know she can. I just want to ask her a few questions and see if I can establish an I.Q. level for her . . ."

Sara's voice trailed off. She looked at the child and was struck again by her exquisite beauty. Cindy did not look retarded. Her features were not deformed. Only the blank, empty eyes of the child suggested that in some way she was lost to this world.

Sara moved the small tape recorder closer to the child and asked softly, "What is your name?"

The girl did not look up from the drawing, but she did reply. A short burst of screeching noise.

"Cindy, I want to ask you some questions." On a notepad, Sara wrote down the questions in the order she asked them. "Cindy, how much is 8,346 times 5,721?" She paused and again Cindy screeched. The noise was sharp and meaningless, but Sara continued softly. "Cindy, in which months during 1998 will the seventh fall on a Wednesday?"

Again Cindy screeched harshly. Santucci's detectives glanced at each other, almost embarrassed to be witnessing this exhibition of the child's illness. But Sara ignored their skepticism; she knew autistic children were capable of astounding mental feats and she wanted to test Cindy's ability. The questioning continued for another five minutes and when she was done, Sara shut off the tape recorder and sat back with a sigh.

"Well?" asked Santucci. "You call that an I.Q. test? No normal kid could possibly know those answers."

Sara shook her head. "I know how it looks. But I'm convinced that those sounds are not random. I want to play the tape back and see if there's any way to make sense of it." Sara smiled up at Pearl Delp. "Thank you for letting me talk to Cindy," she said.

"It's gibberish," Tom stated. They had gone back to Sara's house and Tom had set the Sony on her study desk and played the tape again. Cindy's replies came back clearly but it was all incoherent to them.

"Perhaps it's another language," Marcia suggested. "Is it possible that she knows a foreign language, after all?"

"Yes. There are six-year-old autistic children who can speak French, Spanish, Japanese, Arabic, and Hebrew, but can't say a complete English sentence." Sara shook her head. "But this is different."

She walked to the windows and stood there with her arms crossed, staring out at the cold day. From that side of the house, she could see the top of the ridge, and the slope of wild highland behind the Village. There were plans to landscape that hill in the spring and plant a small park of pine, walnut, and birch trees, but now the long grass grew wild. It would have to be cut, she thought distractedly, or it could catch fire, especially now in the last dry days of late autumn. Then Sara heard Tom say, "We'll never be able to reach that kid, to understand her." He sounded tired and defeated.

Sara turned from the windows. She was shaking her head and disagreeing. "Cindy is functioning on her own wavelength," Sara said. "It's our problem that we can't communicate with her."

"Well, what do we do?" Tom asked, sounding impatient. "We ask her a question and she screeches back at us."

"I don't know what we do," Sara sighed. "I just want to get some sleep. My whole body is exhausted."

"Tom," Marcia said nicely, interjecting herself into the conversation. "Would you do me a favor and drive over to Neil's and pick up Benjamin?" She smiled sweetly at the reporter.

"Oh, sure." Tom glanced between the two women, sensing immediately that for some reason they wanted him out of the house.

"You'll be all right?" he asked halfheartedly.

"Yes, we'll be fine." Marcia walked with Tom to the front door, asking him to take Benjamin back to her house. "I'll be home within a few minutes, just wait for me." When she returned to the livingroom Sara said, "We're due for another attack, aren't we?"

Marcia nodded. "I think so. If I've guessed right on the times." There was fear in the smaller woman's brown eyes.

"It may not happen," Sara said hopefully.

"Yes, it will," Marcia answered. She began to pace, to use the length of the livingroom as her track. She was too frightened to sit, to wait for the attack as if it were a burst of gunfire. Any feeling of perverse pleasure she had gotten from the first orgasms had passed. The last one she had experienced the night before had been violent and painful.

"Come, sit," Sara asked, "it will be easier."

"No, it won't."

"Relax," she said. "Let your body accept the assault. It will be less traumatizing."

Marcia swung around. "It isn't an orgasm, is it, Sara?"

Sara hesitated, unsure of what to say. She didn't know any more than Marcia, but before she could reply, the fierce bolt of pleasure and pain struck her, left her gasping. Sara saw Marcia seize the back of a chair and crumple to her knees, and she herself stumbled forward and hit the rug, her legs weak and rubbery.

"Sara!" Marcia cried, but Sara could not go to her. Her body trembled and shook and went wet with sweat as the pulse ran the length of her body and hit with a massive explosion deep inside. There was no longer any pleasure in the attack. It felt as if her mind was on fire and Sara gasped with pain, seizing her head, as if to squeeze out the flame.

Sara pulled herself to her feet and then, resting against the arm of the chair, exclaimed, "God, my head! It feels as if it has been ripped apart." She leaned over and without warning vomited on the rug. She cried out in pain and humiliation.

"It's all right, Sara." Marcia said reassuringly. She

had pulled herself up and into a chair. There was more blood in her nostrils and on her lips, and she could see a smear of blood on Sara's face, but it wasn't the blood that frightened her now.

"It's getting worse, Sara," she whispered, "it's getting more violent."

Sara nodded. Her head hurt her too much for her to speak, but she realized, too, that it was getting worse. Next time she realized, none of them would be able to stand the assault on their minds.

eighteen

The pain woke Peggy, drove her from the deep groggy sleep of the injection and she stumbled from the bed, staggering and confused as the attack came again, driving a wedge of pain from the base of her neck up through her skull. It felt as if her forehead had caught on fire.

Reeling with the pain, Peggy pushed through the nursery door and into Amy's room. Bright, flashing lines of color now zigzagged across her eyes and she could see nothing else. The lights distorted her vision and suddenly she felt sick. At the doorway, she leaned against the frame and vomited into the room.

She was sure she was dying. The fierce pain whipped inside her head, knocking her off-balance and sending her spinning across the dark nursery grabbing for the walls and furniture. Peggy struck the hayrack crib, shoving it into the wall, and hung onto its high sides, then slid to the floor. She could feel blood in her mouth, its taste sweet and warm.

And then the pain stopped. Peggy leaned against the crib, breathless and bleeding. Her vision had cleared and she looked across the empty nursery, dark in the late afternoon. It was over. The attack was over and she was safe and alive. She pulled herself up, using the wooden slats of the crib for support and stood, bracing herself against the side of the hayrack.

Then she saw the girl. The long-legged daughter of the farmer was curled up in the deep, quilted bottom of the hayrack, sucking her thumb and staring off, her dark eyes fathomless.

"Get out! Get out of there," Peggy yelled, but the child did not move or even cringe. She lay lost in her own world.

"What do you want?" Peggy shouted, enraged that the young girl was in Amy's crib, soiling it with the filth and the stench of her father's farm. "Get out of this crib! Out of my house!" She grabbed Cindy by the collar of her dress, tried to pull her over the high wooden railing, but Cindy was too heavy, too tall, and she screeched and fought as Peggy tried to wrestle her from the crib.

Cindy's strength startled Peggy, but she wouldn't let go. She had the girl in her grip and she wrenched at her crazily, bending her body over the railing.

The child was screeching. Her high, thin-pitched voice shrieked in Peggy's ear as the girl struggled to free herself from the stranglehold, and her long, thin adolescent arms swung wildly at Peggy, striking her at the back of the head, on her shoulders.

"Goddamn it!" With one quick, sudden motion, she slapped Cindy hard on the face, snapping the child's head back. She hated the girl; hated her for being in Amy's crib, hated her just for being alive. And with both hands, she seized Cindy by the neck, her fingers closing convulsively, squeezing the soft, smooth skin of the child. Peggy pressed harder and her strong hands tightened, as if Cindy's throat was soft dough to be kneaded.

Now Cindy lashed out, her fingers flying to Peggy's face and ripping her skin, drawing blood in fine lines down her puffy cheeks. Then she grabbed Peggy's hair and twisted her head, knocking the woman off-balance.

Peggy lost her hold on Cindy's throat, but when she gained her feet again, she braced her body against the hayrack and, with one enormous effort, yanked Cindy over the high rack and out of the crib.

They tumbled to the floor and Cindy broke free and rolled away from the woman, soundlessly on the nursery rug. Then, hurt and exhausted, she crawled into the far corner of the bedroom, drew her legs up, and curled her body into a tight ball. Her high, insistent screeching had stopped and in the dark nursery corner she began to whimper and whine.

For a moment Peggy lay panting on the rug. There was blood on her lips. She could taste it on her tongue, could smell her own vomit in her mouth and on her clothes. Her body hurt. Her arms ached from wrestling Cindy.

Peggy rolled over and spotted the girl crouched in the far corner of the room. She would have to kill her, just as she had killed her husband. She remembered how she had done it, the knife flashing in the bright light of the basement as the blade sliced through the air. Then the memory went vague and she shook her head, confused and hurting still from the attack. She forced herself to concentrate, to remember where she was and what she had to do.

Amy needed her. She had to nurse her baby, and Peggy pulled herself up to her knees, staggered to her feet and went to the crib.

"Yes, my darling," Peggy cooed and shaped her arms around the quilted bundle at the bottom of the crib. She slipped her nightgown off her right shoulder and lifted the bundle to her naked breast. "There, darling," she whispered. "Don't cry." She bent forward to kiss the infant's face and realized the baby was gone, the quilted blanket was empty. She began to cry and, turning, confused, from the crib, she spotted Cindy crouched in the corner.

"You!" Peggy screamed. "Where is my baby?"

She ran to the child, grabbed her long blond hair and jerked Cindy, screeching, from the safe corner. Furiously she kicked at the girl, and Cindy, still screeching, turned and, grabbing the woman's leg, bit her left calf, drawing blood with her teeth.

"Goddamn you!" Peggy bent down and swung wildly, screaming and swearing at Cindy. Out of control, she was intent now on killing the girl.

Cindy raised her hands to shield her head from the beating. She was screeching at Peggy in the same high, piercing voice, as if she were a tropical bird in a rain forest, and Peggy screamed back at her, shouting, "Where's Amy? What have you done with my baby?" She kicked once more and this time Cindy reached out, grabbed Peggy's leg and sent her sprawling. Instantly Cindy was on top of her.

Looking up, Peggy saw that Cindy's vacant eyes were brilliant with flashing colored lights, and that her face was violently changing expressions. Its passive, bored vagueness shifted rapidly, as if she were watching the girl on speeded-up film. Cindy was at once angry, snarling, growling, then suddenly sweet and loving.

Cindy's bizarre, explosive reaction startled Peggy, shook her back to reality, and she saw she was in danger. Her own insane rage shifted quickly to fear, and she struggled to get out from between the legs of the child.

Yet Cindy did not attack. Instead she grabbed her own head with both hands, doubled over with pain, and screeched. The innocent, empty face was distorted and she was sobbing. Cindy screeched again, high, long and piercing.

Peggy tried once more to get away, but this time Cindy grabbed her clothes and held on desperately, as if she were drowning.

"Get away!" Peggy yelled, hitting the child, knocking her over with the force of the blow. Still the young girl clung to Peggy's nightgown, her nails dug into the nylon folds of the skirt. Peggy yanked the gown down to her waist, then over her hips and pulled free. She rolled over, in a panic to get away from Cindy, to lock herself in her own room.

Peggy stood, and was struck once more, this time by a violent bolt to her head. The pain went up the back of her head, cut through the soft mass of cerebrum, dividing the hemispheres, and drove deep into the hypothalamus. Peggy could smell the cell tissues and nerve fibers of her brain burning like fall foliage. The smell of death in her nostrils was the last memory of her life.

Downstairs in his laboratory, Kevin Volt heard the muffled noise from the second floor and in the early evening, he walked upstairs to check on his wife.

He was exhausted. After working on the beam for eight hours, he was fatigued to the point of numbness. Still he had not solved the problem and by week's end he had to demonstrate some results.

On the second floor, at the end of the hall, he stopped, pressed his ear against her doorway, and listened. She would still be sleeping, he reasoned, and he unlocked the bedroom door and pushed it open.

In the waning light of dusk, Kevin saw immediately that Peggy's bed was empty. Instantly wary, he swung the door wide and back against the wall, making sure she was not waiting for him behind it. Then he moved into the room, closing and locking the door behind him.

The small bolt clicked loudly as he tumbled the lock.

His shoulder blades pressed against the wood of the door, Kevin surveyed the room. He was wearing a Lacoste tennis shirt, khaki slacks, and his Nike running shoes. The rubbery web soles were soundless on the carpet of their bedroom.

She had to be here, he told himself. There was no need to worry about her escaping. There was no way she could get away to tell the others. Her little games were even exciting. He looked forward to disciplining her.

Still he did not start out toward the center of the room, where the twilight cast a blanket of light across the double bed. He kept to the walls, walked toward the built-in closets. He was thinking quickly, deciding where she might hide in the bedroom. There were so few choices: under the bed itself, the bathroom, but, more likely, he guessed, the walk-in closet. She would be crouched there, like a disobedient child in the dark corner, in among her dozens of shoes.

He had left the plastic syringe and the sedative on the dresser, and in the semidarkness, he broke open the package and filled the syringe, holding it high in one hand, as he easily slid open the door of the closet.

"Peggy, come out of there!" he demanded, yanking apart the dresses. In the dark closet the only sound was the swash of clothes on the rack as he pushed them back and forth, searching for his wife. She was not there.

Kevin looked back at the bedroom and saw the mistake he had made. The door to the nursery was open. Now he was alarmed. He had been locked in his basement laboratory the entire day; Peggy could have been out of the house for hours. He rushed around the bed and to the door of the nursery.

Dimly, amidst the silhouetted furniture, he made out the crumpled form of his wife, huddled in the oversized crib.

"Peggy! For Christ's sake!" He set down the syringe on the dresser and crossed the room, thinking only: she is sicker than I had imagined.

He went quickly forward and reached down over the high sides to pull her from the crib and only then did he see that she was naked, her face tucked into her crossed arms and hidden from sight.

"Peggy!" He touched her bare skin and it was cold and clammy under his fingers. "Peggy!" He leaned forward and caught the strong, unmistakable odor of excrement.

Her shoulders and breasts were smeared with blood. It was caked to her body like copper mud. "Oh, Christ," he whispered and forced himself to reach out and pull her hair away from her face. The long brown strands had caught in the dried blood and he had to jerk the hair free to see his wife's face. Peggy's eyes were open and she looked surprised, as if whatever had struck her had been more startling than painful. The blood had gushed from her nostrils and poured into her gasping mouth, choking her to death in its thick swill.

And then Kevin realized it was not excrement he smelled, but the soft cell tissues of her cerebrum. Smeared across her face and matted in her hair was the gray matter of Peggy Volt's brain.

By turning her head slightly, Sara could see the digital clock on her desk. It was a little after six in the afternoon. She had been sound asleep on the library couch for nearly six hours and she woke to the thought that she was due for another attack.

Still she did not move. The realization of the imminent attack paralyzed her. The last one had been more vicious than ever before. Each one, she now understood, was becoming increasingly violent and destructive, and she wondered how long she could endure them.

Sara threw off the heavy quilt and stood. Her feet touched the floor as the digital clock changed to six-ten and she tumbled forward in pain, struck this time from behind. A driving pain drove up through her head as if her mind had been severed into its two hemispheres. She could no longer see. Bright, violent lines of color zigzagged across her eyes. In a moment, she knew, she would be sick.

She lay quietly, waiting for Cindy to appear. The child had to be loose, and somewhere near the house, perhaps in the house itself. She should have gone with Tom into the city. Why was she in the Village enduring such pain? Why was she trying to save this girl? And then she was hit again, a driving, blind light spinning through her mind, blinding and stunning her before pushing her over the brink into unconsciousness.

When she woke she was still sprawled on the rug, her fingers clutching the deep pile. She rolled over and breathed deeply. She was all right, she realized. She had lived through another attack, and she pulled herself up. Blood stained the pale blue of the rug, and she could feel blood on her face and in her hair.

Sara used the bathroom downstairs to wipe her face and clean her hair, and when she came out into the kitchen, the telephone rang.

"Are you okay?" It was Marcia calling, her voice weak and weaping.

"I am now."

"Oh, God, Sara, I can't take another one." She started to cry into the phone."

"It's all right now, Marcia. We have another eight hours before the next one."

"No, Sara, the next will be in six hours. They're coming faster. And then it will be five! Four!" Marcia kept sobbing.

"Marcia! Stop it!" Sara ordered. The hysteria of the other woman had forced Sara to calm down; someone, she knew, had to take control. "Marcia, call everyone," she directed. "Get them together. We're going to leave before the next attack. Have everyone pack an overnight bag and meet at the barn."

"Where will we go?" Marcia asked meekly, like a child. It comforted her to be told what to do, to have the decision made for her.

"We'll worry about that later. Somewhere. Anywhere away from this place. Now get on the telephone and call. See if everyone else is okay. I'll be down as soon as I can."

"Come now! Please, Sara, I'm afraid to be alone in this house with just Benjamin."

"I'll be there soon. There's something I have to do here first. Just get hold of the others. Don't worry, Marcia. We're safe for awhile. Bye." And then she hung up before Marcia could protest.

Sara stood for a moment in the hallway, listening for sound. She heard nothing, but that didn't matter. The child had always been silent when she hid in the house, and Sara knew she had to be upstairs, curled up as she usually was in the damp shower.

Sara stood at the bottom of the stairs, trying to control herself. She took several deep breaths and calmed down her racing heart, then slowly, forcing herself to climb the stairs one at a time, she went up to search for Cindy in the dark house.

She looked in the guest rooms first, then went into her own room. Bruce Delp had not yet fixed the windows and her bedroom was freezing. The wind blew through the broken windows and chilled her as she searched the bathroom, closets, and under the bed for the child.

Sara was still shaking from the cold and her own fear when she came back downstairs and into the kitchen to telephone Bruce Delp.

"He's not here, Miss Marks," Pearl Delp said. "He's out looking for Cindy. We were fixing to sit down for dinner and she went to wash up and got out through the bathroom window."

Sara sighed. She had been right. "And when was this, Mrs. Delp?" Sara asked, being careful to contain her anger. The blundering incompetence of Cindy's parents and the local police was exasperating.

"About two hours ago. My husband, he called that detective, and they got people looking in the fields. You ain't seen her, have you, Miss?"

"No, Mrs. Delp, but your husband said he would repair my windows this afternoon and he hasn't. I would like very much if he'd call me the moment he gets home. I can't stay in this house." Sara could hear her voice shouting at the woman, and she stopped talking. Her body was trembling from the cold, her fear, and her anger.

"He's awful worried about that girl, Miss Marks," the woman replied.

"Yes, I understand. And I'm sorry I shouted at you, but it's just that we're all under a great deal of tension because of Cindy."

"It's all my fault," Pearl Delp answered softly.

"I'm sorry," Sara began.

"It's my fault Cindy is this way."

"It's not your fault, Mrs. Delp. Autism can affect anyone's child. Five children out of every ten thousand are autistic."

"I'm being punished," the farmer's wife continued stubbornly. "You see, me and Bruce we had to get married. Cindy, she's a love child. God is punishing us for breaking His commandment."

"Mrs. Delp!" Sara spoke over the woman's sobbing. "You are not responsible. Believe me. I am a doctor, Mrs. Delp, and I know that nothing you and your husband did caused Cindy to be stricken with autism." Sara stopped and listened while Pearl Delp stopped her crying and regained her breath. Then she heard Pearl Delp say coldly, "You don't know, Miss. You may be a doctor, but you're a stranger here. I have lived with that child for twelve years and she ain't normal."

"Yes, I know Cindy is autistic."

"She ain't autistic," the woman shouted back. Her voice was deep and raw. "This child of mine ain't normal. She kills animals. I've seen her with my own eyes. She'll put her hands on them and they'll go crazy in the fields, run wild, bang themselves against trees and fence posts. Don't you tell me about my daughter, Miss. That child ain't right. That child's a killer, and no doctor like yourself is going to stop her from killing more." She slammed down the receiver.

Sara stood still, giving herself time to stop trembling and calm down. Then she shook her head and said out loud as if to reassure herself, "No!" The force and sound of her own voice in the silent house startled her and she left the kitchen and went back into the study, locking herself inside.

In the study, she used the extension to ring Tom in the city. He answered on the first ring, as if he had been expecting the call and she explained quickly what had happened to her and the other women.

"We have to leave, Tom. These attacks are getting worse. I'm afraid of the next one."

"Where's the girl?"

"She's loose in the Village. I just telephoned Pearl Delp."

"What's wrong with those people? Where's Santucci?"

"He's here. They're looking for her."

"Sara, I'll be out there within the hour. Where will you be?"

"At Marcia's. I'm afraid to stay in this house by myself."

"Good. If you're right and Cindy has fixated on you, then she'll be back. Get out of that house."

"Okay! Okay!" His excitement and worry frightened her. She had a sudden vision of Cindy creeping into the house and coming to get her. "I'll just pack a few things."

"Don't!" Tom shouted. "You don't need anything. You can get what you need for work tomorrow morning, when I'm with you. Just leave the house."

"All right, I'm leaving!" Sara shouted, upset with him for being so domineering.

"I just care about you," Tom replied. His voice had softened.

"I'm sorry, Tom. Please hurry. I do want to have you here." There were tears in her eyes.

"I'll get there as soon as I can. Good-bye, sweetheart."

"Bye." Suddenly she missed him terribly and wanted him with her. It made her feel warm, knowing he cared so much for her. Sara sighed and hung up the phone.

For a moment she did not move, but only listened to the silence of the large, empty house. It was dark outside and she had not turned on a light in the study. She reached over and snapped on the desk lamp. Its soft glow cast more shadows than light in the oak panelled room.

Then quickly, frantically, she collected her work off the desk and stuffed the papers and books into her briefcase. Tomorrow was Monday and she had done no reading all weekend. Her job had been the last thing on her mind since the week before when Helen Severt ran to her with her daughter already dead in her arms.

Sara looked up and glanced around the study, looking for anything more she needed to take with her, and spotted the file of material on autism she had brought home from NIH.

There must be something, she thought, among all those research papers and medical studies that would give her an insight into handling Cindy, something that would tell her how to reach the child.

She suddenly stopped packing papers into her briefcase and, moving the file to her desk, began to search through the documents, quickly scanning each report for the clue she had overlooked the week before.

It took twenty minutes of hasty reading before she spotted an interoffice memo that startled her, and she pulled it from the stack and read it through once more.

A bizarre breakthrough happened yesterday at the lab which I thought you should be aware of. It concerns Danny Riley. As you know from his case history, the child has never spoken, but continually emits a high, screeching noise.

While I was tape recording another child's voice at the lab, Danny was playing in the same room. I did not realize I had picked up his squeaking voice, until I played back the tape this morning.

This was unimportant to my work, but when I accidentally played the tape at a slower speed, at 3.3 inches per second, Danny's screeching became immediately clear and understandable.

The boy has been speaking perfect English all these years, *but at twice to three times normal speed.*

Sara picked up the small tape recorder, took out the cassette, and walked over to her own larger stereo and recording components. She slipped in the tape and spun it back to her first question to the child.

"What is your name?"

Sara stopped the machine, slowed it down to 3.3 inches per second and pushed playback. Her fingers were trembling and she held her breath as Cindy replied in clear and audible English, "77, N28, 16, 39, W11, 48."

Sara stopped the recorder and quickly jotted down the numbers, then she shifted the speed back to normal and listened to her next question.

"Cindy, how much is 8,346 times 5,721?"

Again Sara stopped the machine and reset the speed, then pushed playback. Cindy's voice replied, "47,747,466" without hesitation.

"Cindy, in which months during 1998 will the seventh fall on a Wednesday?" Sara had asked next.

"January and October," Cindy replied, her voice soft and timid on the slow-speed tape.

Sara stopped the machine once more. Her hands were still shaking, but this time from her excitement. She leaned against the bookcase and thought what she would do next.

She had to take the cassette with her and play it for Tom and Marcia. Also, they needed to talk to Cindy. Then she remembered she had asked Cindy one last question while at the farm house and turned on the tape recorder and played back the exchange.

"Cindy, who killed these little girls?" she heard herself asking.

Sara slowed the recorder's speed and listened carefully as Cindy, her high, screeching voice altered to a slower speed, answered clearly, "We did."

nineteen

"We did," Cindy answered coolly.

Sara reached over and stopped the tape, then looked up at Marcia and Tom.

"Why *we*?" Tom asked immediately and began to nervously pace around Marcia Fleming's livingroom.

"She might have meant her father," Marcia said. "That could explain what happened to the girl in the woods, the child with her head smashed."

"I think we should let Santucci worry about that," Tom answered. He wanted to get the detective involved at once, and he wanted to get Sara off the farm and out of the Village.

"Wait just a minute," Sara replied. "Tom, what do you think the numbers mean? She handed him the slip of paper where she had jotted them down.

77N281639W1148

He frowned and then said, "She seems to be giving them in sets of two. I thought she paused, for example, after seventy-seven." He rewrote the numbers, spacing them on the notepad.

77   N28   16   39   W11   48

"What do you think they look like now?" He handed the paper back to Sara.

She shook her head, saying, "It's not a phone number or a street address." She passed the slip of paper to Marcia.

"But it might be this," Marcia said, studying the list for a moment, then taking Tom's pen and writing the numbers down one more time.

77   N28'   16"

39   W11'   48"

"Longitude and latitude?" Tom asked, looking up.

"I think so."

"What does it mean when you ask a twelve-year-old child her name and she replies with longitude and latitude?" Tom asked. "I mean, is this kid crazy?

"And if she isn't crazy," he went on, "if all that's wrong with her is that she talks at twice normal speed, then what about the murders? She told you she killed those children. Do you believe her, Sara?"

He was watching Sara as he asked the question. He could see in her face that she did not want to believe what she heard on the tape. It hurt him to watch her, to see how much she was suffering for the child. She cared for the young girl more than he had realized, and he wished to God he had been wrong about Cindy.

Sara shook her head. She did not know what to believe.

"Well, it's police work anyway," he answered.

"Come on, you two; it's almost eight-thirty."

"Let Marcia and me worry about when we leave the Village, Tom," Sara said quietly. "This is more important." She stared across the coffee table at Marcia and said, "Let's ask Cindy what she meant by *'We did.'* "

"There's only one problem," Tom interjected. "Where is she?"

"Neil might be able to help us make more sense of her answers," Marcia said.

"How?" Sara asked.

"These numbers . . . the longitude and latitude, if that's what they are. He has maps at home, and I bet there's a connection between this farm and these numbers." She was already standing, moving toward the telephone. "Everything that has happened to us so far—the killings, the attacks—have occurred on land that was the old Delp farm." Marcia held up the slip of paper with the list of numbers. "There's a connection— somehow, somewhere!—with Cindy."

On the cold, raw night, with the wind whipping up from the river and funneling into the natural amphitheater, it was hard for her to run, to follow the thin cowpath along the ridge. Still she ran, her long legs racing along the top of the ridge, carrying in her arms the small lamb.

The animal's bleating was the only sound on the hillside, but it went unheard in the Village below. The cold wind blew the cry away from the houses and toward the woods beyond the property line.

Yet she could see them searching for her. There were men canvassing the Village streets, working systematically up the hillside, their flashlights bright as stars in a summer sky, and dimly she understood that soon they'd find her, trap her here on the ridge, and she hurried on.

"It's here!" Marcia announced, coming back into the

livingroom. "Neil said that on his survey map of the Village these numbers correspond to a spot on the valley ridge. He said to come by his house and he'll show us."

"How's Benjy?" Sara asked.

"Fine, but exhausted. Neil said he fell asleep in front of the T.V. about an hour ago. I'm going to leave him at Neil's for tonight."

"Okay, fine!" Sara was on her feet, ready to leave. "Let's go."

"What do you think you're going to prove out there?" Tom asked, still upset by their decision.

"We'll find Cindy," Sara replied. "And she'll give us whatever answers we need. The police have most of the county force looking for her in the Village, but they won't find her there. She's already given us the answer to that one. We'll find her on the ridge." Sara saw that he was still frowning. "Come on, Tom, it's worth a try."

"Sara, it's you and Marcia who are in danger." He glanced nervously at his watch. Sara's stubbornness and determination frustrated him. He had not met many women who were so self-willed.

Sara smiled, pleased by his concern for her safety but determined to do it her own way. "We're going to be okay, Tom," she answered, and for the first time in the last several days, she really believed they would be.

The child ran past the Indian mound to the edge of the woods, then through the trees until she found the circle, and there in the middle of the ring of stones she knelt on the fall leaves. The terrified animal tried to scurry away; its thin, black legs kicked at the dirt, and again its bleating filled the silent night.

She clung to the lamb, wove her fingers into its short, tight fleece and held the sheep captive. Then, rocking back and forth, she looked up with her blank eyes and scanned the empty night sky, searching it like an unfocused telescope.

Her head began to ache then, and fierce, ragged bits of bright, colored lights zigzagged across the wide pupils of her eyes. The lines of light swirled inside her brain, tore through the cerebrum, and spun around in her head, leaving her dizzy and sick.

With difficulty, she raised the bleating lamb up above her head, poised it there, and then, panting out with effort, swung the small animal down, smashing it on the sharp edge of the stone, ripping a hole through the tiny head of the sheep and spraying blood and brains over a wide circle in the woods.

Her long fingers were still laced into the oily fleece, now wet with blood, and the small animal jerked its life away.

Reverently Cindy placed the dead lamb on the wet leaves, and calmly washed her hands in the fresh blood. Then, cupping her fingers, she collected the final, sputtering warm liquid of the sheep and, standing, carried the sacrificial blood up the rise to the ancient chamber high over the banks of the river.

The telephone rang before they could leave the house.

"That might be Santucci," Tom said. "I told him to call here. Should I get it, Marcia?" When she nodded, he went to the phone and, picking it up, said, "Marcia Fleming's residence."

"Is that you, Tom?" Santucci's tone was casual, and Tom had come to recognize that this deliberate manner meant trouble.

"Yes, Joe? What is it?"

"We got another murder."

"Shit!" Tom sighed. He ran his hand through his thick, black hair; then he picked up the phone off the foyer table and paced in the hallway.

"What's wrong?" Sara asked. She had come to the archway leading into the livingroom and stood there, braced against the wall, as if she, too, expected the worst.

Tom cupped the mouthpiece of the phone and whispered, "It's Santucci. There's been another murder." Tom paused and watched the fear fill Sara's eyes. The endless night and day attacks, and the deaths of the children, had wrecked the women.

Santucci mumbled something and Tom asked impatiently, "What did you say, Joe?"

"It's Peggy Volt. Her husband found the body stuffed into the baby's crib." He continued to speak in his quiet, even tone, as if reading a newspaper aloud.

"How?" Tom asked, raising his voice, trying to break through the seeming indifference of the detective. "How was she killed?"

"We're not sure. The body was nude. She might have been killed elsewhere and moved."

"What about the husband? Is he a suspect?" Tom had taken out a small notepad and begun to jot down the detective's answers. He was a reporter again, doing his job.

"We've questioned him," Santucci answered and then lowered his voice confidentially. "He didn't do it. I think you were right about this one, Tom."

"What's that?" Tom was having trouble understanding the detective.

"I think you're right. I think it was the girl. We found a piece of her clothing in the bedroom. Her old man has identified it." The detective sounded disgruntled. He was not someone who liked admitting his mistakes.

"We have more evidence here, Joe," Tom replied. It did not make him feel better knowing that he was right, that the strange, retarded child was a killer, and he explained to Santucci about the tape, and how Cindy had answered Sara's question about who killed the children.

"I better hear that. Stay at the house. I'm coming over."

"There's more," Tom went on, and told Santucci about the numbers, and how Sara thought Cindy was hiding out up on the ridge of the valley. "We were on our way up there."

"Okay, I'll get my men and floodlights; we'll meet you there." Santucci was no longer belligerent. He had been wrong about the girl, and Tom Dine had been right.

Tom, still stunned by the detective's news, moved slowly away from the telephone.

"Who is it?" Sara asked.

"Peggy Volt." He couldn't look at her.

"Peggy, too." Sara turned from him.

"How?" Marcia asked quickly.

"Santucci doesn't know. She was found nude in the baby's crib . . . stuffed into the crib."

"They'll kill us all," Marcia whispered.

"No, they won't," Sara replied quickly. She knew she had to be positive and forceful.

"Santucci told me they found some of Cindy's clothes at the Volts'," Tom went on, in what he hoped was a neutral voice.

"It wasn't her," Sara answered back.

"She already told us she killed them, Sara!"

"Whoever is causing these attacks," Marcia interrupted, "has got to be much more sophisticated than this twelve-year-old child, or her farmer father. I think Bruce Delp is capable of brute force, of murder, but not this!"

"Marcia's right!" Tom agreed with excitement. "I think this kid has some sort of psychic powers. I keep remembering how her eyes seemed to blaze with color when I trapped her in the hayloft." He turned quickly to Sara, saying, "Remember what I told you, that these autistic children have an unnatural ability to concentrate, to focus their minds."

Sara nodded. "Yes, but you're saying something much more bizarre—that her power of concentration can, number one, burn the cells and nerve fibers of the brain, and, two, cause these brutal attacks."

"Mind control," Tom answered. "It's been proven from the research into psychokinesis that people like Uri Geller, for example, can bend metal just by the concentration of the mind. Well, Cindy Delp has that power. Only," he added, "hers is a killer mind."

She left a trail of lamb's blood in the woods, on the thin path at the edge of the valley, and in the long grass that grew wild near the ancient site. Here the child stopped and circled the mound, easily finding in the dark the small mouth of the chamber. Centuries of neglect had reduced the entrance to a small tunnel, barely large enough for her to squeeze through into the cold stone room.

She stood and, reaching up over the old entrance to the giant lintel that faced the autumn sky, she marked the stone with her sacrifice, drew in blood the slanting lines, marking the granite with the eye of Bel.

Tom led them out of the Village, and up through the fields to the crest of the hill. They all had flashlights and there was enough light among them to locate the mound quickly. It rose like a slight blemish on the thin edge of the valley. Beyond it were more open fields and woods, all descending in a gentle roll of landscape.

But the mound—even covered with long grass and dirt—was noticeable to the untrained eye, once you knew you were looking for it. At Neil Cohoe's house, they had all looked silently at the section of the ridge Neil had marked on the survey map. Then Marcia announced quietly, suppressing her excitement, "The mound. The Indian mound where Benjy and Debbie were picking flowers the day it happened. That's the only thing it could be, on that section of the ridge."

The tunnel entrance was more difficult to find in the dark, and they made it even more so by trampling down the grass in their haphazard search. It was Sara who finally discovered it, stumbling down into the large opening as if she had come upon a gopher hole.

"It's too small for me," Tom said, clearing away the grass. He looked at both of the women.

"I won't go in there!" Marcia protested immediately. She even backed away from the others. "Just because I'm the smallest. . . ."

"Fine, we'll wait for Santucci," Tom answered, pleased with that decision. He did not want either of them inside the mound.

"I'll go," Sara said, and immediately slipped off her jacket.

"Sara, that's not necessary!" Tom objected. "If Cindy isn't inside, some wild animal probably is. This is Santucci's job, not yours."

"Let me take your flashlight, Tom?" Sara asked. "It has a stronger beam." She was only wearing jeans and a flannel shirt, and was immediately cold from the night wind on the hillside.

"Sara, don't!" Marcia said, feeling guilty that Sara wasn't afraid to crawl into the dark tunnel.

"I want to talk to Cindy, now that we know how to reach her," Sara responded calmly. "If Santucci gets hold of her first, she'll be put under arrest for the murder. We'll never know what she has been trying to tell me. And this," she sighed, "is my only chance. Look!" Sara pointed down the hill. In the dark they could see a dozen beams of flashlights, all converging, all climbing through the open field toward them.

"Then I'll go with you!" Marcia said suddenly.

"Marcia, that's all right."

"No, I won't let you go alone. We don't know what's inside; you might need me. Only," Marcia took a deep breath, "you go first."

Sara dropped to her knees, and shining the flashlight before her into the tight, dark hole, she crept forward. The tunnel was only a few feet wide and tight on her body; she had to twist and use her feet to kick herself forward and into the chamber.

The room was larger than she had expected and when she swung the wide beam around the room, she saw it was also clean and bare with the snugness of an attic. Then she turned the light toward the small entrance and helped Marcia scramble inside.

"This isn't an Indian burial site," Marcia announced after she had searched the room with her light. "It's incredible, I know, but what I think we're actually standing in is an ancient temple observatory."

"It's a what . . . ?" Sara turned her flashlight on Marcia. Marcia's mouth was open and she was shaking her head, baffled by the discovery.

"I realize it sounds outrageous," Marcia continued, "and I'm not positive—I'll have to do some measuring—but what this is, this chamber, is an astronomical observatory. The Celts used temples like this to mark the equinoctial days, and the summer and winter solstices. The opening faces east and it was from here that the Druid priests observed the sunrise of each new season. I'll call the Smithsonian in the morning and have a team of archaeologists and epigraphists assigned to this site." Marcia spoke rapidly, planning ahead.

"It still doesn't help us with Cindy," Sara responded.

"I know, Sara, but try to appreciate this. We might be standing in a Celtic temple built over three thousand years ago. This spot on the hill may have been a Druidic astronomical observatory before the Algonquins lived in the Appalachian mountains.

"The typical Celtic temple is like this one—a rectangle with a narrow entrance doorway in the middle of the eastern wall, and a smoke hole for the altar on the western wall. There are no window openings and the only light comes from the doorway.

"These people made a cult of sun worship. The sun meant everything to them: warmth, the growth of vegetation, and, after winter, spring and the birth of wild animals. They worshipped and feared the sun and kept track of it in ways that don't mean very much to us."

"Is it possible, then," Sara asked, coming closer through the dark, "that there might be some connection between Cindy's obsession with the Bel monogram and the Celts' observation of the sun?"

"Yes, it seems to be tying together. We ask her name and she gives us the longitude and latitude of this place. Perhaps she thinks she's acting at the will of this sun god Bel."

"How could Cindy be responding to some ancient, prehistoric ritual?" Sara demanded.

"Sara, in certain places farmers today still plant under a waxing moon and harvest under a waning moon. These traditions—folklore, superstitions—still prevail, and actually I don't think it is any more farfetched or preposterous than supposing that Cindy has psychokinetic powers."

"I'm sorry. I didn't mean to jump all over you. I'm just feeling the strain of tonight." Sara sighed, then added, "Let's get out of this place." She spun her flashlight around and searched for the small dirt hole in the entrance. In the total darkness of the chamber, she was disoriented. "Where's the entrance?" she asked angrily. A small ball of panic sped through her body and caught in her throat, and she wildly flipped the beam of light back and forth across the walls of the long, narrow cave. "Marcia!" she called.

"Sara!" Marcia touched her arm and she jumped involuntarily.

"Let's get out of here. This place is getting to me."

"Wait a second!" Marcia said. "I think I saw something." She took the flashlight and moved the beam of light slowly along the wall. "There!" she exclaimed. "See those marks!" Marcia moved closer, keeping the light fixed on the dark stains above the tunnel.

"These are new," Marcia said, reaching up and touching the damp, slanting lines drawn on the lintel stone. "It's blood," she whispered.

"Does it mean anything?" Sara asked, and again she felt a wave of fear, realizing she was alone with Marcia in the chamber.

"Yes, Marcia answered, concentrating on the blood markings. "This is the Ogam inscription, the one I told you about earlier."

She stepped back suddenly, away from the lintel, and the beam of the flashlight cast her face into shadows.

"What does it say?" Sara asked quickly, frightened by Marcia's reaction.

"It says," Marcia began, beaming the light on each slanted line as she read, "G-L-N F-G."

"Meaning?"

"Pay heed to Bel. His eye is the sun."

On the butcher block table of Sara's kitchen, Marcia began to draw simple line sketches on sheets of drafting paper, explaining to the others as she worked.

"Throughout all the phases of the Bronze Age in Europe, worship of the sun was a common religious practice, and sites where solar worship occurred were indicated by engraved signs representing the sun—a wheel, a checkerboard, and at times a ladderlike symbol.

"Also rocks were set with astronomical meaning. I'm sure there were rocks here that were keyed to stars and sunrises, but over the centuries, they've been removed to build the farmhouse and barns."

"I think I've seen some of these rocks," Tom interrupted. He took his small map of the Village and opened it on the table.

"Can you pinpoint where that girl's body was found beyond Neil's house?"

Sara leaned over the table and pointed to the wooded area beyond lot 75.

"There were huge rocks near the girl," Tom went on, speaking quickly. "I'm sure they formed a circle under those oak trees. They didn't seem important at the time, but they'd have religious significance, wouldn't they?''

"Yes, of course. Rings of Stone. Not many have been found in the United States. They are quite common in Ireland, and I've seen pictures of some in Connecticut, but the giant rings, such as Stonehenge, are found only in England.

"They're called Druids' circles and probably were used for religious and magical rites. Where was that girl killed?''

"Right here." He pointed to a dark spot on the map.

"What are the other X-marks for?" Marcia asked.

"Oh, I was fooling around, trying to find if there was a graphic pattern in the deaths and the attacks on the women. And you can see the lines are like spokes of a wheel, pointing toward the Indian mound.''

For a moment Marcia studied the Xs on Tom's map, then she slipped a thin piece of drafting paper over the map and, pressing lightly with a black magic marker, drew another set of lines connecting the X-marks. She lifted the drafting paper off the map and placed it flat on the table.

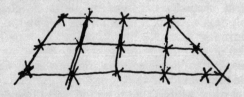

"It looks almost like a checkerboard," Tom responded.

"That's right. A symbol of sun worship."

"Another sun reference," Sara said, sighing, "but still none of it makes sense."

"Oh, it makes sense. We're just having a difficult time accepting the truth: that Renaissance Village is built at the exact location where once—sometime be-

tween 800 and 100 B.C.—a Celtic population built that
rock chamber to chart the skies and pay homage to their
sun god, Bel.

"This hillside, I'm sure, is another Mystery Hill, full
of underground passages, standing monoliths, temple
chambers, and Bronze Age Inscriptions."

"But you said earlier, Marcia, that no one, not even
the experts, were able to decode Mystery Hill."

"Yes, but now we have a key they didn't have. A
walking, talking Rosetta Stone." Marcia's eyes were
bright with anticipation.

"Cindy? But how?" Sara asked. "These monu-
ments—this chamber, the ring of stones—are over three
thousand years old. How could she understand them?"

"The language. Cindy can write Ogam script. You've
seen her."

"But that doesn't prove anything. Autistic children
are able to achieve remarkable tasks, sometimes totally
unrelated to their lives.

"I read about a boy who could run through a Walter
Cronkite news telecast verbatim, complete with pauses,
foreign reports, and commercials. He'd do the different
voices, and also hummed the background music as he
breathed. Actually this type of autism is common.
There's even a technical term for his behavior, delayed
echolalia."

"You'd like that, wouldn't you, Sara?" Marcia
answered. "A plausible, scientific answer to Cindy's
strange behavior."

"I'm sorry, Marcia, but my mind doesn't work quite
like yours. I can't take such large leaps of the
imagination. Perhaps if I knew more about archaeology." Sara shrugged and shook her head. "I'm sorry,
but I don't believe this child is somehow linked to the
Celts who sailed to America in 800 B.C."

"Reincarnation?" Marcia asked wryly.

"Oh, come on!" Sara crossed her arms and walked
away from the table. "You're a scholar, Marcia, not a

believer in transmigration.'' Then Sara turned back to the smaller woman and said forcefully, with all the conviction of her training, ''The child is sick. Cindy Delp is an autistic savant suffering from neurological and biochemical imbalance, but it's possible she can be cured through megavitamin therapy and an anti-allergic diet. And once this nightmare is over, I'm going to see she gets proper therapy.''

''Once this nightmare is over, you might not have the chance,'' Tom replied calmly. The women looked quickly at him and he went on, ''You said yourself the next attack could be fatal.'' He glanced at his watch. ''Well, we'll soon see.''

twenty

"The child won't hurt me," Sara answered. "I've been with her during two stress periods and she hasn't attacked me. I've seen the look in her poor eyes. This girl is trying to reach me, and I cannot run away from her. I'm going to find her, wherever she is hiding on this farm."

"Sara, I know you believe that she won't hurt you. And I agree: Cindy wouldn't hurt you intentionally, but she can't control herself." Tom kept talking, but he could see in how she stood—her arms crossed, her head up and her jaw squared—that she had made the decision, and he knew she wouldn't be swayed. But still he went on. "Sara, the power she has will destroy your mind, burn the cell tissues as it did in those children. As I'm sure she did to Peggy Volt."

"I'll be all right, Tom. She won't hurt me." Sara smiled to make it easier, to show both him and Marcia that she wasn't afraid.

"I'm staying, too," Marcia volunteered.

"No, Marcia," Sara protested. "There is no reason for you to risk your life."

"You're both crazy!" Tom raised his voice and glanced at his watch. "You've got less than twenty minutes," he warned.

"I'll call the barn," Marcia went on, "and tell the others to leave without us." She went into the hallway to telephone.

"Come on, you two!" Tom pleaded. He was frightened, and his fear made him panic slightly. "Sara, if I have to, I'll carry you out of this house and off the farm. The same for you, Marcia!" He was standing in the middle of the kitchen with his feet spread apart and both hands on his hips. He looked wild and out of control.

"Sit down, please," she asked Tom, and slid herself into one of the kitchen chairs.

"Fifteen minutes," Tom announced, still standing.

"Tom, I'm not leaving. I'm going to find that child and solve this mystery. I am going to find out why we are being attacked."

"Sara, she'll kill you." His voice softened and he stepped over to where she was sitting and crouched down beside her. She was wearing boots and jeans and was sitting sideways in the chair.

"Please, don't fight me. I need your help."

"I'm not fighting you; I just don't want to lose you." He took hold of her hand and kissed her fingers.

He looked sad and worried and, Sara thought, adorable.

"You won't lose me," she whispered and, leaning forward, kissed him softly on his lips. She could smell his body and the scent sent a sudden rush through her, as if he had just unbuttoned her blouse and touched her breast.

"I'm not leaving you," he answered. "If you're going to stay in this Village and hunt the girl down, then

I'm staying with you. You might need me."

"I do need you." She touched his cheek again and he turned his face and playfully grabbed her forefinger in his mouth, holding it gently between his teeth and growling.

"Don't," she laughed, trying to pull her finger away, but he wouldn't let go. As he growled again his eyes lost their cold, dark-weather look. He was having fun holding her at bay, and he realized that they hadn't shared one amusing moment since they'd met.

"Please, Tom, it's late." She tugged her finger once more and he opened his mouth and let her loose as Marcia came back into the kitchen to tell them that the women at the barn had already left for Washington, D.C.

"So it's just us, Sara."

"And Cindy Delp," Tom added.

"Yes, Cindy Delp," Sara answered and then bounded out of the chair, saying, "We can, I think, help ourselves against the attack." Going into the study, she picked up her medical bag and returned to the kitchen. She snapped it open and removed syringes and two small vials.

"This is a composition of several drugs, including demerol hydrochloride. What it should do is deaden our reactions; it could be dangerous, but, given the circumstances this is a quick and perhaps effective way of surviving the next attack. I'll fix another syringe, Tom, and if we go into shock just jab us with another 20cc of this."

"But, Sara, I don't know how!"

"Oh, come on," she smiled at him, "be a big boy. After all, it's Marcia and I who are taking all the chances. Ready, Marcia?" She held up the syringe.

Marcia took a deep breath. "I guess. I mean, no, but. . . ." She shrugged. "Do you want me to bend over or something?"

"No, just roll up your right sleeve and let me swab it

with alcohol. There will be a severe but temporary withdrawal from reality. A general numbing of your body. We both should be numb for between five to ten minutes."

"What happens is that the drug shuts down certain neurotransmitters in the central nervous system and the brain. It also closes off any desire for sex. At least in mice." She shrugged and smiled.

"Six minutes," Tom announced.

"Go ahead, Sara." Marcia held up her arm, exposing the soft, white underside of her forearm for the injection, then turned her head away so she wouldn't see the needle being jabbed easily into the thin, blue vein.

Sara waited a moment to see Marcia's reaction. Quietly and slowly, she explained to Marcia how the drug was affecting her, telling her to sit down and make herself comfortable. "Don't fight it, Marcia."

"Three minutes, Sara," Tom reported. He had begun to pace nervously back and forth.

"Okay," Sara replied calmly. She had time, she knew and she carefully fixed the second syringe, then swathed her own left arm. "Would you like to practice, Tom?"

"Sara, I can't," Tom protested. He backed away.

She smiled, then glanced at Marcia, who was now sitting in the kitchen chair, her head back and her eyes closed.

"How do you feel, Marcia?"

"Fine." Her voice was soft and slow.

Sara lifted her arm, tightened the rubber tourniquet, then turned her vein up and in a smooth motion slowly squeezed the drug into her blood stream. She was light-headed before she set the syringe down and loosened the rubber tourniquet.

"Are you okay?" Tom asked.

"Yes." She had difficulty making her tongue form the word.

"Easy, honey." He was behind her, helping her to the chair.

She felt as if the air had become oppressively heavy and was crushing down on her body, breaking apart her soft bones. She sat exhausted in the chair, pulling each breath up and out. She could still hear Tom. He seemed to be speaking, but his voice was far away, as if separated from her by an ocean.

He was looking away, pointing towards the kitchen windows, and shouting at her. Slowly, with great effort, she moved her head, looked in the direction he was pointing, and there in the dark window, pressed against the glass, was Cindy Delp.

twenty-one

By the time Tom unlocked the kitchen door and got outside, Cindy had made it across the backyard, heading for the rocky hillside beyond Sara's property. She ran fast, with the wild, long stride of an animal pursued.

He realized at once where she was heading—to the curtain of dark trees on the hillside—and he sprinted across the terrace, cutting off her flight.

At the edge of the yard he dove for her, bringing her down with an open-field tackle. They rolled over in the wet grass while she screeched and kicked, but he had her arms wrapped tightly around her slight body, bear-hugging the young girl. This time she wouldn't get away from him.

When he had wrestled her into submission, she wouldn't stand, and he grabbed her arm and dragged the screeching child across the yard and back to the house.

In the lighted kitchen doorway, he saw Sara and

Marcia. He pushed the sulking adolescent ahead of him into the house, saying, "Are you okay?"

They nodded, still unsteady on their feet, and Sara answered, "I'm not sure if it was the drug or if we just weren't attacked this time."

"Oh, you were attacked, or at least she tried." He had hold of the slumping child, holding her roughly at arm's length, as if for example, and added angrily, "Why else would she be here?"

"Please, Tom," Sara said, "you're hurting her. Let go of her arm."

"No, she'll only run away."

"But what are you going to do with her?"

"Ask her some questions. This time we're going to find out the truth about this kid." He pushed her ahead of him toward the study. "We're going to find out how she is killing these children and attacking you."

"Try again," Tom said. "Play it at a different speed."

Sara reset the large reel, saying, "This is 3.3 inches per second." Then she started the tape of Cindy's screeching. Her words were still muddled and incoherent.

"Maybe we should tape her again," Marcia suggested, glancing over at Cindy. The child sat on the floor, quietly playing with a black magic marker, endlessly drawing the monogram of the eye of Bel on posterboard paper.

"Try it at a faster tape speed," Tom said instead. "Maybe that's the problem."

Again Sara set the short tape they had made of Cindy's screeching. "This is 15 inches per second, twice the normal speed." "She turned the switch and Cindy's voice came through clear and comprehensible.

"2444504.5."

"Christ, more numbers." Tom sighed. "Do they mean anything to either of you?"

Marcia shook her head. "They could mean anything. She's the only one who knows."

"Well, let's ask her." Tom said. "She gave us these numbers for a reason. If she does want to communicate, as Sara thinks, then she'll tell us." He positioned a new roll of tape on the machine.

Sara moved closer to Cindy, careful not to disturb her with any sudden movement. When she was sitting next to her, she spoke softly, pulled the child's attention away from the drawings and showed her the list of numbers.

"Cindy, who gave you these numbers?"

The child screeched in Sara's ear.

"Do you have that, Tom?" Sara asked, not turning away from Cindy. She kept searching the blank black eyes, searching for some hint in the faraway look of the child, but Cindy's eyes were empty and fathomless.

Behind her, Tom played back the tape.

"The smaller dog," Cindy's voice answered.

"Cindy, what is the smaller dog?"

Tom played back the tape and again Cindy rattled off a list of numbers.

"We're not getting anywhere," Tom said, studying the numbers. "Maybe we should call Santucci and tell him we have Cindy." He glanced at the women.

"Wait. Not yet, Tom." Sara said, then asked, "If someone said smaller dog to you, what would it suggest?"

"Maybe it's her dog. A family reference," Tom replied. "We could telephone Delp and see if Cindy had a dog."

"No, not Cindy. What does the term or name *smaller dog* mean?" It was not wild speculation on Sara's part. Something was tugging at her memory.

Marcia shook her head.

"Isn't *smaller dog* an astronomical term?" Tom asked. "Like the Great Bear and the Smaller Bear?"

"Of course!" Marcia jumped up. "Canis Minor, the

smaller dog—like Ursa Major and Ursa Minor. Lots of planets and star clusters are named after animals.'' She snapped her fingers excitedly. ''We have to get Neil involved in this. He's an astronomer. He can tell us what Cindy is talking about.''

Neil Cohoe opened a copy of the *American Ephemeris*, spreading the star atlas on the desk in Sara's study. ''What were the numbers that Cindy gave you when she mentioned *smaller dog*?'' he asked.

''These,'' Sara said, showing him the list.

He studied them a moment, and then explained. ''If she used the term smaller dog in connection with these numbers, then they'd make sense as the right ascension and declination, the way we locate the position of planets and stars in the sky. Declination and right ascension are equivalent to terrestrial latitude and longitude. Any other numbers?''

''Yes, this list. She was screeching these numbers when Tom brought her into the house . . . 2444504.5.''

''Well, we have to assume that it, too, is astronomial, and. . . .'' he opened another astronomy reference book and flipped rapidly through its long tables of data. ''That number looks like a Julian date. That's simply the astronomical way of counting days. Unlike our normal Gregorian calendar, the Julian date is a continuous counting of days from January 1, 4713, B.C., and that would mean . . .'' he paused at one column and ran his finger down the listing, saying, ''2444504.5 is September twenty-second.'' He looked up at the others, adding, ''That's the autumnal equinox. It falls on the twenty-second this year.''

''Tomorrow,'' Marcia whispered.

''Yes, sunrise tomorrow.'' Neil replied.

''It must have some meaning,'' Sara said. ''I mean, it seems to be coming together. The deaths, our attacks, the finding of the prehistoric chamber focus on the equinox, and all of Cindy's strange numbers, the terrestrial latitude and longitude. Yet still we haven't any idea why.'' She looked around the room.

"Let's ask her,'' Neil answered. "Each time you've asked her something, she's responded, right?''

They nodded.

"Okay, let's see what she knows.''

On a sheet of posterboard, Neil quickly drew a diagram, explaining as he did, "This denotes the fundamental formula of spherical trigonometry which is essential in determining planetary motion and other astronomical data. If Cindy can explain this formula, then we know she's using planetary explanations as her points of reference.'' He held up the diagram, saying, "What is this formula, Cindy?''

For a moment it seemed as if Cindy wasn't paying attention. Her blank eyes floated unresponsively over the drawing and Sara thought how ridiculous it was even to think of showing the diagram to Cindy, or any child. Then Cindy picked up her magic marker and went back to her poster card doodles. At first it appeared she was writing at random and then on the bottom of the white sheet Sara saw her carefully print, *"cos* a = *cos* b *cos* c + *sin* b *sin* c *cos* A.''

Quickly Neil asked, "Cindy, what's the Gaussian Gravitational Constant?''

Again at the bottom of the white sheet she carefully printed, "0.01720209895.''

Neil glanced at the others, saying, "She's right. Now this information is simple, and common to anyone involved with astronomy. If she's truly autistic she could still have learned it all, memorized it, by reading a few books, studying a star atlas.''

"Ask her something more,'' Sara said quickly. "Ask what all these numbers and astronomical data mean. Most autistic children can't reason. They only know information. Well, let's see if she can think.''

Neil nodded, and then to the child, asked, "Cindy, who told you these numbers?"

Cindy screeched, and they played back her answer: "The smaller dog."

"And who is the smaller dog?"

"The eye of Bel."

Neil looked at the others, confused by the reply.

"Go on, Neil," Marcia urged, "we'll explain later."

"Who is Bel, Cindy?"

Cindy looked up, her head flopping over as if she couldn't control herself, and the black depthless eyes rolled loose in their sockets. Sara blinked, momentarily unsure of what she was seeing. Cindy's eyes were spinning wildly, then blazing with color. Marcia grabbed Sara's arm, whispering, "Do you see?"

"Yes." Sara went down on her knees and crawled toward where the child was sitting on the floor. Perhaps they had pushed her too far, she thought, and Cindy was reacting, experiencing a seizure.

"Who is Bel?" Neil repeated loudly, and Sara spun towards him, signaling for him to stop, that the young girl had gone into shock, when Cindy looked back at the group, her pale, fair skin scarlet with fear, her eyes enlarged and bright with the violent light that zigzagged across her retinas. She screeched. Again and again, her voice louder and louder, shrill and terrifying. The shrieking crushed them with sound.

Sara was shouting, telling Neil to stop the questioning. Then she rushed Cindy, took the trembling child into her arms, and hugged Cindy against her breast, blocking out for the moment the terrible noise of the outside world.

"Listen," Tom instructed, when Cindy had calmed down and slipped again into her silent, secret self. He flipped on the tape recorder, playing back her screeching on the slower speed.

On a pad of paper, Neil quickly wrote down the string of new numbers, the setting of terrestrial latitude and longitude.

Then he frowned.

"What is it?" Marcia asked, seeing his puzzled reaction.

He shook his head and opened the atlas, fingering through the pages, then stopped and asked Tom to play the tape once more, before replying, "Well, these numbers she has quoted are accurate, in the sense that they are a correct ascension and declination. Mathematically, there *is* such a spot just outside our solar system." He turned the book around, pointing to a spot near Capricornus. "Here it is, outside the orbits of Pluto and Neptune, and part of the Capricorn constellation, approximately 3,666 million miles from the sun. The problem is—" Neil paused, as if to get their full attention—"if you look to where I'm pointing on this atlas, to the planetary latitude and longitude that Cindy gave us, what do you see?"

"Nothing," Sara answered.

"That's right. No planet, star, or nebulae." Neil closed the large atlas and moved it aside.

The others glanced at each other, then Marcia asked, "Well, what does it all mean? Why those numbers, then?"

Neil shrugged and adjusted his glasses, speaking thoughtfully as he watched the silent child. "We look up into the sky at night and see perhaps a thousand or two thousand stars but we really don't begin to comprehend the magnitude of space. We know of about 250 billion stars in space, so maybe we've overlooked one or two. . . ."

The others glanced around the room.

"What are you suggesting . . . that Cindy is somehow connected with an unknown star or planet at the edge of the universe?"

Neil nodded towards the child on the floor. "I'm not suggesting anything. She is. These are her terrestrial alignments." He lifted his notepad with the numbers jotted down, as if producing evidence.

"Incredible," Marcia whispered.

"Oh, for God's sake!" Sara protested. She pulled herself up from the floor and began to pace nervously in the study.

"What are we talking about?" Tom asked. "Extraterrestrial life?"

Neil shrugged, unsure of what to say, then he answered, speaking slowly. "Someone gave this girl these astronomical numbers. Now let's assume for a moment that it was some form of extraterrestrial life. It's not as farfetched as we might think," he said, glancing at the group. "If only one percent of the stars in our galaxy have conditions suitable for life, that would mean 2.5 billion planets or stars could have technological civilizations like ours.

"Now we usually assume these civilizations would visit us in some sort of space ship, a flying saucer for example. But they won't.

"Carl Sagan, and other astrophysicists, are convinced that the first communication will be some sort of space probe, terrestrial radar maybe, or microwave, perhaps a laser beam of ultraviolet light.

"There is even a likelihood that another advanced civilization has already reached earth and is watching us now, collecting data, and sending it all back out into space."

"A relay system?" Tom asked.

"Yes, something like that. For example, it might work this way." On the white posterboard, Neil drew a rough outline, explaining, "The information is relayed from here on earth, this Village, to the 'eye of Bel'—in this case, the star Canis Minor—toward the rim of our solar system and the Capricorn constellation, some four million miles from the sun."

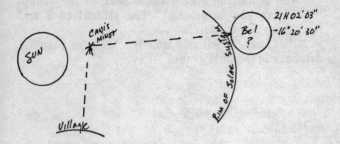

"His eye is the sun," Marcia said slowly. "My God, it is unbelievable."

"We assume that other civilizations discovered us when we ourselves became aware that there might be life out in space," Neil went on. "But more likely we have been watched for billions of years, perhaps from the time when life on earth was no more than simple organisms like jellyfish."

"And that might explain why primitive man has always been attracted to the sun," Marcia added quickly, picking up on Neil's line of thinking. "This 'eye,' so close to the sun, had a meaning for them; it was their link with outer space, other galaxies. And yet they didn't have the technology or knowledge to know why."

"But now we do have that technology. We do know how they are watching us," Neil answered. He was leaning forward, growing more excited as he reasoned out what was happening.

"How?" Tom interrupted, frowning. "Maybe you two understand how it's being done, but I don't."

"A databank," Neil said quickly. "A computer that they have planted on Earth to use as a listening post. A way for this advanced civilization out in space to watch our progress, monitor our earthly activities." He sat back and then nodded toward Cindy.

"Wait a minute!" Sara came back to the group. "What are you suggesting?" She glanced back and forth from Neil to Marcia.

"It's Cindy," Neil said quietly. "They've placed a databank in the child's mind."

twenty-two

"Do you think she's been sent here to kill us?" Tom asked the question quietly, and Neil answered in the same tone.

"No, she wasn't sent here. My guess would be that, for some reason, she was picked, selected, and her brain was altered, probably chemical realignment, to operate as a computer for this 'eye of Bel'."

"Stop it, please!" Sara protested. "I'm tired of this cosmic connection nonsense." She was furious now, and her voice rose and lashed out at the others. "You people are scientists. Marcia, Neil, how can you even contemplate such a bizarre chain of science fiction answers? Cindy is an autistic savant, not a space cadet! We're not helping her or ourselves with such speculation. And besides, we're going to be attacked again. It's almost time."

But Tom was not paying attention to her. Nor were Marcia and Neil. Cindy had stood and moved away from the desk, and begun to circle the study, moving towards Sara. She moved slowly, awkwardly, her feet tripping over each other.

The child was not threatening. She was tall and thin with the gangly body of a preadolescent, and a pale, beautiful face, lifeless as marble.

Yet now her eyes were focusing. The black pupils narrowed and locked onto Sara. She came steadily forward, singling Sara out, cutting her out from the others.

Sara could feel herself in retreat, stumbling back and growing alarmed. Still Cindy did not make a sudden move. Her lovely, angelic face was only tilted up, as if she were listening to some faraway sound. Yet the dark, narrow, laserlike focus of her dark eyes bore into Sara, held her as if she were caught in a rifle's sights.

"Tom," Sara whispered, as she tried to dodge Cindy's gaze. "Tom, please!" Sara raised her voice and backed herself against the oak wall of the room.

Sara tried to look away, to find Tom across the study, but she was too afraid to take her eyes from the child. Cindy was within arm's length, bearing silently down on her, and from the corner of her eye, Sara saw Tom approach, moving quickly around behind Cindy, getting into position, and she thought: I'll be okay; Tom will take care of me. She had just realized that all the while she had been holding her breath, when Cindy jumped forward, seized her by the shoulders and threw her against the wall.

Tom dove for the girl, grabbed her around the waist and tore Cindy loose. The two of them stumbled over each other, then Tom tripped on the rug and they both hit the floor. He lost his hold on Cindy and she quickly scrambled away.

Cindy whirled around, confused and off-center, as if her sense of equilibrium was damaged, until her dark eyes spotted Sara. Holding fast on her, as if Sara, trembling with fear against the wall, was an anchor of reality in her world, she sprang forward once more, seized Sara by the shoulders, dug her nails into Sara's body, and screeched out.

The shrilling ripped Sara's ear and she jerked away as Tom recovered and once more grabbed Cindy and pulled her into his arms, locking her against his body.

It was several minutes before they could play back the tape of Cindy's outburst. What they heard was Cindy crying out, begging Sara in the words and voice of a terrified child, "Help me, Sara, before I kill you."

twenty-three

"How can I help her?" Sara asked, looking at the others. Her voice had softened and once more she was afraid. Afraid she could not help Cindy Delp.

"Get Santucci," Tom suggested immediately. "Let's have her locked up. She needs to be institutionalized."

"That's not helping, Tom." Marcia said quietly. She looked over at Neil. "Any suggestions?"

Neil shook his head. "Maybe Sara's right, maybe the child is only autistic. If that's the case, then what can any of us do?" He shrugged and, taking off his glasses, wiped the lens clean, watching Cindy as she once more played with the posterboard and the mysterious drawing of Bel.

"Well, what if she isn't autistic," Marcia asked, sitting forward in her chair. "What if she is being controlled and her mind is a databank? How can we find out for sure?"

Neil's head popped back, understanding at once what

had to be done. He jumped to his feet. "Of course! Her mind is simply a computer."

"And?" asked Sara.

"Well, we just" he paused, planning quickly—"we just link her with a computer artificially intelligent enough to understand the girl."

"But is that possible?" Tom asked.

"Yes, I think so. Sara? Can you link her brain waves to a computer?"

Sara nodded slowly, not sure whether she was willing to go along with the attempt. "Yes, it's possible," she began slowly, "I've done it with head trauma patients at Harvard. They are linked to a computer through an EEG. It's a way of finding out the severity of neurological damage. But how could we do it? And where?"

"The Naval Observatory. Its computer contains everything we know about space. We'll take Cindy into Washington. . . ."

"That's impossible now." Tom spoke up. "Santucci has the police at every gate. I was stopped, coming into the Village, and I'm sure they won't let us out, not with Cindy."

"What about Kevin Volt's computer?" Marcia asked. She looked up at Neil. "Remember, he showed us his home computer down in his lab."

"Possibly. If it's sophisticated enough, I can link it by phone to the Naval Observatory, and we can read out the results on his terminal." He began to nod his head enthusiastically. "It's worth a try. Sara, what do you think?"

She began to shake her head, still protesting, and Marcia spoke out.

"Sara, we all want to help Cindy; we all want to find out what is happening to us here, who's attacking us."

"But, Marcia, he just lost his wife and child and we're going to barge into his home with Cindy? The police think she's the killer; they're already searching for her!"

"If Cindy is the killer, we'll know soon enough. If this child's brain is a databank, programmed to kill us, then we'll know. Let's find out finally what is in that child's mind."

twenty-four

In the basement laboratory of Kevin Volt's house, Sara worked quickly, improvising with his equipment and her medical instruments to implant the monitoring electrodes.

"What I'm doing," she explained to Kevin and the others, "is placing the needles bilaterally on parasagittal planes approximately one-centimeter medial to the midorbital lines. And I'm going to place an anterior pair of electrodes two centimeters above the supraorbital ridges. Now when the current is passed from the right anterior to the left posterior electrode, we should pick up her brain waves and intercept any databank within her brain."

"What do you think is in there?" Kevin asked. "A computer chip?"

Sara had never liked Peggy's husband, but even so she was shocked by how quickly he had become absorbed in their experiment, apparently forgetting the tragedy that had taken place in his home that afternoon.

"No, I wouldn't think so," Neil answered, watching Sara work on the docile child. "All they'd really have to do is rearrange the chemistry in her brain, use her cells as the databank. What do you think, Sara? You've done psychopharmacological research at Harvard."

"If they have restructured her brain as a computer databank, then they're using the neurotransmitters. Those are the chemicals that carry nerve impulses between cells, but they're pretty mysterious. We know the function of fewer than five percent of these neuro-transmitters." Sara stepped back from the girl and nodded to Neil. "Okay, she's ready."

Neil placed the telephone receiver into the computer saddle, then dialed the Naval Observatory.

"We'll be on line in a moment," he added, saying to everyone, "What we're doing in effect is linking her mind to the Naval Observatory computer. It will quiz Cindy, ask her a series of questions.

"Would you turn on your terminal, Kevin?" Neil asked, and all of them looked to the screen, all except Sara, who sat by the child, holding Cindy's hands in hers.

"We won't hear the questions," Neil continued, "but on the terminal screen we'll see Cindy, or the databank, responding to the questions." And on the screen a series of numbers and formulas were instantly displayed.

"That's Kepler's laws," Neil said quickly, his voice tensing up with his own excitement. "These are basic laws of astronomy. They relate to the planet Earth and its movement around the sun.

"The observatory computer is a vast warehouse of astronomical data. It's questioning her randomly now, discovering what level of intelligence it's dealing with."

More answers were printed out on the screen, and more formulas running in long, complex configura-tions. Neil leaned closer to the screen, concentrating on the display.

"I'm running a video tape, as well," Kevin said quietly. "We'll have a recording of this."

Neil nodded, then explained, without taking his eyes from the terminal.

"She's explaining the orbital velocity of Phobos, that's the angular velocity of Phobos around Mars. The theory is that it's increasing. Now to understand and explain that, Cindy would have to have at least a Ph.D. in astronomy."

Sara glanced over at the screen, saw the display of numbers, the child's incredible thought pattern, then back at Cindy. The young girl sat quietly, her pale face blank and passive, her dark eyes unresponsive to the world around her.

"There must be some logical explanation!" Kevin stated. His full attention was now riveted to the display and he glanced at the farm girl, thinking: who is this child?

"She's dealing with questions of the origin of the solar system," Neil spoke up, his voice once more registering amazement. "She is answering questions about thermal structure, planetary magnetic fields." He gestured to the screen. "I'm sorry. I'm not that familiar with astrophysics. We can have it all checked later, run her replies back through the computer and verify them."

"But why?" Tom asked, awed himself by the child's ability. "How could it happen that this girl was implanted with a databank?"

"It must be the location, this Village," Marcia suggested. "The temple and the worship of Bel mean this spot on the Potomac has always been significant to people, and for reasons they wouldn't understand. We have no idea how many other 'autistic' children might have lived here in the last three thousand years; we only know about Cindy."

"And she's trying to kill us all," Tom answered.

"It's not Cindy; she isn't in control of her actions,"

Neil answered. "There must be another reason for these deaths," and then he saw what it was. "Look!" he shouted, pointing to the terminal screen.

They all saw the digital numbers flashing erratically on the terminal screen. Sara glanced back at Cindy. The child still sat quietly, unmoved and silent in the chair.

"The databank," Neil whispered. He and Kevin were the only ones who immediately understood what was occurring. "It's malfunctioning. That's what's happening! They're trying to reach Cindy, trying to correct the databank."

He spun around and his voice quickly rose with excitement. "They're trying to find her, to correct her brain, and it's the probes from outer space that are killing the children and causing your attacks. The probes must be sweeping the Village like a radar scope, but for some reason—maybe because of the malfunction of the databank—they can't find her."

"Of course," Marcia said, understanding Neil's theory. "And since the probes are locked into a female's hypothalamus, that's why it's only *us* that are being attacked. Benjy was never really in danger." She stopped, stared at the child, and then added slowly, "But, Neil, you're wrong. They aren't trying to correct Cindy's mind. They're trying to destroy that databank in her brain, destroy her."

For a moment no one spoke. They stared back at the computer terminal, at the same flashing digital numbers that swept again and again across the screen.

"What will happen?" Tom asked.

Neil shrugged. "If Marcia is right, and I'm afraid she is, then they'll keep probing, more and more frequently, until the databank is destroyed."

"And the child killed," Sara added.

Tom stared at the others, frowning and uncertain. "Can't we do something? Save her?"

"How?" Neil asked.

"We could deprogram her," Sara answered. "We

can change the chemical composition in Cindy's brain, alter the neurotransmitters and break the cell link they're using to control her mind.''

"Sara, is that possible?" Marcia asked, moving closer to her.

"Yes, in theory. Chemicals bridge the gap between the nerves. If Cindy's brain is functioning like a computer, then in theory we could inject her with psychotropic drugs, alter her consciousness, and break their databank, free the child.

"We do know already that active agents like choline, lecithin, vasopressin, and others do promote intelligence, while a drug like scopolamine can cause learning deficiencies.''

Sara paused a moment and ran quickly through her mind the experiments she had done at NIH, how they had taken monkeys and caused a depletion of acetylcholine activity and produced a loss of memory, then used dimethylaminoethanol p-acetamidobenzoate to regain the acetylcholine levels and normalize the animals.

"We have done this on laboratory animals," she said to the others, explaining, "and once the databank is wiped out, I'll use choline and lecithin to reestablish the child's intelligence.''

"Wait a minute!" Kevin interrupted. "I mean, why do that?" He stared at the others, then said forcefully, "Look, this child's link with an extraterrestrial force is more important than she is. You can't just go experimenting. Christ, don't you realize what you have here? Neil, come on, this isn't just some sick kid." He gestured toward the terminal screen. "I saw what she was able to achieve. My people can protect her; we can use her to reach this other life source.''

Kevin was thinking rapidly, planning ahead. The discovery of this child, he knew immediately, was far more important than the covert operation he was developing in the Village. He had had the go ahead from the Agency to develop a microwave and laser beam listening capability in the Village, a way for the CIA to tap the private lives of all the people who worked in the White House and at the State Department.

He had worried before about Peggy telling the community; she had been appalled by his deliberate bugging of their neighbors. But those experiments were insignificant compared to what the others had stumbled upon, this child who was linked to outer space, to another planet. If he brought her in to Langley, it could be the making of him.

"No, Kevin, we can't wait; we can't take the chance." As she spoke Sara began to unlink the child from the computer. "And you should understand, Kevin. You've lost a family because of what they are trying to do to Cindy."

Kevin was on his feet, shouting, "I'm taking charge of this child." He grabbed Cindy, pulled her loose from Sara's hands and stepped past the others, moving quickly towards the door, dragging the girl with him.

It was Cindy herself who stopped him. She whirled around in his grasp and broke loose, fell against the laboratory table and, when he grabbed for her again, she locked her eyes on his. They could see the wide, dark eyes focus and the brilliant flash of light. Kevin's hands shot to his face and he stumbled away, crying with pain as he hit the basement floor.

Tom reached him first, held his body as it convulsed on the floor, shook and then froze. Slowly and with difficulty, Tom pried Kevin's hands from his face. His eyes were wide, as if they had witnessed a revelation, and blood poured from his nostrils, filling his gasping mouth.

twenty-five

"She's a killer," Sara whispered as she watched Cindy back into the corner of the laboratory, slide down on the floor, then, crouched like a hunted animal, scan them with her blank eyes.

"No," Neil reasoned, "she's only the instrument; they've obviously programmed her to react violently if threatened. She has the ability, the power of concentration, to destroy minds."

"Like she did to that little girl in the woods," Tom added.

"And Peggy Volt."

"But why the baby?" Sara asked, tears in her eyes.

Neil shook his head. "It's impossible for us to know now, but I'd say she didn't harm the baby. She's only struck out, it seems, at people she thought were threatening her. Debbie and the baby were probably killed by the probe when it swept the Village. You and Marcia and the other women were strong enough to withstand the attacks; Amy and Debbie weren't.''

"It's getting closer," Sara said softly, "that's why the assaults are much more violent. This probe is like cannon fire; it's finding the range.''

"It's the autumnal equinox, of course!" Neil exclaimed, breaking into the conversation. "That's why the twenty-second of September was programmed in her mind.''

The others stared at him, waited for an explanation.

"This morning—at the equinox—the earth, this valley, must be in a direct line with Bel. For a few moments, at sunrise, it will have an open window to the Village. The probe will be able to lock in on Cindy's databank directly; it won't have to sweep the valley searching for her. It will be able to destroy the databank directly.''

Sara went to Cindy, wanting to protect her. But the child did not seem alarmed; as usual, she sat vacantly scanning the room. Then Sara realized what was happening. Cindy's beautiful black eyes were recording all their movements. Everything they said and did was being relayed to the rising sun, the eye of Bel, and from there 3,666 million miles to the edge of the universe.

Their lives and Cindy's, she now realized, depended on how long it took for the information to reach outer space, be comprehended by this intelligent life, and their violent reply sent back to Earth and the Village.

"Hurry!" Sara directed. "We have to take her back to my house. All my drugs are at home. We have to break this link, destroy her databank, before sunrise.'' She moved quickly to Cindy and gently lifted the tall girl, speaking to the others as she did. "It will have to be a massive assault of psychotropic drugs if we're going to have a chance of saving her.''

They had made it up the stairs and outside into the backyard of the Volt house when the first pulse struck the Village. Tom looked down across the Village and in the thin first light of day saw the ball of blazing red light appearing like a lost meteorite in the eastern sky. He did not even have time to shout a warning before the blazing ball hit the house like summer lightning, breaking glass as the roaring burst of energy ripped a twelve inch hole in the ceiling and roof, then soared back into the empty sky.

Another followed, tearing more holes in the frame house as it swept out of the cloudless sky, cut a bright swatch of light through the house, and disappeared into the atmosphere. Already the Volt home was on fire.

"They know what we are going to do," Sara shouted, hugging the child closer. From where she stood high up in the Village, she could see more brilliant flashes of light striking the Village, sweeping out of the vast sky, cutting like colored scythes through the streets, hitting the houses around the cul-de-sac. Farther down the hillside other homes were on fire. The blazing lights that flashed from out of the early morning light were changing colors, from deep blues to oranges and violets. Each light was a long, thin knife of color cutting through the sky, hitting the houses one at a time, slicing through the rooms, then soaring up again into the empty sky and disappearing from sight.

Sara could see her neighbors in their bed clothes rushing into the streets, herding their children before them, then falling to the ground as a beam of light tore out of the heavens and swooped across the valley, striking whatever crossed its path.

"I have to find Benjy," Marcia shouted, seeing how the fire was spreading, from one cul-de-sac to the next.

"Go with her, Neil," Tom said. "We'll meet you at Sara's." He grabbed Cindy's other arm and the three of them raced across the Village as all around them the locomotive roar of the bright beams of light sped through the sky.

In her own kitchen, Sara hurriedly filled several syringes with the liquefied chemicals from the laboratory, setting them in a row on the butcher block table.

"You're going to have to help me, Tom," Sara ordered. "We haven't time for me to do it all." She handed him two small syringes, saying, "Just jab her thigh. You're less likely to do damage and the muscles will absorb the medication."

Sara bent over the child and speaking softly, reassuringly, lifted Cindy's arm. The child followed her motion without interest as Sara swabbed her forearm and easily jabbed the skin. Tom held one syringe ready in his hand, but Sara could see he was unable to use it.

"Never mind," she said, pulling the syringe from his unsteady fingers. Then, turning back to Cindy, she found a second vein in the girl's thin arm. She had filled the syringe with 50 cc of chlorpromazine and haloperidol, drugs that were known to relieve hallucinations and chronic psychosis, and to block the neurotransmitter dopamine, one of the primary transmitters of nerve impulses.

Cindy's arm flinched and she jerked from Sara's grasp. She glanced up at Cindy as she readied the third syringe. The girl's eyes had begun to focus, to concentrate on Sara.

"Tom, grab her!" Sara ordered and lifting Cindy's dirty skirt, jabbed another needle into Cindy's right thigh.

Cindy swung wildly at Sara, caught her on the side of the head, then seized her by the neck, digging her nails deep into Sara's throat and drawing blood.

Sara dropped her syringes and grabbed Cindy's wrists, tried to pull the powerful hands from her throat. She could see Cindy's startled eyes, see the bright zigzagging lines shoot across her retinas. The girl would kill her, she realized.

Then Tom grabbed Cindy. He pulled her hands from Sara's throat and wrestled Cindy to the floor, using his size and weight to pin her down.

For a full fifteen seconds they lay locked in that position. Then Sara said, "All right, Tom, let her go." It would be only moments, she knew, before the full impact of the chemicals reached the child's muscles, nerves, and brain.

Tom rolled off the sprawled girl and Cindy scrambled to her feet, stumbling awkwardly around the room.

"She'll kill us," Tom yelled.

"No, we're all right. The scopolamine causes partial paralysis. Whatever she is being signaled can't be carried out. She won't have any control over her muscles." Sara did not take her eyes from the child as Cindy tried to move forward, to come after them, the need to kill still programmed in her databank brain.

She fell against the kitchen chair, swayed precariously, stumbled forward in hesitant steps. They kept backing away, giving the child room to maneuver.

It hurt Sara to watch the drugged child, to know she had injected Cindy as she might one of the white mice in her laboratory. Now she began to fear she had made a mistake, that the massive dose of untested psychotropic drug compounds would kill the child.

In the middle of the kitchen floor Cindy stopped. Her feet apart, keeping her unsteady balance, she raised her hands and gripped her head. She tried to speak and a thin screech escaped her lips.

Oh, God, Sara thought, her strength leaving her. I've failed again, another child I could not save.

A fireball hit the house. A roaring locomotive noise of bright light ripped through the house, smashing a round hole from one wall through the next, then crashing into the kitchen and out the back, spraying glass and wood and plaster over them all.

Sara screamed and reached for Cindy, pulling the frightened child to her arms, then fell quickly to the floor as another blazing beam struck the house, ripping the walls apart and soaring off through the ceiling and roof. She rolled over with Cindy in her arms and slid

beneath the butcher block table as the second floor of
the building gave way and crashed into the kitchen.

Cindy was crying hysterically but it took Sara only a
moment to realize she was all right, that neither one of
them were injured, and then she thought of Tom and
cried out for him.

He was only a few feet from her, trapped beneath
part of the kitchen ceiling, and Sara tore loose from
Cindy and crawled to his side. Another ball of bright-
colored energy swooped through the wrecked house,
destroying more of the structure, but Sara disregarded it
and cleared some of the loose debris from Tom's face.

He was bleeding and unconscious, but he was alive.
She had to get help; she could not move the heavy wood
off his body.

Again the soaring ball of light roared into the house,
smashing a path of flaming destruction, still seeking
Cindy.

She could not keep the child here, Sara thought
quickly. She had to get Cindy away from the Village.
That was the only way she could save Tom and the
others. Once Cindy was gone, they would leave the
Village alone.

Quickly she kissed Tom on his lips, then crawled back
and pulled Cindy out from beneath the table and led the
child out of the wrecked house.

"You have to run, Cindy," she instructed. Taking
her by the hand and crossing the backyard, Sara
climbed the hillside towards the ridge of the Village and
the stone temple of Bel. Drugged and disoriented, Cindy
stumbled as she ran, and Sara had to half drag, half
carry the girl up the hill.

They were more vulnerable now, Sara knew, but she
saw also that the streaking balls of light were still attacking the Village. From the crest of the hill, she saw
that the roaring jets of brilliant light were not random
and irregular, but instead they were systematically
destroying the new houses of the subdivision, moving in

a deliberate pattern up the farm road and into the new cul-de-sacs.

Already they had set on fire the homes on Chaucer Drive and Montesi Court, and the flames from the burning frame houses had spread to the long dry grass in the open field beyond the construction. Encouraged by the roaring winds of the extraterrestrial attacks, the fire had moved quickly up the hillside toward the top of the ridge.

The flames had built up a wall of fire across the open field and from where Sara stood at the site of the mound, she saw that all of Renaissance Village was aflame, from the crest of the hill to the shore of the Potomac.

Still the bright pulsing beams from space continued to zigzag across the Village. Sara spotted in the distance a cluster of her neighbors on Petrarch Court, all huddled together in the center of the cul-de-sac with their houses in flames around them. She saw a single, looping orange beam rip out of the sky, drop down in a long, graceful swoop and drive through the huddle of people, scattering their bodies like trash.

"Oh, God!" she cried, and grabbing the child, pushed her down and into the tunnel of the ancient temple. The first beam struck the top of the mound, burning a hole through the grass and dirt that for centuries had concealed and encased the stone temple. Sara felt the quiver of the ground, then the blast of after-shock. She pushed the child forward and into the large chamber.

Another streak of careening light burst from the sky and hit the temple mound, boring a hole through the dirt and striking the slabs of granite that formed the roof of the long, rectangular building. Inside Sara attempted to stand, but the second wave of after-shock toppled her once more.

Cindy screamed and Sara went to her, pulled the child closer. It was a mistake, she now realized, to hide in the temple. It would be destroyed, too, and the heavy slabs of granite would crush them to death. And then she heard Cindy whisper, "Sara, take the pain away."

Sara pushed the child away and looked into the blank, black eyes of the autistic child. The drugs had helped some, cured Cindy of her speech problem, but the databank memory was still programmed, otherwise Cindy would not remember who Sara was. It hadn't worked; she had not been able to wipe the child's mind clean.

And millions of miles in space a final fireball of energy zeroed in on the Village, locked itself to the fading signal of the databank and sped through the galaxies until it hit the thick, heavy atmosphere, crashed the ionosphere, and broke into dazzling colors as it raced on, now less than seventy-five miles from earth.

Sara crawled out of the temple, still holding tightly to the child. The fire had swept past the ridge, leaving the dirt charred and the ground hot. Below her the Village was a bonfire of destruction. It was all over, she thought, in a moment it would be all over.

She saw the last blazing pulse speed towards earth like a shooting star, flying straight forward on its final programmed mission. It would destroy them both, Sara realized, but still she clung to the child.

She watched the hurling bright red light as it swooped to ground level and swept along the Potomac as the first thin slip of sunrise broke the flat horizon. The autumn equinox, she thought, and closed her eyes to wait.

"Oh, look!" the child cried out with delight.

Sara opened her eyes to catch a flash of the blazing pulse sail harmlessly over their heads.

"Isn't it pretty?" Cindy asked, smiling gleefully at Sara, her dark eyes bright with excitement.

Sara turned to follow the disappearing ball of light. The drugs had worked in time. Cindy was free and the window for the eye of Bel closed.

"Yes, darling, it is pretty." Sara whispered, and with the child watched the beautiful ball of colored light roar across the high ridge of the ancient valley, and disappear into the first bright day of autumn.

epilogue

Spring, 1981

Sara crossed Mount Auburn Street against traffic and hurried into Ferdinand's for lunch. She was early on purpose, but Sam was already waiting at the table and she smiled wryly, thinking, she could never anticipate him. Punctual to a fault, he had taken away her advantage.

"Welcome home," he said, standing quickly and kissing her on the cheek. She knew by the sound of his voice that he was tense, that this first meeting wasn't going to be easy on him, either.

"You've lost weight," she commented as she sat down. She took a long look, staring openly as if to evaluate him, to make a decision about how well he had fared since she left him.

"And . . . and you." He smiled. "You look as always—beautiful."

Embarrassed, Sara glanced away from his steady gaze. It wasn't like Sam to be complimentary. It cost him something, and she wondered what he expected in return.

"I read about what happened," Sam started, not knowing where to begin. "There was a long article in the *Globe*, and I saw some T.V. reports. How many people were actually killed?"

"Over a hundred."

"It seems incredible that there could be that much destruction. A total housing project. A village!" Sam kept shaking his head. He looked worried, as if he were somehow responsible. "The *Globe* called it some kind of meteorological phenomenon."

"Well, the brush fire caused most of the damage. The houses all had shingled roofs and the flames swept from one cul-de-sac to the next. Also, the Village was five miles from the closest town and it took over thirty minutes for the firemen to reach us." Sara sighed, weary of the silent deception. She knew she could not yet reveal what had really happened at Renaissance Village, but she did not like concealing the truth, especially from Sam.

"Thank God, at least you're okay." He reached out and, as if spontaneously, seized her hand, then watched her face, waited for some response, some slight signal that his concern meant something to her.

"Yes, I'm all right." She slowly withdrew her hand and reached immediately for the menu. "And how are you, Sam?" she asked. "How is the book?"

"Oh, as good as I can expect. I've been slowed by the usual research problems. You know, experiments that end up going nowhere. In December I lost a solid month tracking down the wrong enzymes."

She looked at him then. He seemed exhausted and she could see traces of gray hair at his temples that hadn't been there when she left him.

"What about NIH?" he said.

"Oh, I've left—I resigned just before the first of the year. I moved to a little farm outside Culpeper,

Virginia, and went into practice with an older doctor in town.''

She looked up at Sam and saw that the news had surprised him.

"It sounds pretty remote," he said carefully. "Aren't you lonely?"

"Well, I'm living with someone, a writer who used to be with *The Washington Post*. He's working on a book now, about what happened to us in the Village."

"Is this serious, this relationship?"

"Yes," she said, "it is serious," and just saying it made her feel good, and she realized there were no emotional ghosts waiting for her here at Harvard. On that wave of security, she continued to talk, to explain how she had first met Tom, and what had actually happened at Renaissance Village. She talked in a rush, while Sam's eyes widened in astonishment.

"Cindy's parent were killed in the attack and the state granted me legal custody of her. It was then I decided Cindy was more important than my work at NIH. Most of all she needed a safe, secure environment." Sara shrugged, then admitted, "And I think that's what I needed, too. So I went looking for a place near the Blue Ridge Mountains.

"Cindy is doing fine. I spend as much time as possible with her, and so does Tom. We've arranged for a student from the local community college to tutor her. She's not able to handle public school yet. The gaps in her education are tremendous."

"And there's no residual evidence of what happened to her?" he asked, still skeptical, still the same devil's advocate he had always been.

"I thought at first she had been freed—and she is, really; she isn't in any danger—but occasionally I'll see her solve a math problem, for example, with phenomenal ease. Some sort of memory, perhaps, is still lodged in her brain cells. Or maybe she simply is gifted. It's too soon to tell."

"Incredible, Sara! If this crazy story is true, you have to do more research on this girl." Sam leaned forward across the small table, his voice rising with excitement.

"No! Cindy is going to be left alone. She's suffered enough. It was like a long nightmare for her and I'm not going to drag back to her consciousness all the terror she experienced."

Sara's outburst silenced and surprised Sam. She had never been this forceful when they had lived together. He saw there was a sureness about her, a confidence that had been lacking. He saw it in her eyes, in the way her mouth was set.

"Then don't you worry about your friend's book? Isn't it going to draw attention to you and the girl?" he asked defensively.

"No, we can protect Cindy. We've thought it all out; that's one advantage of living out in Virginia. Besides, Tom's book is important. It can help us. It can help others."

"Others? What do you mean?"

"I think—we think—there are others," Sara answered, keeping her voice down, as if sharing a secret.

"Others? You mean, more children programmed like Cindy?"

Sara nodded. "There is a group of us involved . . . Marcia Cohoe, an epigraphist from the Smithsonian, and her husband Neil, who's at the Naval Observatory. We've begun to study children with autistic disorders, children with special perceptual problems. It may be that they, too, have been reached as Cindy was. It's too early to say, but our preliminary findings look positive. The next step is to mount a full-scale investigation, but we can't do that on our own. That's why I'm in Boston; I'm trying to see if any of the foundations here will give us research money."

"You actually believe all this, Sara," Sam whispered, shaking his head. "You really believe this autistic child was controlled by a databank from outer space?" He kept shaking his head in disbelief. "I mean, Sara, you must. . . ."

She let him talk, listened to his voice drone on while she concentrated on her salad. It had been a terrible mistake to tell him the story. How could he possibly understand what had happened to her and Tom?

"Sam, just promise you won't tell anyone," she interrupted, "especially here at Harvard. I don't care if you don't—can't—believe this, but it's important that for the moment no one be aware of what we're doing. You can see yourself that it's too sensational, too far-fetched, and any sort of publicity would be detrimental. I only told you because you're my friend, and a scientist. I thought you'd understand." She was leaning forward, staring hard at him. The look in her eyes told him she was deadly serious.

Sam nodded and absentmindedly picked up his fork and began to eat. For a moment both of them were silent and then Sam asked, speaking speculatively, "If all of this is true, Sara, if this girl is—was—a databank, then what are you going to do next fall?"

Sara paused, glanced at Sam, unsure of what he meant.

"The autumnal equinox," Sam answered. "Won't that space window to this extraterrestrial life be open? Won't they come searching for Cindy? And if there *is* some sort of residual data in her brain cells, won't they find her?"

"No, they won't." Sara shook her head. "We don't live in the valley, and that's the place where the eye of Bel made its contact with Earth—on the land that became the Delps' farm. The ancient settlers of America discovered this; that's why they built the temple in that valley."

Sam set down his knife and fork and stared at Sara. "But you just said you thought other autistic children might also be controlled like Cindy. That means the force from Bel must make contact with Earth in other

places—*lots* of other places; there's no telling where, or
how many. They could go anywhere, attack anyone's
brain, and they could find Cindy again, wherever she is
in the world.'' He stopped abruptly, seeing the fear fill
her eyes.

"Are you okay, Sara . . . ?" Sam reached for her
hand, but Sara pulled away, trembling with fear, then
stood abruptly and, collecting her coat and briefcase,
rushed from the restaurant.

She ran headlong into the busy street as if pursued by
the truth of Sam's question, and only the blare of car
horns and screeching tires brought her back to reality.

Sara spun around in the heavy Cambridge traffic,
momentarily unsure which way to turn, then stopped
and stared into the bright spring sky over Boston. Sam
was right. They would come again to search for Cindy.
In the fall of the year when the Northern Hemisphere
was once more aligned with the eye of Bel they would
come to kill Cindy. They would come again to kill her
child.

TURN THE PAGE
FOR MORE TERROR . . .

John Coyne's phenomenal bestsellers have rocketed him
to the top rank of America's new masters of horror,
along with Peter Straub and Stephen King.

On the following pages are chilling excerpts from THE
LEGACY, his novel of a young California couple who
inherit an ancient terror . . . and THE PIERCING, the
story of a young woman, a tormented priest, and a
miracle from Hell.

The Legacy

Maggie fled the Grand Hall, afraid to go to her bedroom alone. Instead she headed for the fire-lit library, a warm and cozy room, close enough to Pete to call him if she needed help.

She immediately switched on every lamp, bathing the room in light. Yet even with all the lamps shining, the library was haunted by shadows. The whole house seemed haunted, even the whole of England, and she suddenly missed the sunny openness of California.

Walking to the fireplace, she heaved more logs on the flame. The dry wood caught quickly, and in a few minutes the fire blazed so intensely that she had to step away from the heat.

It was then that she noticed the portrait of the young woman. The girl was Maggie's age, dressed in the same square-necked black gown, with the same long brown hair swept up off her neck and fastened with a gold headpiece set with pearls. She wore only two pieces of jewelry, a heavy lavaliere around her neck and the signet ring of Ravenshurst. In her hands she clutched a thin, leather-bound book.

"She's quite beautiful, isn't she?" Karl's voice startled her. She hadn't noticed when he'd slipped into the library and stood watching her studying the portrait.

Maggie was too stunned to answer him. Seeing her likeness in the sixteenth-century portrait was eerie but exciting, like discovering an unknown twin.

"Do you admire the ring on her finger?" the German persisted. He moved closer, dragging his bad leg across the thick carpet. Maggie could hear him approach, his shuffling step driving a wedge of fear through her. She had to force herself to keep from screaming for Pete.

Too frightened to turn, she could feel him close behind her, could hear his heavy breathing and smell his breath, rancid with tobacco and whiskey.

He spoke softly in her ear, as if telling her a filthy story. "She lived here. When she was just your age, she was dragged from this house and burned at the stake by order of Queen Elizabeth the First. Her name was Margaret, too—Margaret Walsingham."

Maggie flinched and spun around to Karl. Her eyes widened and she stared at him.

"My mother's name was Walsingham," she cried without thinking. But then it was too late. Too late to heed Pete's warning not to tell these people anything which could be used against her.

Karl looked up at the portrait and continued. "This Margaret Walsingham was succeeded by her illegitimate son, who inherited all her wealth and power. And so it has been ever since, as prescribed in a book she wrote—called *The Legacy*."

He slipped the small leather-bound book from his suit pocket and pressed it into her hands, closing her fingers around it.

"I want you to read this, so you will fully understand what has been happening here." He glanced at the door, to make sure no one could hear them, then said, "I heard you ask Jacques if our group is involved with the . . . the occult . . ."

Maggie looked intently at the German. "Well, is it?" She held up the book that Karl had just given her. "And while we're at it, just what is the legacy . . . ?"

Karl looked again toward the library door, then whispered, "You *must* read Margaret's book. It will explain the inexplicable happenings at Ravenshurst. You will learn the meaning of Maria's death."

"It was an accident . . ."

Karl shook his head. "Expert swimmers like Maria do not hit their heads on the bottom of pools."

"Clive killed her, didn't he?" Maggie asked bluntly.

Again Karl shook his head. "Then why is Clive now dead? Tell me, Margaret, what did he eat this evening?"

She thought a moment. "Ham, for sure, and some pâté. His plate was full. I think he took mostly vegetables . . ."

"Any chicken?"

"No. I remember. When Arthur asked him, he said he had too much food on his plate."

"Well, he choked on a chicken bone," Karl replied. "Adams pulled a splinter from his throat."

"Oh, God." She could still see Clive stretched out on the table, gasping for breath, his legs jerking up and kicking the table as he tried to stay alive. "But that's not possible," she protested. "He didn't eat any chicken."

"It happened nevertheless, Margaret." He gestured toward the book clutched in her hands and urged, "Read that and you'll understand. Remember, too, who your only friend is at Ravenshurst."

But it was not Karl who was her friend. Of everyone at Ravenshurst, only Pete could be trusted. She backed awkwardly away, mumbling, "Excuse me . . . I must . . ." Then she turned and rushed from the library, desperate to find Pete.

Karl watched her go and allowed himself the luxury

of a small, tight smile. He had played that very nicely. Very nicely, indeed. He went to the bar and poured himself a brandy. He had not eaten anything; not after seeing what Adams had done to Clive. But he continued to drink, despite the fact that the liquor would dull him when he most needed to be alert.

Jacques was the killer, Karl was sure of that. Sly, insidious Jacques with his fine manners and soft voice. The French gentleman. The connoisseur. Karl snorted. The bloody murderer. It had to be Jacques and Adams working together. The proper, condescending Nurse Adams. Another killer in their midst.

He could still see her cold-bloodedly cutting Clive's throat. And the blood. Quart after quart of hot, hissing blood pouring from the incision. Karl could still smell it, taste it, and he quickly gulped the brandy to wash the taste away.

Jacques and Adams had worked it all out. One final weekend when they would kill off everyone else Jason had written into his will. Maria and Clive already were gone, and those who survived would be attacked one by one, like sheep singled out by wolves.

That had been their plan. Quite smart. Karl snorted again, amused.

Jacques had been the one who told him to read Margaret Walsingham's diary, page by page. He agreed with Barbara that it was all nonsense, a book of lies and superstitions. Jacques and his talk of the occult! Jacques would have them believe the devil was among them. Karl smiled as he sipped his brandy.

Let Jacques believe that Karl Liebknecht, survivor of the Hitler Youth Corps, the Western Front, and the terrible years of the Occupation, was frightened of ghosts and devils. It served his purposes perfectly to have all the others believe that. Just as it had been a master stroke to convince Maggie Walsh that she was a true descendant of Margaret Walsingham. Tomorrow morning, when the helicopter landed on the lawn, he would be the only one waiting.

He strolled over to the fireplace, warming himself as he watched the beautiful gold vermilion of the flames. The Americans would have to die. Especially the young man, who was already pressing for an investigation. With any luck, Jacques or Adams would handle that problem for him.

Karl stared at the fire as he made his decision. If Jacques did not eliminate the Americans, then he would have to do it. He already knew he was not afraid to kill. It would not inconvenience him if, before the weekend was over, it was necessary to kill again.

The fire was dying. Karl leaned over and threw another log onto the blaze. The fire hissed and a small log tumbled forward onto the firestone. Karl lifted it and sent it back with the tongs. For a moment, he stayed crouched before the flames, enjoying the perverse thrill of the intense burning. He was thinking of Jason. The old man had hung onto life longer than he was useful, and as Karl was damning him for living, the fire struck him.

The flame bellowed out of the hearth in a rolling cloud of heat. It licked his bare skin, blinded his eyes, and burned his lips and tongue as if a searing poker had been jammed between his teeth. His shriek of pain caught in his throat and he fell back onto the floor, the flames following, covering his body like a blanket.

The fire burned his clothes first. It reduced his shoes to warped rubber, melted his watch, his fine jewelry. The gold cigarette case burst open and the ink in his fountain pen shriveled away in the tube.

He did not lose consciousness immediately. He felt the white flame envelop his body and burn away his eyebrows and silvery hair. He heard his own skin crackle like grease on a skillet as the flame ran up his sleeves to his armpits and burned a path across his chest. He felt the flame as it spread over his body, seizing his soft genitals and then burning down the length of his thighs. He was dead before the fire began to roast his remains.

He burned for ten minutes. The fire did not spread; it consumed only the body of Karl Liebknecht, leaving the library untouched. His body curled, shrinking like a log on the hearth, as his limbs jerked and contracted and finally broke off from his trunk like dried, rotten branches.

The smell of burnt flesh was intense, but that, too, was contained within the room, not even spreading when Adams opened the door and stepped inside, locking it behind her until her work was done.

By now the charred remains were only a small lump, blackened and unrecognizable. The fine silvery hair was gone, the elegant features obliterated, the rangy body reduced to a compact heap which smoldered like a charcoal pit.

Adams paused to study the charred mass. The sight itself did not upset her, but the thick smoke and the dense odor made her eyes water. She blinked rapidly as she went about her work, opening the windows to clear away the smell and the smoke. Then, emptying the wood from the iron bucket, she took up the tongs and meticulously collected the remains, stacking them like peat. It took her only one heavy load to clean Karl Liebknecht's corpse from the library of Ravenshurst.

The Piercing

Father Matt Driscoll reached over and pulled the small white envelope from the church's collection basket. It stood out like a marker among the brown Saint John of the Cross tidings. The white envelope was sealed and across the front the word PRIEST had been printed in crude lettering, as if scribbled by an illiterate.

It was late in the evening and the pastor had just sat down at the kitchen table of the rectory to count the collection from Ash Wednesday's masses. Usually his young assistant did it, but Father Kinsella had gone off to visit a sick parishioner and left him the job.

Father Driscoll finished his scotch and turned the white envelope over in his thick fingers. For some inexplicable reason the letter made him apprehensive.

He tapped the envelope against the kitchen table thoughtfully. He'd open the envelope, then pour himself another drink. As he tore open the sealed flap, a sudden, violent electric bolt ripped through his fingers and up his arm. He cried out and dropped the letter.

For a moment he sat stunned, massaging his forearm and studying the envelope, wondering if it might be a practical joke put into the collection basket by one of the elementary school kids.

Cautiously he touched the envelope again. This time there was no shock and he sighed and slid out the letter. It was a single sheet of paper with the crudely written message:

FOR CHRIST'S SAKE
BETTY SUE WADKINS

And under the lettering a dark stain the size of a dime.

The priest lifted the slip of paper and sniffed the dark stain. It smelled like perfume, but looked to him like blood. He'd been in the war; he didn't need anyone to tell him what blood looked like. Father Driscoll leaned back in the kitchen chair and stared at the message.

He knew the Wadkins' name. There was a large clan of them outside of town, up in the hills near Blue Haze Ridge. Over the years he had heard stories about them, rumors of people disappearing while hunting near their land, but they were just mountain stories and he hadn't paid much attention to them. Besides, the Wadkins were Baptists; they didn't belong to his parish. Very few people in the area did.

Father Driscoll decided to disregard the note. Slipping the letter and envelope into his shirt pocket, he went back to counting the collection, but he was at it for just a few minutes when he began to feel hot and feverish. He stood up, and taking his glass to the kitchen, reached up to the top of the cabinets and took down the scotch bottle from where it was hidden behind the detergent boxes.

Perhaps he was getting the flu, he thought as he poured himself another drink. The Swine Flu, he hoped. He wouldn't mind dying from the flu. It would be an honorable way to go; better than some of his suicide schemes. Then again, it might only be the whiskey. Another drink and he'd feel fine. He'd lie down for a while and get some rest, then finish the collection.

The pastor left the kitchen, shutting off lights as he walked, and went along the dark hallway to his room. There were only the two of them living in the rectory and he could have had any of the bedrooms on the second floor, but he rather liked the privacy and closeness of this small room. He had crowded all his possessions into it and used the space as both his office and bedroom.

He tried to sleep, but it was too hot in the house. Father Kinsella, he decided, must have turned up the heat. The young priest's bedroom was at the back of the rectory and he was always complaining about the cold. The boy had thin blood, the pastor thought.

Father Driscoll sat up on the edge of the bed and wiped the perspiration off his forehead.

His shirt began to itch and he stood to take off his clothes. He was unbuttoning his shirt when he felt the blood. The shirt pocket was wet and he touched himself carefully, his hand shaking at the discovery. There was no pain in his chest, but the fresh blood continued to spread, soaking the shirt and staining the white cotton.

He jerked the shirt loose from his trousers and off his shoulders. The front was completely stained and dripping with blood. He reached into the pocket and pulled out the envelope. It was hot in his fingers and soaking wet. The blood pumped through the open flap and gushed into the priest's hand.

Father Driscoll was not afraid. He held the bleeding envelope and watched as the blood blistered the soft flesh of his palm. That there could be no natural explanation for what he saw did not disturb him. The old priest had spent his whole life preaching about miracles, and now in his fingers was the proof. He began to pray.

Then, holding the envelope before him like the Holy Eucharist, he moved toward the door. Blood seeped through his fingers and dripped to the hardwood floor. He would have to wipe it up later with holy water, but first he had to place the bleeding envelope in the chapel, near the Blessed Sacrament.

He cupped his hands and let the drops fill his palms. The skin sizzled as the blood touched him and he staggered from the pain, but he held on to the envelope and went down the dark hallway into the chapel of the rectory.

When he entered the room a soft glow haloed the envelope and he did not need a light to find his way. He carried the bleeding note to the front, genuflected before the altar, and placed the note in the paten, a small, shallow silver dish. The thin envelope floated free in the blood. Then, slowly, the dripping stopped and the soft glow dimmed. Father Driscoll touched his fingers. The blood had dried and the blisters had shriveled up. The pain was gone.

Father Kinsella was in the dark kitchen, peering into the open refrigerator. He had a carton of milk in one hand and was reaching for the bologna. In the frame of the light, he looked like a young thief.

"Oh, Father, something wonderful has happened to us!" the pastor exclaimed as he burst into the room and flipped on the overhead light.

"What's that, Father?" The young priest smiled at the old man, then took out the bologna and shut the refrigerator door with his elbow.

"I found this letter in the collection basket," the pastor went on. "A small white envelope addressed to PRIEST, and when I opened it there was a slip of paper and a message. An obscure message, really, just a few awkwardly printed words. It said, 'For Christ's Sake,' and was signed by a girl named Betty Sue Wadkins. I think she might be one of that clan up on Blue Haze Ridge, those Baptists.''

Father Driscoll was breathing fast and he grabbed the back of a kitchen chair for support, then rushed on with his story, telling how he had found blood on his undershirt.

Father Kinsella had only been half listening, and when the pastor stopped, waiting for a reaction, he realized he had lost the point of the story. "What blood?" he asked.

"The envelope!" The old priest leaned across the kitchen table, shouting at him. "The envelope was bleeding, for Christ's sake!"

Father Kinsella tried to stay calm. When he had come up to the mountain parish and met Matt Driscoll he had known it would come to this: that someday he'd have to arrange for the old man to leave the parish. The Bishop had hinted as much: Father Driscoll had a drinking problem. But it had happened so soon, and Father Kinsella hadn't seen it coming.

On campus the college girls—Catholic and non-Catholic—had crowded into the chapel for his morning masses, and when he stepped to the pulpit and swept the pews with his eyes the soft gray color of dusk he had sent thrills through them. In his first year as the campus chaplain, six women converted to Catholicism.

"I'm telling you, son, that envelope bled in these fingers." Father Driscoll raised his hands as if they were proof. "Look in the chapel if you don't believe me. It's a miracle!"

Father Kinsella sipped the glass of milk and kept watching the pastor, wondering what he should do next. He hadn't moved from where he stood, leaning against the kitchen sink.

Father Driscoll shot him a glance. "You don't believe, I suppose, in miracles?"

"Not in Mossy Creek." He kept smiling, trying to keep it light.

"Maybe if you believed a little more in the simple teachings of the Church and the power of Jesus Christ, you wouldn't have gotten yourself into such a fix at the university." Father Driscoll did not look at the young man as he spoke, and for a moment there was silence between them.

"You know, Father, that I asked for this assignment," the young priest finally answered.

"Under pressure," the pastor retorted. "I know what you were up to at that university."

"I had my options."

"Like what? Leaving the priesthood?"

"Yes, like leaving the order," he answered softly.

They never discussed why Father Kinsella had been transferred. When the young priest had come to the mountain parish, Father Driscoll accepted him without a protest. He knew he had no clout at the Chancery and couldn't have stopped the assignment even if he had wanted to. They were both exiles in this remote corner of the diocese.

The old priest slowly pulled his aching body from the chair. He was stiff from the kneeling. "I'm going into the chapel," he announced, as if defying Father Kinsella with his own conviction.

"Okay, Father." The young priest grinned. "Let's have a look." He shook his head and finished off the glass of milk.

"Suit yourself." Father Driscoll no longer cared. The boy either believed or he didn't. Father Driscoll knew that once someone lost the faith it wasn't easily gained again.

"Show me, Father, and then let's get some sleep. It's late enough." Father Kinsella followed the pastor down the hallway and into the chapel, flipping on the light as he entered.

"There's no need for lights," Father Driscoll whispered and moved forward, supporting himself by grabbing the pews as he went toward the altar. At the front of the chapel he genuflected and the pain in his leg made him gasp.

"Easy, Father!" The young priest grabbed the arm of the pastor.

Father Driscoll motioned toward the sacristy. "Look for yourself. On the altar."

Father Kinsella stepped onto the altar platform and saw the white envelope in the silver dish before the tabernacle. The flap was open and the envelope was spotless. He reached out, touched it, and was thrown back against the front pew as if hit by a bolt of electricity. He slipped dazed to the floor.

"Are you all right, son?" Father Driscoll put his arm under the priest to help him up.

"What was that?" The priest shook his head, a little dazed.

"The envelope! I felt a shock myself when I first touched it, but nothing like that! Are you all right?"

". . . . . short in the wiring . . ."

"There must be a shor . . . . power of

"No, it's the envelope. I told you! It's the power of God."

Father Kinsella pulled himself up. "More likely it's the Duke Power Company, Father."

Father Driscoll left him and went to the altar. "Look for yourself! See what I told you!" His face beamed.

Father Kinsella stepped onto the altar, being careful where he walked, and looked again. Now the silver paten was filled with blood and the envelope was soaked red. He reached into the dish and plucked out the envelope. There was no shock this time, but blood pumped out of the open flap and ran through his fingers.

He pulled the slip of paper from the envelope and saw where the blood gushed from the dime-size mark. Then, pressing the heel of his hand against the flowing blood, he squeezed the spot as if applying a tourniquet. His fingers blistered and pus ran from the sores, but slowly he cut off the flow of sweet-smelling blood. He dropped the slip of paper and the bloody envelope into the silver paten. He could hear Father Driscoll whisper that he would be all right, that the blisters would heal. But it was not the blisters that terrified the young priest: it was the slip of paper that bled like an open heart in his hands.